MW01591684

Bill,

THANKS FOR BEING

A FRIEND ... ENJOY

JEB

UNFORGIVABLE ACTS

Also by Jeb Browning

Halo School Series

Halo School – The Holy Nails

MFB Black Ops Series

Asset Recovery (coming soon)

UNFORGIVABLE ACTS

A Thriller by
JEB BROWNING

This book is a work of fiction. Names, characters, dialogue and incidents either are products of the author's imagination or are used fictitiously. Any resemblance to actual events or persons, living or dead, is entirely coincidental.

Copyright © 2018 by J.E. Barbara.

All rights reserved, including the right to reproduce this book or portions thereof in any form whatsoever.

ISBN: 978-1-7084758-9-5 (paperback)

Published by: Bayshore Publishing House

Cover Art by: Barbara Ann Devine

DEDICATION

I would like to dedicate this novel to my family. I thank them for their love and support in my writings.

ACKNOWLEDGMENTS

I would like to thank former Monroe County District Attorney Howard R. Relin for his help in understanding the DA's procedures and protocol for specific situations involving crime and prosecution.

A big thank you goes to Monroe County Deputy Sheriff Patrick M. O'Flynn for his help and guidance with police procedure. Congratulations on becoming sheriff.

Many thanks to the [City of] Rochester Police Department, especially the Maplewood and Campbell Street Sections. They were very kind with their insightful contributions.

Ann C. Barbara and Teresa Bishop, both have been nurses for many years, helped me with some of the medical research for this book and I thank you for your contributions.

Thanks to Lina Tang Esq. and Michelle Brown for their contributions in the editing and story development of this book.

A special thank you to Ken Firmender; his advice and help in both story and line editing were invaluable. Ken is an adjunct English professor at Housatonic Community College.

A special thanks to Barbara Ann Devine for using her artistic skills in designing the cover of this book. Working with her was a pleasure.

Finally, thanks to M.R. Callahan, who has worked for the United States in agencies whose acronyms most people have never heard of, and will never hear of. He covertly handled Black Ops independent contractors for many years.

INTRODUCTORY NOTES

Some of the battle scenes in this book are based on actual battles. Most of the locations described in this book are actual places.

Many of the scenes were inspired by real life events that happened to me or people close to me.

Most of the weapons are currently in use by the U.S. military.

Many of the events described in the Thousand Islands Region are based in fact.

More detailed information on these and other events in this book can be found in the Author's Notes.

CHAPTER 1

Base of the Hindu Kush Mountains, Afghanistan

Under the cover of darkness, as the brilliant desert stars danced in the sky, the MFB black ops team set up an ambush twenty miles into the desert just below the Hindu Kush Mountains, hideout of a high-ranking Al Qaeda operative named Eljazir Abdul El Karazim.

According to CIA intel, El Karazim planned to disrupt an upcoming OPEC summit with a car bombing. Commander Michael Callaghan and his men had been hunting El Karazim and his men for two weeks. The previous week they'd been able to paint his caravan with a geosynchronous satellite ping and had been tracking his movements ever since.

Michael Callaghan watched the caravan of twenty terrorists descending the mountain road on his 3-D satellite monitor. His team was solid. They had grown up together and all had served in various branches of Special Forces before joining Michael in the MFB black ops. Together they had accomplished missions for the president all over the world.

Michael had reservations about his cousin Mitch Connors joining this one. Mitch got married a month ago and found out on the morning of their departure that his new bride was pregnant. Michael had tried to talk him out of coming, but Mitch wouldn't have it. Even his brother—Michael's second-in-command, Lieutenant (LT) Greg Connors—tried unsuccessfully to talk Mitch into sitting this one out.

The men waited three hours for the terrorist and his armed caravan to arrive. With new attack Hummers on each side of the road and the sand deployment systems engaged, the assault vehicles looked like sand dunes. In the moonless desert night, his men waited like messengers of death, concealed in the darkness and shadows. Commander Callaghan checked the monitor and clocked El Karazim's caravan heading their way. He notified his men and the team dragged a dead camel they'd found earlier into the middle of the road.

They heard the caravan before it came into view. When it made the turn onto their stretch of road, the lead truck skidded to a stop. After some shouted discussion, six men climbed down to move the camel. They were in no hurry and most took the opportunity to stretch and move around. Finally, the men used some thick hemp rope to secure the animal to a winch on the front of the truck.

The MFB team was viewing their targets through night vision monocular units attached to their helmets that gave the terrorists a ghostly green hue. Callaghan squinted and studied every detail in front of him. He watched his prey like a mountain lion, hidden in the night, a shadow waiting to pounce. This is what the United States government taught Michael Callaghan to do. This is what the United States government needed Michael to do. These were bad men, as bad as they come. Men who had killed thousands of innocent people and made promises on behalf of Allah that they were not empowered to make.

Out of nowhere, a small herd of goats tended by a lone boy appeared out of the darkness and began crossing the road. Commander Callaghan held his breath, hoping the boy and his goats would pass before the terrorists finished moving the camel.

A shout from El Karazim's vehicle and two of the terrorists picked up their AK-74s, the next generation of the trusty AK-47, and stopped the boy. The boy shook his head vehemently several times before the terrorists opened fire on his herd. They killed seven goats before the herd scattered.

Commander Callaghan whispered into his throat mic. "Hold your fire." Callaghan knew his men hated the way the boy had been treated.

From the back seat of the second vehicle, El Karazim smiled, lit a cigarette and sucked the Turkish tobacco smoke deep into his lungs. He thought about the virgin he'd had the night before. She was a plump little girl that smelled like jasmine. He blew a plume of smoke rings, rolled down his window and spit a chunk of phlegm into the desert air. So far, his mission had been a success. He had recruited nineteen faithfuls, fucked a virgin, and now had fresh goat meat for his men. His lips curved upward as his thoughts returned to the night before. He took a long drag.

As the camel was being winched from the road, Commander Callaghan searched the desert with his night vision monocular, relieved the boy and his remaining goats had moved off as fast as they could. Commander Callaghan gave the order through his throat mic for LT and JR to begin the assault.

From behind two sand dunes fifty yards up the road, LT and JR roared out on high-speed attack motorcycles. Dressed in black, with night vision binoculars and Kevlar vests with ceramic plates, their sound suppressed bikes raced toward the enemy. Within seconds, they were inside the enemy's perimeter. They opened fire with silenced MP5 9x19mm submachine guns, taking out the lead truck's headlights first. More bullets spiraled through the air, leaving streaks of light trailing behind them as they found their marks. The six terrorists moving the camel crumpled and dropped.

Commander Callaghan watched LT and JR from one of the Hummers. LT pulled an incendiary grenade from his vest and tossed it into the back of the third truck as he raced past. The explosion rocked the truck and it burst into flame. Six men crawled or rolled out of the burning truck, half dead and on fire. When the remaining terrorists took the bait and jumped out of their vehicles to shoot at the motorcycles roaring past them, Michael gave the order to open fire.

He held his breath while the enemy fired on LT and JR. He concentrated one of the Hummer's 20mm M61A1 Gatling guns on the terrorists that were targeting his men. Out of the corner of his eye, he saw LT take a hit and go down.

Callaghan turned to Ace and yelled, "LT is hit. Focus your fire on the men around the last truck."

Ace turned his six-barreled Gatling gun and together they took out the men in and around the last vehicle. The 20mm armor-piercing incendiary rounds ripped the truck apart and killed a dozen newly recruited terrorists.

Mitch and Lou unleashed a barrage of fire on El Karazim's men from their armored Hummer on the other side of the road, unleashing hell on the desert around them.

Commander Callaghan saw a terrorist take aim with an RPG. Callaghan swung his Gatling gun as the rocket-propelled grenade took flight. Firing over six thousand rounds per minute, the Gatling gun peppered the air with 20mm rounds trying to hit the needle in the haystack. The RPG exploded just feet away from the attack Hummer. The quarter-inch steel plates, ballistic foam and Kevlar reinforcement saved Callaghan's life, but the vehicle shook from the blast.

Commander Callaghan realized that his ammo-belt was empty and his gun barrel was still spinning. He quickly reloaded and continued his assault, sweat pouring from his body. He mopped sweat from his brow. He knew he'd been only seconds from certain death when he hit the RPG in mid-air.

The terrorists fired wildly into the night, bullets pinged off the attack Hummer and empty shell casings littered the floor at Callaghan's feet. Two more of the terrorists fired RPGs. Both went wide and high. Russian AK-74s lit up the night. Some of the rounds bounced off the armored Hummers and others went high. El Karazim pulled an ivory handled Colt nine-millimeter pistol from its holster, ducked and took refuge on the floor in the back seat of his vehicle. He screamed at his driver to get out and aid his comrades in the fight.

When the terrorists stopped firing, Commander Callaghan gave the order to cease-fire. As the smoke cleared Ace, Lou, and Mitch, carrying MP5 submachine guns, checked the bodies to make sure the terrorists were dead. The only person in the caravan still alive was El Karazim.

Commander Callaghan grabbed a medic bag and ran toward LT. JR turned his bike around and raced back toward his fallen comrade. They arrived at the same time.

LT was lying on his right side, holding his left leg. Blood was pouring from the front and rear of his thigh. "LT, hang in there, buddy. You're going to be okay." Callaghan dumped the contents of the medic bag onto the road.

"I'm fine. Really. It's just a flesh wound."

Commander Callaghan tore open LT's pants and examined the wound with his fingers. "It feels like a through and through. I have just the thing to fix you up, my friend." He reached for the QuickClot gel and removed the packing from the tube. The gel was a new product developed by MFB's R&D to help stop bleeding in the field.

Holding a flashlight in one hand, JD pulled out a single dose morphine syringe, ripped off the wrapper with his teeth, jabbed it into LT's leg and depressed the plunger with his thumb. "This should help with the pain."

"Thanks JR," LT grunted through clenched teeth.

Michael handed the tube of gel to JR and pulled his bowie knife from the leather sheath attached to his left shoulder. Carefully cutting the pants away from the wound, Michael exposed the bullet hole.

Taking back the tube of gel, Michael stared intently at LT and said, "This may hurt a bit, even with the morphine, but it'll stop the bleeding."

LT ground his teeth. "Ready when you are, Commander."

Michael put the tube just inside the wound on the back of LT's leg and swiftly squeezed gel directly into the hole. He emptied the tube into the wound.

"Whatever that was, it's getting really warm inside my leg," he said. "Hey, look at that—some of that stuff is oozing out of the front."

Michael could see that the bleeding had stopped. "Son-of-a-b, this shit really works." He smiled at LT. "How does your leg feel now?"

LT Connors didn't even have to think about it. "It doesn't hurt like it did before. It feels like a really bad Charley horse."

"Do you think you can walk?" Michael knew they had to get moving before more trouble headed their way.

"Sure thing, let's go." LT stood up and stretched his leg. "I feel ten times better. Just a bit of a leg cramp."

When Cool Hand Lou and Mitch arrived at El Karazim's vehicle, they found him hunkered down on the floor. He had urinated in his pants and was crying. Mitch opened the door and El Karazim emptied his six-round revolver into him. Four of the bullets embedded in Mitch's flak jacket, one round splintered, sending fragments into his neck, and the last round sliced through his carotid artery.

Mitch staggered backward, clutching his neck, and went down.

When Michael, LT, and JR heard the gunshots, they turned with weapons raised.

"It's my brother. Mitch has been hit." LT was using his night vision binoculars.

The three men climbed aboard the motorcycles and raced back to the rest of the team. When they arrived, Ace was applying pressure to Mitch's wound and Lou had El Karazim pinned to the ground with a knee on his neck.

LT jumped off the motorcycle before it came to a stop and ran to his brother. "Mitch, I'm here now." He knelt down and pulled his brother's head onto his lap.

Michael followed with the medical kit, his dropped bike spinning on the side of the sandy road. One look at the blood pouring out of Mitch's neck and Michael knew a bullet had hit his carotid artery.

He pulled a scalpel and a clamp from the med-kit and got to work. "I need to stop the bleeding by clamping the artery on the proximal end, cut the artery evenly on both sides and try to sew it together." Michael knew Mitch only had two to four minutes if he couldn't repair the artery.

LT grabbed a morphine syringe and stabbed Mitch in the shoulder. "Hang in there, little brother. We're going to get you fixed up."

Mitch looked into his brother's eyes. "Promise me you'll look after my boy."

"Stop talking like that." LT angrily wiped a tear from his eye.

Callaghan was trying to cut the skin around the artery so he could apply a clamp, but the gushing blood made everything slippery.

Mitch began to fade in and out of consciousness, claiming he could see his dead mother and she was smiling at him.

LT shook him. "Stay with me, Mitch, your wife and baby need you." Tears slid down his face. "I need you."

"Hold him steady, LT. We're trying to work here." Michael was fighting back his own emotions, trying to focus on his task. He had to save his cousin's life. Michael was an only child but had grown up with Mitch and LT.

Mitch scrabbled at his brother as if he was blind. "Are you there, Greg? Is Michael here?"

LT held his brother's face still and stroked it gently. "We're both here, Mitch, we're both with you."

Mitch reached a bloody hand and found his brother's face. "Promise me that you'll look after Gabby and the baby."

LT caught his brother's hand. It felt cold and weak. "I promise, little brother. Now you stay with me." LT's tears fell on his brother's face.

Michael had secured clamps on the carotid artery, yet blood continued to pour onto Mitch's chest. "What the hell?" Callaghan searched Mitch's neck for another wound.

"I'm so cold." Mitch shivered, his voice hollow and distant.

"Mitch, stay with me." LT took off his jacket and covered his brother's chest. Ace followed suit.

Mitch's eyes fixed on a distant object.

Michael found a second wound. "Son of a bitch!" He shook his head at LT. "There's another neck wound."

Mitch found Michael's eyes. "Don't worry, cuz, it isn't your fault."

Michael knew. "I shouldn't have let you come."

Mitch's limp bloody hand found Michael's. With his last breath, Mitch whispered, "You couldn't have stopped me, I was always going to die at your side."

For the next few minutes, the only sound was LT's grief.

Time ceased to matter and the men paid respects to their fallen brother-in-arms. Several were whispering prayers, others wiped tears or rested a hand on Mitch, their way of saying goodbye.

Everyone's mood was somber. Everyone except El Karazim.

"You Americans make me sick. You weep like children over the loss of one man. I have lost over twenty men on this night."

In a conversational voice, LT said, "I'm going to kill him." LT gently released his brother's head and lunged at the terrorist.

Michael caught him and held him back. "LT, you can't."

LT tried to shake him off. "Let go of me, I'm going to kill him for what he did to my brother." LT pulled his Ka-Bar knife. "He knew he was being taken prisoner. What he did to Mitch is unforgivable."

"I can't let you do that. He acted like a terrorist. If you kill him, the mission is a failure. We owe it to our country, and we owe it to Mitch." He let go of LT. "Mitch was as much a brother to me as he was to you." Michael searched LT's eyes. "If you kill him, Mitch died in vain."

LT choked back a sob and said, "Let's clean this place up and take our brother home."

According to the final mission report, the ambush went off as planned. All four terrorist vehicles had been destroyed, nineteen armed guards and one driver were killed, and that was the tally.

The MFB team arranged for a small group of anti-Taliban and government loyalists to swoop in, scoop up El Karazim, and take him to a cave hidden in the mountains.

With cleanup complete, the MFB team retrieved El Karazim and put him on a CIA black plane, which took him to a U.S. black site on an abandoned oilrig south of the Bering Strait. The loyalists publicly took credit for capturing El Karazim and killing his men, thereby bolstering their notoriety while keeping the MFB's involvement secret. To further the ruse, the loyalists waited two weeks then claimed to have executed El Karazim for his crimes against the Afghani people.

The MFB transported Mitch's body to the military base in Qandahar where their plane, the Hawkeye, was waiting. The CIA created a file for Sergeant Mitchell David Connors, who had died in a military training exercise. His body would be transported back to the States when the paperwork cleared.

The Hawkeye lifted off the ground as the sun began to rise.

CHAPTER 2

The warm summer sun sparkled and danced across Jeff Kane's glossy mahogany desk in his home office.

Although it was Saturday morning, Jeff Kane and his secretary Ann Chantel still had work to finish before Jeff left that evening for the National Manufacturers Product Show in Chicago. Jeff was shuffling papers. At six feet tall he towered over Ann's petite five foot four. Ann admired him from the corner of her eye and decided he was especially sexy today.

Jeff was very aware of the auburn-haired woman next to him. Her emerald green eyes and soft lips were part of the reason he'd hired her in the first place. She smelled like vanilla and her lips were wet and inviting. He dropped his paperwork on the desk and pulled her to him. As their tongues slowly twirled around each other, he could feel her hips rubbing up against his groin. This sent his imagination racing. Jeff could picture himself having Ann on top of his desk, fondling her breasts, filling her with passion beyond her control. He slid his hands down her back and over her ass. He squeezed firmly and felt the bulge in his pants growing harder.

The squeaky hinge on the screen door whined a warning that someone was about to enter. Jeff and Ann bolted apart as the inside door opened and Jeff's sister Amanda walked in with both arms full of boxes and shopping bags that carried the names of several upscale department stores in Rochester, New York. Jeff's wife, Cathy, who also had her arms full of goodies from their shopping excursion, was right behind her. Had the cumbersome boxes not slowed Amanda down, she would have caught Jeff and Ann still in each other's arms. Amanda saw them stepping away from each other, and knowing her brother, she knew what was going on.

"Is it nippy in here, Ann?" Amanda said, eyeing Ann's chest.

"Hello, ladies, how was shopping?" Jeff tried to ignore his sister's remark.

"Great. We found some really good sales, and I even talked Amanda into buying some new clothes for the products show." Cathy's brow furrowed, her eyes darting from Jeff to Ann.

"Ann and I were just finishing up some last-minute details on the Minnesota acquisition. I need Ann to have all of the papers in order for me when I get back tomorrow night, so I'll be ready for my Monday morning flight out," Jeff offered, trying to explain Ann's presence. "I think we're about done, Ann. So, if you could make those changes to the contract we discussed and have it ready for me by tomorrow night, I'd appreciate it." Jeff used his professional voice.

"I'll have everything typed up, and I'll see you then." Ann gathered up her paperwork and nodded politely to Cathy and Amanda on her way out. Her face turned red when she caught Cathy staring at her erect nipples, which she promptly covered with the file folders in her hand.

"What made you use the back door to my office? Why are you even *in* my office?" Jeff's hands went to his hips.

"I bought you a surprise for your office, and it's much too heavy to lug all the way from the front door," Cathy replied defensively. "Now, I want you to sit at your desk and keep your eyes closed until I tell you to open them."

"All right, fine." Jeff sat down and tried not to think about Ann.

A few minutes later, Amanda and Cathy struggled up the steps and into his office. Cathy said, "You can open your eyes now."

Jeff opened his eyes to a large wooden globe on a mahogany stand with gold tipped legs. "I love it."

He rose to get a better look at his gift. Sliding his hands over the carved landmasses, he found the crease that followed the equator. He smiled and expertly opened the globe and revealed a bottle of twelve-year-old scotch and two crystal glasses. He didn't notice when his wife and sister left.

On Saturday evening at 6:00 p.m., Cathy Kane finished packing Jeff's suitcase just the way he liked it. She lugged it down the stairs for him to take to the waiting car in their circular drive. Jeff took the bag and neither one spoke a word. The driver loaded his suitcase, laptop and briefcase into the trunk, and Jeff slid into the back seat of the limousine.

Cathy returned to their master bedroom and cursed. "What will you bring home this time, my dear, a new product line for the company? Or maybe another venereal disease for the wife?" She shook her head and a tear ran down her cheek. "What a bastard I married."

She pictured Ann's erect nipples. "He must think I'm a complete idiot."

Cathy had been married to Jeff Kane for more years than she cared to remember. She had raised their two kids practically by herself. She had tended to his every need, want, and desire. Yet he still cheated on her with every floozy that crossed his path. It was time to end this miserable life of servitude.

"Your time is coming. You're going to get what you deserve. I promise." Cathy was planning a trip to her hometown, where there were plenty of eligible men and a dozen or so were connected to the mafia. She knew people too.

CHAPTER 3

Commander Michael Callaghan was in the satellite observation room of MFB Black Ops Headquarters, a cave system in Rochester, New York—also known as HQ. He had been stateside again for all of six hours. He was watching firefights between Afghani soldiers and Taliban forces in three different positions, switching between two geosynchronous satellites orbiting twenty-two thousand two hundred thirty-six feet above the Earth, belonging to the MFB. The combined coverage provided him with a complete overview of the bloodbath, and from his vantage point, he could discern the battle strategies of each side. Watching it was necessary even though it flooded his mind with sights and sounds of the last mission.

He watched tensely, clenching and unclenching his fists as men raced toward certain death. Sweat trickled down his back. He could feel a rush of adrenaline wash over him like the high tide. His right hand instinctively drifted to his hip where his Glock 30-45 caliber silenced pistol normally rested, only today he was unarmed.

Michael knew the MFB Black Ops' capture of El Karazim—which Afghani soldiers were happy to take credit for—was the reason this battle had begun. He felt a more than a little guilt as he watched men die.

"Commander…" Second Lieutenant Jamie Thurston was trying to get Michael's attention.

He felt a tug on his arm, and with the speed of a predator attacking its prey, he spun on his heels.

"Commander, I'm sorry to bother you, but POTUS is on hold for you."

Michael nodded at the West Point graduate and headed toward his office. He sat down in a tall leather-backed chair behind a desk devoid of any personal objects. Michael often wondered if he would ever have family pictures of his own to display on his desk.

He cleared his throat and picked up the phone. "Good morning, Mr. President. I'm sorry to keep you waiting."

"I'm glad you're back. I've read your debriefing. I see you lost one of your men and another one took a bullet. Is he all right?" POTUS and Michael had served together and now Michael was a trusted member of the president's kitchen cabinet.

Michael leaned back in his leather chair. "He'll be okay."

"I wanted to thank you and your team for getting El Karazim for us. After some persuasive techniques were applied, he became most cooperative and forthright with intel."

POTUS waited for a reply. Michael didn't offer one.

"Are you okay, Michael? You sound exhausted. I know you've only been back a few hours. Maybe you should go home and relax for a few days."

Michael nodded. "Perhaps you're right, Mr. President."

"When you get around to it, send me a bill so I can get you guys paid." POTUS paused for a moment. "Michael, I'm sorry for your loss, and thanks again. Your country owes you a debt of gratitude."

Michael almost smiled. "Thank you, Mr. President."

When he hung up the secure phone, Michael decided to pack it in and head home. He checked on his team and headed down the tunnel toward the elevator.

After entering his security code and undergoing a retinal scan, the steel doors opened and Michael stepped inside. There were no buttons. The motion activated sensor closed the doors and the elevator accelerated upward.

When it stopped, a computer-generated female voice declared, "There is no activity within the security perimeter, Commander Callaghan."

Michael opened the door and stepped out of what looked like a towering pine tree with branches that blocked any view from overhead. The doors closed automatically and Michael walked down a path to a rural road and crossed it to an abandoned and boarded up house owned by MFB. He entered a code on a hidden keypad and at his feet, concealed doors parted, revealing a stairwell.

He took the stairs down to his 1984 Harley FXSB Low Rider Shovelhead, one of only 2,876 made, and one of the last 469 bikes made in cherry red. His all-leather seat and backrest were in pristine condition. The Navy SEAL insignia adorned the left side of the gas tank. On the right side, a simple MFB in glossy black.

He secured the stairwell and after checking the security monitors, he started the bike and rode up the ramp and out through the cluttered garage. It felt good to have the wind on his face, the rumble of his bike under him and the freedom of the road. He thought having a few drinks with Greg over the next couple of days was a great idea and was glad they'd decided to attend the National Manufacturers Product Show to blow off some steam.

What he didn't know was that relaxing wasn't an option. He was about to face his biggest fear in Chicago.

CHAPTER 4

At home in Rochester, Michael stowed his gear, showered, and mixed a strong Jim Beam and ginger. He pulled his field journal from his bag and to begin the ritual that he performed after every mission. In the walk-in closet, he ignored the switch on the wall and pulled chain hanging from the light three times then pulled it down and held it. The wall pivoted open.

The hidden room revealed the history of Michael's family, including heirlooms. Some of the relics were priceless and had been in his family since the tenth century. Michael felt pride every time he entered this room.

An oil rendering of a king in rich green and crimson robes and a polished silver chest plate engraved with the family crest had pride of place. The portrait was of King Ceallachan of Munster, Michael's ancestor, painted in 952 A.D. Michael bore a strong resemblance to the king. He had the same hairline, build, facial expression, and even the same crooked smile.

The rest of the wall space was filled with ancient scrolls, tapestries, paintings and many portraits of Callaghan clansmen, depicting heroes and great battles. Ancient steel helmets with bands of velvet and feathers, greatswords, lances, and daggers of all sizes were locked in wood and glass display cases. Coats of arms of varying age and design were scattered about the cavernous room. There were trunks full of Gaelic golden coins, silver and gold candleholders, cabinets that held ancient plateware, and silverware of all shapes and sizes.

Lastly, on a plinth, a scroll describing a great battle in 1172 when Anglo-Norman invaders under the command of Strongbow defeated the Callaghan king. Lands were lost and treaties signed. Battered but not beaten, life went on for the Callaghan clan.

Michael liked to walk through this room because the history, legends, and wealth on display made him feel surrounded by his ancestors… he no longer felt alone. He really needed it today, after losing Mitch.

Michael put the field journal from his recent op on a shelf and pulled out a leatherbound journal of parchment with the field notes of his great-great-grandfather, Mike Callaghan, for whom he was named. Returning to his bedroom, Michael sat in the wing chair and rubbed his hand across the leather cover. Instead of reading the journal now, as was his custom, Michael tucked it in the top drawer of his nightstand until he felt more like himself. Mitch's death had hit him hard. With a heavy heart, he decided to pack for the product show.

Unbeknownst to Michael, there were hidden dangers lurking in Chicago.

CHAPTER 5

Amanda Kane and her director of marketing at Kane Wholesale, Michelle Jargen, checked into their suites at the Intercontinental Chicago Magnificent Mile Hotel. Besides its peaked glass roof, historic entrance, and opulent interior, the hotel also offered views of Lincoln Park and the downtown skyline. After freshening up a bit and unpacking, they were on their way into Mickey's Bar and Grill.

Once past the bouncers, they walked through a second set of doors and into the bar. The bar was straight ahead and stretched into a sixty-foot semicircle.

Amanda and Michelle ordered their drinks and began watching the crowd and chatting casually. They were just finishing a conversation about marketing strategies they planned to use for the upcoming Minnesota acquisition, when Amanda sat up as if she'd been struck by lightning.

Michelle turned her head and scanned the room. "Who are you looking at?"

"The man I'm going to marry." Amanda could feel her temperature rising. "*If* he can pass the test and prove he'll be faithful to me."

"Which man are you looking at?" Michelle's eyes widened with excitement; she'd never heard Amanda talk like this.

"Do you see the two men standing next to the third and fourth bar stools on the other side of the bar?" Amanda took a sip of her drink through a thin straw. "They're both about six feet tall. One has dark brown hair, a mustache, and is dressed very nicely. The other is clean-shaven with sandy blond hair. His white pants make his butt look fantastic." Her face flushed. "Most importantly, I don't see a wedding ring on either of them."

Michelle said, "The blond is hot. Both of them are, for that matter. Do you think they've seen us yet?" Not waiting for a response, Michelle continued, "Do you think we can get their attention?"

"I don't know. Do you think I'm his type?"

"You're definitely his type."

Amanda considered that briefly. "I don't know… what if he doesn't find me attractive?" Amanda couldn't keep her eyes off him.

"Look at you—tall and blonde, great skin, long legs and a killer figure. Who could resist you?" Although Michelle was stroking her boss's ego, she was telling the truth.

Michelle put her drink down and turned toward Amanda. "We've been watching them, and not once have they stopped talking and scoped for women. That tells me he isn't a womanizer."

"Good point. Okay, how can we meet them?" Amanda had a note of impatience in her voice.

"Watch and learn." Michelle reached out and grabbed the first person that walked by.

"Excuse me, sir," Michelle said to the tall dark-skinned man wearing a black three-piece suit, black silk shirt and black wingtip shoes, "I wonder if you would be so kind as to help us with a small problem?"

"How could any man refuse two beautiful ladies such as you?" He bowed slightly, and then his face broke into a large toothy grin. "I am Jamaal," he said. "What is it you desire me to assist you with?"

Michelle ignored the grin and his odd accent and asked, "Do you see that man right over there?" Michelle pointed to the mystery man at the other end of the bar. "The man with sandy blond hair, white pants, holding his drink. Well, my friend would like to meet him, but she doesn't think she's pretty enough to get his attention. Do you think you could help us?"

His eyes narrowed as he regarded the stranger. "Sure. I'll be right back." He turned and walked away.

Both women watched intently as he approached Amanda's mystery man and tapped him on the shoulder. "Excuse me for a moment, but there's a woman down there that would like to meet you." Both mystery men turned and looked.

"Could you please come with me for a moment?" Jamaal said. After getting a closer look at both men, he was sure he knew them.

Michael turned to Greg and whispered, "If it looks like there's going to be trouble, watch my back. There may be others."

"After you," he said to the stranger and followed him toward Amanda and Michelle.

Amanda's heart began to beat like a drum solo. She could feel her body tense up. She was tingling all over with excitement.

"He's looking better and better the closer he gets," Amanda whispered to Michelle.

When the two men reached Amanda and Michelle, the dark man stepped aside, noting that Greg was heading toward the restroom. He excused himself and made a call on his cell phone. "Abu, it's me, Jamaal. We have a target of opportunity. Meet me in the men's toilet."

Abu protested, "Can't this wait, my brother? I'm enjoying the company of a new friend." Evidently Abu found the charms of his new companion hypnotic.

"Abu, you foolish man, our target is on his way to the restroom. Now, stop messing with your playmate and move." He snapped his phone shut and followed his quarry.

Greg Connors observed Michael engage the two women in conversation as the dark-skinned man turned and left. "Looks and charm," he commented to no one in particular as he turned and headed toward the restroom. The restroom was empty, and Greg took the urinal on the far wall. Moments later, a tall dark-skinned man entered—the same man who had approached Michael.

A glance told Greg there was no reason to be concerned… yet there was something about the way the man looked. Suddenly it registered. Recent intel had described the signature attire of the terrorist group known as the Black Blade of Allah and this checked all the boxes. Turning in a swift defensive move, Greg deflected the dagger before it sliced open his left kidney.

The dark-skinned man was caught off-guard and staggered backward. "I know who you are, infidel. You, Commander Callaghan and your band of thieves have taken our brother El Karazim and you shall pay with your life!" Jamaal slashed wildly, hoping Abu would arrive soon.

Greg jumped back, dodging the dagger as it sliced the air in front of his throat. He moved closer to the stalls, giving Jamaal less room to swing the blade and asked, "Who told you our names?"

Jamaal ignored the question and thrust the blade at him.

Greg anticipated the move and pulled open a stall door, swinging it to meet the dagger.

As Jamaal tried to dislodge the dagger, Greg jumped up and dropkicked him, both feet striking the center of his chest.

Jamaal slammed into the wall-mounted hand dryer. Wincing in pain, he steadied himself and continued his attack.

Greg blocked a high arcing swing and planted a deadly palm strike against Jamaal's nose. His nasal bones broke and pierced his brain. Death was instantaneous.

The body was face up, and a small amount of blood oozed from his ruined nose. Greg frisked him, looking for identification. He found a passport in the name of Jamaal Aziaya. On the inside of his right wrist was a tattoo of crossed black daggers formed an X below a waning crescent moon—the symbol of the Al Qaeda cell known as the Black Blade of Allah.

Greg stuffed Jamaal's nose with paper towels to stop further drainage. He used more paper towels to wipe a few spots off the floor. Then he dragged the body to the bathroom door and checked to make sure the coast was clear. He picked Jamaal up and carried him out the back door as if he were another patron who'd had too much to drink. Outside, Greg threw him into the dumpster. "That was for Mitch."

When Greg returned to the bar, Michael was still talking to the women. Unbeknownst to Greg, Abu was in the far corner of the bar, still flirting with his sexy new friend.

Greg remembered what Jamaal had said. Somebody must have talked. Damned paid informants, not one of them could be trusted.

Michelle stood up and grabbed Michael by both arms, turning him toward Amanda. "I want you to take a good look at my friend and tell me if you think she's attractive."

Michael wondered if they were call girls looking for a client or something else. "Okay." He carefully looked every inch of Amanda over with a hint of a smirk on his face.

Amanda flushed and closed her eyes, wishing she was somewhere else.

When Michael's eyes reached her face, it was crimson. A deep red, the kind that came from pure embarrassment. He stood there feeling guilty, ashamed for having done such a thing to this woman who obviously wasn't a hooker.

"Well? Do you think she's hot?" Michelle was standing behind Amanda and couldn't see the look on her face.

"Yes. She's very good looking," Michael replied in a quiet voice. "May I ask what your name is?"

Amanda opened her eyes and saw how genuine Michael was being. "Amanda. Amanda Kane." Amanda looked into his golden-brown eyes and her legs felt like Jell-O.

"What's your name?" She tried to regain her composure.

"Michael Callaghan, and it's a pleasure to meet you, Amanda Kane." He held out his hand.

"It's a pleasure to meet you too." They shook hands, a little longer than necessary.

"Amanda, I'm here with a friend of mine, and he's sitting at the bar waiting for me. Would it be all right if we both came back and talked to you two in a little while?" he asked politely.

"Sure, that would be great." She smiled. "Or you could call him and invite him to come over and join us."

Michael pulled his cell phone and asked Greg to grab their drinks and join the table.

Introductions were made and Michael explained that he and Greg were cousins, and Michael's mother had died giving birth to him. Since his father was away a lot on business, Michael grew up with his aunt, uncle, Greg and his brother, Mitch. They were more like brothers and best friends, rather than cousins.

Amanda was thrilled when she learned that Michael was also from Rochester.

She smiled happily and said, "Well, when we get back to Rochester, we should get together."

Michael stared deep into Amanda's eyes and warmth flowed through his body. "I'd like that very much."

Jamaal had failed to answer his cell phone for the last five minutes, and now a thorough search of the restroom revealed a single smudge of blood. Abu studied the floor on his hands and knees and saw the faint scuffmarks left by the fight.

He followed the scuffmarks to the dumpster behind the bar. He let out a cry when he found Jamaal's body and swore he would torture the man responsible and have him beheaded. He called his driver and told him to bring the car around. Abu would ship the body home. Then he and his brothers would have time to grieve. Afterward they would track down the person responsible and exact revenge.

CHAPTER 6

It was 11:30 p.m. Jeff Kane and Joshua Stein, director of distribution at Kane, had checked into their suites at the Intercontinental Chicago Miracle Mile Hotel and before unpacking, they went downstairs to the hotel lounge for a drink. They were on their third.

"So, Josh, tell me, when are you going to find yourself a nice woman to sink your teeth into and take a bite out of life?" Jeff scanned the bar in search of lonely women.

"I've had my eye on someone for quite some time now. Nothing steamy yet, but maybe in the next couple of weeks we'll start getting more serious."

"Great, who's the lucky girl?" Jeff was only half-interested. He set his sights on a blonde woman sitting at the end of the bar.

"Ann Chantel, your secretary. We've been dating for about—"

"Hold it right there." Jeff turned his barstool around to face Joshua. "I don't think it's a good idea for you to be dating Ann. You should break it off right now before it goes any further."

"Don't worry. It won't affect our working relationship. Besides we've been so discreet, nobody at work even knows." Joshua smiled.

"You don't get it. I don't think she's right for you." Jeff's tone was sharp and cut like a knife.

"If it's Ann you're worried about, don't be. I think she really likes me." Joshua was cautious, and realized by the harsh look on Jeff's face that something was very wrong.

"Let me make this real clear. I don't play second fiddle to anyone. You keep your hands off my secretary. Got it?" Jeff's eyes had a hawkish glare. "If I even thought another man was messing with one of my women… I'd kill her first, and then I'd kill him with my bare hands."

Joshua stared at Jeff, wondering why life was so cruel. *Here's a guy with good looks, tons of money, a wife that most guys would kill for, and of all the women in the world, he wants the same one I do. And, to top it all off, he's my BOSS.* "Yes, I got it, loud and clear." A bead of sweat trickled down his hairline. His face was red. His heart felt as heavy as an anvil and his head felt like a nuclear explosion had just gone off.

"Good. Now let's not let a little thing like a woman ruin our night." Jeff smiled and raised his eyebrows a couple of times then turned his attention back to the blonde.

Joshua sat tapping his swizzle stick on the side of his glass and thinking about Ann. As his resentment started to grow, he considered how nice life would be without the arrogant, womanizing, demanding, pompous son-of-a-bitch, Jeff Kane.

CHAPTER 7

It was Sunday evening at five fifty p.m., and Jeff Kane had just arrived at the Rochester International Airport on his return flight from the Chicago Product Show. He was halfway down concourse A to where Ann was waiting for him near the security gate.

The sun was casting long shadows when they left the terminal and headed for Ann's car. On the way, Ann told Jeff how much she missed him and that he was all she could think about. Jeff hardly heard a word she was said. All he could think about was how sexy she looked in her nearly see-through sundress.

"How was your flight?" she asked cheerfully, still trying to engage Jeff in what was currently a one-sided conversation.

"It was a short flight, only about an hour and a half." Jeff smiled as he looked into her eyes for only the second time. "Do you have everything ready for tomorrow?"

"Yes, I did as you asked. All we need is a few signatures and Kane will own another lumberyard." Ann gave a flirtatious wiggle of her shoulders and chest.

"Do you know what I think we should do after the deal is finalized?" Jeff had a boyish grin.

"No, what should we do?" Ann dug her keys out of her purse and unlocked the car.

"I think we should go out to dinner at one of the best restaurants in town, and then head back to our hotel for an evening of fun and pleasure." He cocked his left eyebrow and smiled suggestively.

"Am I going with you to St. Paul to finalize the deal?" Ann asked, ignoring Jeff's innuendo.

"Well, Joshua is still in Chicago at the trade show, and I'll need someone to assist me in finalizing the deal. I was hoping that someone would be you." Jeff stood by the car door waiting for a response.

"Yes! I can't wait. I'll be the best assistant you ever had. I promise." Ann was filled with enthusiasm. This could be her big opportunity to climb up the corporate ladder. If she performed well, maybe that promotion she had been wanting would be within reach.

"That's what I was hoping you'd say." Jeff opened his door and got into the car.

When Ann got in, Jeff reached over, gently cradled her face with both hands, and gave her a long, wet kiss.

The ride to Jeff's estate in Mendon took thirty minutes, during which Jeff reviewed some of the paperwork on the Minnesota deal.

When Ann turned into the large circular driveway, he closed the file and handed Ann a corporate Amex Black card. He told her to get an airline ticket for the same flight he was on and some sexy lingerie.

When the car stopped in front of the large porte-cochère, Jeff leaned over and kissed her, a slow sensual kiss. It was a promise of things to come, and when he stopped, he left her wanting more.

"Thanks for the ride home. I'll meet you at our flight tomorrow morning." Jeff reached into the back seat and retrieved his bags.

"I'll be there with the rest of the file, and together we'll set Minnesota on fire." Ann beamed as Jeff left.

From her bedroom window Cathy Kane watched Ann pull away. She'd seen her husband lean toward Ann before getting out of the car, and although she couldn't see them kiss with her own eyes, she saw it with her heart. Even after the car was long gone, she continued to stare out her bedroom window. A cold stare. The stare of a woman who knew her husband was cheating on her, but couldn't do anything about it. She felt scared, empty, and lonely. Her dreams of a happy life were lost. Most of all, she felt betrayed.

She wanted revenge. Cathy didn't want to take her husband's abuse any longer. It had been going on for years, and she was tired of it. She was waiting for a return call from a friend, and through that friend, she would have her revenge.

Jeff's two kids, Chloe and Jeff Jr., greeted him at the front door. Both children were yelling, "Daddy's home, Daddy's home." Jeff set his luggage on the crimson-colored silk settee his father had brought home from China as a wedding present.

After handing each of his kids a T-shirt that he'd bought at the Rochester airport, Jeff shooed the kids up the stairs and noticed Cathy glaring down at him.

The smile left his face. "Hello, Cat. Was everything all right while I was gone?" His tone was casual and indifferent.

"I thought you were taking a limo home from the airport?" Cathy sneered and started down the stairs.

"I intended to, but Ann finished the paperwork for Minnesota and brought it to me at the airport. I thought that was very conscientious of her, as this is Sunday and I'm leaving at 10:00 tomorrow morning. Now I'll have the evening to make sure the papers are in order." Jeff picked up his luggage and headed into his office without another word.

Monday morning came, and as planned, Jeff and Ann met at the airport and departed to close the new deal for Kane. On Tuesday, Amanda, Michelle, and Joshua returned from the product show and so did Michael and Greg.

When Joshua walked into Kane's corporate headquarters, he asked his secretary to page Ann Chantel. When the news came back that Ann had left with Jeff for St. Paul, Joshua was enraged. It was his job to assist Jeff with new acquisitions. That bitch had betrayed him, and now she was going after his job.

Joshua couldn't let Ann sleep her way into his job. He had to do something about it.

CHAPTER 8

When Thursday morning came, Michael called Amanda for the first time since his return to Rochester. It had taken two days for him to get over his fear of a relationship. He decided that if things didn't feel right, he would bail immediately.

On their first date, Michael and Amanda went to Grisante's for dinner, and then to a movie. By the end of the movie, Michael had his arm around Amanda and she had her head on his shoulder. Their evening together was magical.

A light breeze, a good meal, and a love story framed the warm summer night. They sat for an hour on Amanda's front porch, talking and gazing at the scattered lights that graced the Mendon countryside and the star-filled sky. They ended their first date with a romantic kiss. It was a long, slow kiss, a very exciting kiss. When it was over, Michael had goosebumps on his arms.

"Now I know what I've been waiting for all of my life... a man that kisses as well as you do," Amanda whispered as Michael drove away.

On Michael's drive home, his thoughts turned to his mother, who had died from complications during his birth. He had always felt responsible for her death and that was part of the reason that he'd never been serious with a woman before. His father was devastated when his mother died. Michael often wondered if his father blamed him for the death of his mother and if that was why he sent Michael to live with his cousins, like an orphaned child.

"Perhaps if I take care of Amanda, and never let any harm come to her, it would be kind of like making it up to you, Mom." Michael was pleased at the prospect of some stability and even domestic tranquility in his hectic life. He couldn't have been more wrong even if he drove the wrong way down a one-way street.

When Amanda got up from her porch swing and went into the house, she was thinking about her own mother. Her mother had died after an automobile accident while Amanda was in college. On her deathbed, she made Amanda promise to test the man she wanted to marry. With a heavy heart, Amanda made the promise and kissed her mother for the last time. This was a promise she couldn't break.

As Amanda entered the formal living room, she looked at the portrait of her mother, hanging on the wall above the fireplace. As she looked deep into her mother's soft blue eyes, she remembered her advice about men. *'Never trust a man. You don't have to— you're pretty, you're intelligent, and you have lots of money. So never marry a man without testing him to make sure his love is true, and he won't ever cheat on you.'*

"I remember what you said, Mom, and I'll test him. But this is the right man, I can tell," Amanda whispered to the picture.

Amanda believed that Michael would pass the *test*. At least that's what she kept telling herself.

CHAPTER 9

It took four days of intense bargaining, but Caulkins Lumber now belonged to the Kane Empire. Jeff Kane had finally sealed the deal. Like all hostile takeovers, it had been a long, emotional, and physically draining battle. Jeff pulled out all the stops, and with some last minute underhanded maneuvers, he got the deal he wanted.

He was ready for a fine dinner with an expensive wine, a Jacuzzi bath, and some hot steamy sex. The attraction between Jeff and Ann was so strong that he had opted to bring Ann on this trip instead of his right-hand man, Joshua Stein. Agreeing to go would prove to be the biggest mistake of Ann's life.

Jeff and Ann went back to their hotel suite to celebrate. They ordered dinner from the room service menu of the hotel's five-star restaurant.

"I can't believe the way you handled those people. It was *unbelievable* how you knew just the right things to say when it came to their financial and personal situations. Here's to Jeff Kane, the world's best buyout artist." Ann raised her wine to toast their success.

Even though the two bottles of wine during dinner and the bottle of champagne after dinner left Ann somewhat inebriated, she and Jeff continued to soak up more wine in the bubble-filled Jacuzzi.

Jeff set his glass on the side of the Jacuzzi. "Do you want to see something even more exciting than the way I handled the takeover?"

"Like what?"

"Like the way I handle you." He leaned over, picked her up, and carried her to the luxurious king-size bed.

He put Ann down gently in the center of the bed. He smiled at the sight of her naked body. He started with a long, wet, sensual kiss and then worked his way down her neck, his hot mouth kissing and licking everything.

Ann felt the ecstasy she had dreamed about since their first kiss. She buried her head deeper and deeper into her pillow. She could feel the heat and moisture intensifying within her. Her moaning grew louder and louder as Jeff continued to pleasure her.

He slowly kissed his way up her flat belly and she felt his torso slipping between her legs. The anticipation of what was about to happen between them made her nervous, yet excited. He penetrated her slowly and she let out a soft moan. Ann's desires were coming to the surface, bubbling up from the depths of her soul.

Their lovemaking lasted a few minutes, with Jeff becoming more and more aggressive.

Then it was over. Jeff finished, and a moment later, he was lying next to her, sweating profusely and breathing heavily.

"That was great," Jeff huffed. "I must be really drunk. I would have gone longer, but I got really dizzy."

Thank goodness it's over, Ann thought. "That's okay, you were wonderful, and I really enjoyed your talents." Ann lay there gazing at Jeff's sweaty face.

"God, I'm sweating like a pig. Just look at the alcohol pouring out of my pores. Be a good girl and turn on the AC for me." Jeff was drunk and exhausted.

"No problem, I'll get it right now."

She set the fan on high and the temperature control at medium. When she returned to the bed, she found Jeff fast asleep and still sweating... totally gross. Ann slipped into the bed, closed her eyes, and tried not to think about the sweaty man next to her. The last thing she wondered before she slipped into unconsciousness was how long it would take before Jeff proposed.

CHAPTER 10

Jeff and Ann returned Friday afternoon to Kane's headquarters on the top floor of the Changing Scenes Building in downtown Rochester. The building got its name because the top floor rotated 360 degrees every twenty-four hours. Jeff went straight to his office, called his father and sister, and asked them to meet with him in ten minutes. After unloading his briefcase and reassembling the pertinent paperwork, he left for the conference room.

As people passed the conference room, the faint murmur of voices and an occasional roar of laughter were clue enough to the level of success that Jeff had achieved once again.

George J. Kane sat at the head of the table with a proud smile on his aging face as his son told his tale of conquest. George was a man of sixty-three who looked every year of it. Gray hair had replaced the youthful black and he carried a belly that rippled when he laughed at Jeff's antics.

"You should have been there, Father. The way I handled Ted and Randall Caulkins was like a superbly directed play. As you know, they thought we were going to offer them six million for their little piece of the action. For the first two days, I went along with the charade. I told them that I had a check made out, and all I needed to do was review their books, and the money would be theirs. On the third day I gave them just a little hint that something was amiss." Jeff stopped for a dramatic pause.

"Yes, get to the point," Amanda urged, leaning up to the table in anticipation.

"I called for a meeting at four o'clock. I started the meeting by saying, 'Okay, gentlemen, there's something very wrong here, and unless we get this issue straightened out here and now, I'll be on my way back to Rochester and you'll be out six million dollars.'"

Jeff took a sip of water. "The brothers looked at each other and then Ted said, 'What are you talking about?' I pulled some papers from my file and said, 'First, it appears as if Randall has been skimming profits off the top,' and that's when Randall blurted 'that's outrageous.'

"I got really serious and said, 'I've reviewed your books, Randall. Your cost of goods sold is inflated by two hundred and sixty thousand dollars. The inventory you shipped to your new cottage, and the new addition to your house last year, were charged against several different projects, which falsely increased your cost of goods sold on those projects. And by inflating your cost of goods sold, you reduced your net income for last year by a substantial amount, and that, Randall, is a crime. It's called tax evasion and embezzlement, and is punishable by a fine and potentially jail time.'

"'You have no proof.' Randall looked very nervous.'" Jeff was performing a play-by-play of what was said and done at the meeting.

"And I looked him in the eye and said, 'Sure I do. My people contacted your customers and compared the price of the products you sold them to your sales receipts and they matched. What doesn't match is the cost of those products versus the cost of the same product sold on other jobs during the same period. Someone inflated those job costs in your financial statements to hide the fact that you never paid for the material shipped to your properties. According to delivery tickets for the same period, you shipped two hundred and sixty thousand dollars worth of inventory to yourself. The books don't reflect any billing or payments to or from you.'

"Ted Caulkins started getting belligerent. 'Look here,' he said. 'You can't come to our lumberyard and make accusations like that.'

"So I said, 'Well, Ted, I had hoped this wouldn't be necessary, but, what do you suppose your wife and three daughters would say about your lover?'" He recalled that with a grin.

"'Lover, what are you talking about?' The man went as white as a sheet. I pulled an envelope from my briefcase with pictures of Ted and his lover, and tossed it on the desk in front of him. 'How's this for proof?' I asked."

Jeff produced duplicates of the pictures and placed them on the conference room table in front of Amanda and George. The pictures were of two men having sex in multiple positions while watching gay porn.

"Well, Ted didn't like that at all." Jeff laughed. "Ted got up from the table, walked over and looked me straight in the eye, and said, 'You're a cocksucking snake.'" Jeff looked pointedly at Amanda. "And do you want to know something?"

"Yes, what?" Amanda replied with wide eyes.

"Ted was so mad, I thought he was going to hit me."

"What did you do?" George Kane was getting restless.

"I just looked him straight in the eyes and said, 'I may be a snake, but you, Ted, are the cocksucker.'" Jeff roared with laughter, which also got George rolling. Amanda shook her head in disgust at her brother.

"Just then," Jeff continued through his laughter, "Randall yelled, 'Oh my God, Ted, that's you with a man?'"

"You've got to be kidding. Randall didn't know that Ted was gay?" Amanda was shocked that the brothers had kept such secrets.

"Randall had no idea what Ted was doing."

"So, how did you get them to sign the contracts?" George looked puzzled.

"Well, Ted walked over to Randall, grabbed the pictures and yelled, 'At least I didn't steal from you.'

"Randall was whining, 'Look, Ted, I was going to pay it all back, honest I was.'" Jeff's next words came out slowly, and it had a sobering effect on the three of them. "Then things started to fall apart. Randall freaked out, saying his life was over because they would be going to jail for tax evasion. Then, Ted said he would lose his family because his wife would find out he was bisexual. It was really pathetic. Ted just fell into a chair. Randall ran over to him, but Ted just sat there sobbing."

"What happened?" Amanda whispered.

"I said, 'Listen up, gentlemen. No one is going anywhere, and no one has to find out anything.' Then Ted said, 'What do you mean?' I told them that I wasn't about to pay six million dollars for a company that was worth substantially less. Under the circumstances, I was willing to offer two million dollars, forget about the embezzlement, and surrender the photos with their negatives," Jeff concluded and sat down at the far end of the table.

"Very nicely done, Jeff." George nodded approval and got up to get a drink.

"Thank you, Father," Jeff replied.

"It seems like you were being a bit underhanded. Did it have to be that way?" Amanda was upset about the whole situation. "If you turned over the photos and the negatives, why do you have these copies?"

"Underhanded? You think I was underhanded with them?" Jeff exploded. "How do you think I felt, watching a grown man cry?"

"Hiring a detective to dig up dirt is not only unfair, it's unethical and probably illegal," Amanda said. "What you did is tantamount to blackmail, and that's illegal and it's not the way we want to run this company." Amanda faced off against her younger brother. "What you did to those people is unforgivable."

"You don't get it, do you? You just sit up there on your high horse and wear those rose-colored glasses. Well, let me tell you something. In this world, you take control or it takes control of you. They were like wounded fish in the water, and the first shark that happened by ate them. If it wasn't us, it would have been someone else." Jeff was offended.

"Since when do we condone illegal acts and resort to blackmail to force buyouts? I want no part in any of this and if we need to call legal…" Amanda raised her palms.

Jeff snarled, "Listen, those two guys were only making sixty-five thousand dollars a year, plus a year-end bonus of fifteen grand. I offered them a million each. All they have to do is invest that million wisely, and they'll make more than that every year. I think I was pretty generous with them."

George interjected, "Well, according to their books, over the last two years their profits fell thirty-five percent per year, probably because of the slump in the economy, but their net assets are still worth three and a half million dollars. So we got a good deal."

Amanda shook her head in disapproval.

George said, "Running a successful business isn't easy, Amanda. Jeff, God knows we have enough trouble without looking for it. We need to put our heads together and do the best we can with what we have. In the future, we'll look a little closer at the prospects before we make our move—and let's try to keep our hands clean. Now, we need to get busy, we have a lot of work to do to make our newest acquisition a success."

Jeff didn't tell his father and sister that he had mailed a copy of the pictures to Ted's wife after they signed the deal. That was Ted's punishment for crying like a wuss.

CHAPTER 11

Joshua was sitting in his office with his back to the door, looking northeast, a part of the city plagued with rampant drug abuse, prostitution, and murder.

Sandy, the receptionist, called over Joshua's speakerphone, "Excuse me, Joshua, I don't mean to interrupt, but Jeff and Ann have returned to the office."

Joshua said, "Thank you, Sandy. Could you please ask Ann to come to my office as soon as she's available?" Joshua knew Jeff was a man who didn't practice fidelity, and would make a move on Ann. What he didn't know was whether Ann would reciprocate.

"Sure thing, Joshua, I'll let her know immediately."

Several minutes later, "Did you want to see me about something, Joshua?" It was Ann, and by her tone, she wasn't anxious to see him. Joshua's heart sank.

"Yes, I wanted to review some of the Caulkins Lumber files with you. I'm trying to determine their past purchases versus annual sales so that I can get a handle on what kind of inventory they're going to need."

Ann didn't know what to think. The tone of Joshua's voice was new and worrisome.

"You do have that portion of the file, don't you?" Joshua didn't like playing hardball, but he didn't like Ann being coy either.

"Yes, I have copies of those records," Ann conceded.

"Good, could you please bring them to my office in five minutes?" Joshua needed to look into her eyes and see for himself if there was anything left between them.

"Sure, give me a few minutes to get organized." Ann didn't want a confrontation with Joshua. After all, she was just trying to advance her career.

"Thank you." He hit the disconnect button.

Several minutes later, Ann walked in to Joshua's office with the file. She'd been dreading this moment since she boarded the flight home. She sat down in the leather chair directly across from Joshua, and put the file on his desk.

"So, how was your trip?" Joshua turned from the window, finally acknowledging her.

"Great," Ann blurted without thinking. "I mean, as good as can be expected, considering the nature of the trip. You know what I mean," she hedged.

He noticed some bruising around her neck. "No, what do you mean?"

"Well, it's just that a hostile takeover takes so much out of you." Ann regretted her choice of words as soon as she said them.

"Oh, you mean except for business, everything else went great," he replied sarcastically. "What else did Jeff take out of you?"

Ann's face flushed; she didn't appreciate his remark. "Don't put words in my mouth. I don't appreciate your crude comment."

Joshua smirked. "I didn't put anything in your mouth. You must be thinking of someone else."

"Then what's with your sarcastic bullshit attitude?" Ann was irritated. She rubbed her forehead with the palm of her hand, trying to shake the lingering effects of last night's intoxication. "What are you getting at?"

"The same thing everybody else in the office wants to know. The only thing people have been talking about for four days." He glared.

She folded her arms across her chest and tilted her head. "What, exactly, is that?"

"Did you sleep with Jeff so you could move up the corporate ladder?" Joshua enunciated clearly, fearing he already knew the answer.

"I don't have to answer that. You're being incredibly rude."

"You just did. So, I guess our relationship is over."

"Accusations like that could get you in a lot of trouble with Jeff," Ann threatened. She stood up and walked toward the door.

"That's not an accusation, that's a fact. Besides, what's Jeff going to do, fire the whole office? I hardly think so."

"Even if I did, what gives you the right to give me the third degree like I belong to you?"

"Nothing, I just thought that we had something going, that's all." Joshua was sullen. "Apparently, that was my mistake."

"We didn't have commitments to each other, and I would hardly call a couple of dates a relationship," Ann retorted.

"Like I said, my mistake. Thanks for the file. I'll see you around sometime." Joshua was hurting and motioned for Ann to leave his office.

Ann could feel his pain. She had hoped if this happened, it would be easier.

"Would you like me to review the file with you?"

"No thank you, I can read it for myself. You can go help Jeff now."

"Fine, have it your way." Ann left the office feeling shitty for the way she'd treated Joshua. He was a nice person, and she really did like him, but that was before she knew Jeff Kane was in love with her.

Joshua wasn't about to let Ann sleep her way into his job. She had taken his work and taken credit for it. Jeff was to blame too. He knew Joshua and Ann were dating, but he wouldn't keep his hands off her. Jeff didn't care about anything or anyone, except money.

"I don't have to put up with this shit. Who the hell do these people think they are?" Joshua spoke through clenched teeth. He wanted

42

revenge. "I have options, I know people, and it's time someone was taught a lesson."

CHAPTER 12

POTUS applied some pressure through backchannels and Mitch's body returned home to Rochester in seven days. The wake and funeral were in the traditional Irish manner. Gabby insisted on holding the wake at her and Mitch's house. Greg had the coffin placed near an open widow, someone stayed with him at all times, and Michael stopped all of the clocks and covered the mirrors.

Over two hundred people attended the first night of the wake. Most were men that had served with Mitch, all of them paid their respects to Gabby and in their own way, said goodbye to Mitch. The evening ended with Father Canaan, a cousin, leading the prayer service while Gabby sobbed.

The last night of the wake was different. The first few hours were a continuation of the mourning, and then the atmosphere changed. Michael and the team spread out booze and food for the guests. The forty people that remained were crammed into the large parlor with Mitch's body.

Greg was the first to start. He recalled a time when they were kids and he, Mitch, and Michael went fishing. Mitch had a big bass on the line. In his excitement and eagerness to get the fish in the rowboat, Mitch stood up to grab a net, and at that moment, the large bass broke water and jumped into the air, causing Mitch to stumble and fall overboard. Everyone laughed and toasted Mitch.

Michael recalled the time when a large Holstein calf was born in the cow pasture behind their cottage in Bayshore Estates. After several sightings of the calf running around the cottages, Michael, Greg, Mitch and the rest of the boys in the neighborhood decided to catch the rogue. They searched two cow pastures before finding the calf, which promptly took off, running for its life. Through briar patches, beehives, and crab apple orchards, they chased it at breakneck speeds. When Michael closed the distance to mere feet, he grabbed the calf around the neck and attempted to cowboy wrestle it to the ground. After being dragged for twenty yards, Greg caught up and plowed into the rear end of the bovine, causing a tangle of hooves, arms, and legs to crash to the ground. Shortly thereafter, Mitch, JR, Billy and Lou jumped on the pile in a gang tackle. Once they were all standing, the decision was made to carry the calf back to the cottage. Michael took one front shoulder, Greg took the other and JR and Billy took the rear legs, leaving Lou and Mitch to carry the rump. The boys had barely walked a dozen paces when Mitch let out a blood-curdling yell. When Michael and Greg turned to see what had happened, Mitch was covered in dung from his chin to his knees.

The room erupted with laughter and the celebration of Mitch's life continued. Everyone, including Gabby, took turns recalling happy memories, drinking and celebrating Mitch's life.

The wake lasted all night and the following morning they buried Mitch.

The burial service took place at Calvary Cemetery with an early morning mist swirling like ghosts around the headstones. Father Canaan performed the service and when he was finished, seven members of the local Army Reserve in their dress uniforms gave a twenty-one-gun salute, and with all the ceremony befitting a fallen comrade, they folded the flag that draped the coffin and gave it to Gabby. Taps bugled in the background. Two men playing "Flowers in the Forest" on bagpipes followed the military ceremony. As the sun began to burn off the swirling mist, another cousin, Mary-Brigitte, belted out an astounding rendition of "Amazing Grace."

Greg ended the burial service and they lowered the casket into the ground singing "Danny Boy." There wasn't a dry eye as the mourners dropped flowers on top of the casket and left the cemetery. Greg and Michael rode home in the limousine with Gabby. During the ride, Michael handed her an envelope and told her that it was Mitch's profit-sharing disbursement. He also explained that their medical and dental benefits would continue in perpetuity. Gabby knew that if she ever needed anything, she could call on Greg and Michael, and they would always be there for her. What she didn't know was the check that Michael gave her was for six million dollars and the majority of the money came from Michael's personal funds.

CHAPTER 13

Michael dropped Gabby and Greg off first, then returned home. After disabling the ground sensors and security alarms by remote control, he entered his house, went upstairs to his bedroom, and changed. He sat in the wingchair next to his bed and thought about the events of the last few days, which triggered the memory of the journal in his nightstand. Perhaps the field notes would reveal some strategy or tactic that could help save the lives of his men in the future. When Michael opened the one-hundred-year-old document describing a great battle in the East China Sea, he could almost smell the surf as he began to read.

JULY 15, 1863

STRAIT OF SHIMONOSEKI, EAST CHINA SEA, JAPAN
Both steam engines and the finest sails power the U.S.S. *Wyoming*, a wooden hulled screw sloop. The mighty ship was anchored south of a small island just outside the Strait of Shimonoseki, a narrow gateway to the East China Sea off the coast of Japan. Commander Mike Callaghan, second in command, was alone in his stateroom reviewing the latest report describing how one of the *Daimyos* (great feudal lords), Lord Mori Takachika of the *Choshu Clan*, had sent his private navy to take control of the Strait of Shimonoseki. This violated the Treaty of 1854 between Japan's

de facto rulers—a military dynasty called the *Tokugawa Shogunate*—and the United States.

The Treaty of Kanagawa proclaimed bilateral peace between the United States and the Emperor of Japan. It also opened two Japanese ports to U.S. ships for provisioning, guaranteed safe haven for shipwrecked sailors, and permitted the appointment of resident U.S. consuls in Japan. Internal warring between the local warlords and Japan's emperor had led to murder and arson committed by master-less samurai called *Ronin* and had spread to many of Japan's cities. When the U.S. Consulate in Tokyo was burned to the ground, American Consul Robert Pryun retreated to Yokohama. He then dispatched orders to the U.S.S. *Wyoming* to break off its hunt for the Confederate raider C.S.S. *Alabama* and to retake control of the Strait of Shimonoseki and its ports to protect American interests. By the time the orders reached the U.S.S. *Wyoming*, the intelligence was two weeks old. It stated: *At last report, the Japanese had three merchant ships outfitted with cannons and six shore batteries protecting the strait. Two of the ships are anchored on the east side of the strait and the third ship is anchored on the west side.*

The *Wyoming*'s commodore, David McDougal, had called for a meeting of the ship's officers regarding these orders. Commander Callaghan was gravely concerned with the mission they were about to undertake. After rolling up various maps of the region and heading to the commodore's quarters, he began formulating a bold and dangerous plan.

Commodore David McDougal was five feet six inches and barrel-chested, with white hair and a matching beard that stood in contrast to the man on his left, Commander Callaghan. Mike Callaghan, with his muscular six-foot-two-inch frame and wavy blond hair, towered over the ship's captain. Despite the disparity in height, they both had a commanding presence, which helped them to lead the sailors.

All of the ship's officers gathered around the map table as the commodore laid out his plan. "Men, we face formidable defenses. There are at least twenty cannons aboard three warships, backed by six shore batteries. The shore batteries are located atop the hills and line both sides of the strait. At first light tomorrow, we're to going to stoke the steam engines, sail into the strait, and take control of the port. It will be a bloody battle, but I believe our men are the best trained and most experienced sailors in the Pacific."

The commodore pulled a long swallow from his wine glass. Wiping his mouth with a napkin, he continued, "We will open fire on the two ships anchored on the east side of the strait on the way in. Then we will reverse engines, come to a stop between the two ships, and using them shields, open fire on the shore batteries. Once we have disabled the batteries, we will turn hard about and open fire on the third ship as we head for open water. If we can sink her, we will be able to retake this crucial port and waterway."

When the commodore finished, there were several moments of dead silence, as the officers realized how lacking in detail the plan was. Then everyone started talking at the same time. Many of the officers were shaking their heads over what was seen as a poorly conceived mission.

A young lieutenant named Collins raised his voice above the din. "Commodore, what if we don't silence the ships before we pull up to them? We will be sitting ducks and facing cannons on both sides. Moreover, what about the shore batteries? They could blast us out of the water. Are we supposed to ignore them? This strait looks very narrow on the map. Their cannons could hull us before we even get to the anchored ships. This is suicide."

"Now, lads, this is no time to panic." The commodore raised his hands. "We must keep our heads in the face of adversity, and we must make certain we take out the cannons on those two ships." He ignored Collins's question.

"Commodore, even if we make direct hits to their cannons, which would be incredibly difficult when sailing at full speed, we could be boarded and engaged in hand-to-hand combat before we have a chance to sink their ships." Collins wasn't letting up, and clearly panic had taken over.

The commodore countered, "I have faith in our superior combat skills should that occur."

At this, the officers began to argue.

Commander Callaghan raised his hand and silenced them. "Commodore, I have a plan I would like to discuss, with your permission."

"Of course, Callaghan, by all means, share your thoughts." Commodore McDougal knew his options were limited, but they had their orders, and one didn't receive promotions and earn a place in Washington without following orders.

"We're facing firepower far superior to ours, yet we must retake the port. Therefore, I suggest we even the odds." Callaghan pointed to the map of the strait and the harbor. "If we can silence the cannons on at least one of the warships before we are fired on, I believe we have a chance. Our reports state that three ships are anchored here, here, and here. By taking out the cannons on the ship closest to the eastern shore before we engage in battle, we can focus all our guns on the ship next to it during our approach and we'll have a chance to retake the port."

"How do we do that?" The commodore seemed intrigued by this suggestion.

Callaghan, known as a brilliant war strategist, said, "We have a man with sealed containers of gunpowder swim into the harbor under the cloak of darkness, climb aboard the ship, and place two containers in each cannon. When the cannons are fired, the extra powder in the bores will form a plug and their cannons will blow up. This will not only stop them from firing on us but also cause fires aboard their ship and sow confusion. The smoke from the fires will help hide us from the shore batteries."

The room was silent as the officers considered the new suggestion. "It might work, if we have the element of surprise on our side," Collins agreed. "But that would require someone to swim at least three miles each way while lugging a dozen two-pound tins of gunpowder, and who could do that?"

"I will," Callaghan volunteered. "I'll swim with the current on the rising tide on my way, dragging the tins of gunpowder in a net. Once I've planted the gunpowder aboard the ship, I'll swim back at high tide when there is no current, *and* I'll have a scouting report so we can better ready ourselves for our attack. We will have firsthand knowledge of the enemy position instead of a two-week-old report." Callaghan was confident, even though his suggestion seemed incredible. Still, everyone knew Commander Callaghan had done many things in the past that were thought to be impossible. "If anyone has any better ideas, I'm all ears."

The commodore broke the silence. "Well, it's settled then. You had better start preparing. You're nearly out of time before the currents change. Collins, I want you to make certain the tins are waterproof and have them ready to go in forty minutes."

The sun was beginning to set, casting the sky in orange and pink hues when Commander Callaghan stepped on the top deck. He was wearing a tight black undershirt and a pair of black trousers. He had one knife strapped to his left forearm and a second strapped to his right leg. The entire crew of one hundred and ninety-eight men had formed two lines leading to the bow. As Callaghan walked between them, he received handshakes, pats on the back and well wishes from every man aboard.

Commodore McDougal waited with Lieutenant Collins at the end of the line. "I don't have to tell you, Callaghan, that if you get caught, the U.S. Navy will disavow any connection to you. This is strictly an off-the-books operation," the commodore whispered as he shook hands with Callaghan.

"Of course, sir. I'm a Canadian privateer looking to relieve a ship of some of its bounty, that's all."

The commodore stepped aside and Commander Callaghan dove off the bow of the ship. A cargo net loaded with gunpowder was waiting for him in the water. He untied the net from the boat's forward lines and started off with his cargo in tow.

Lieutenant Collins and Commodore McDougal watched Commander Callaghan swim away. "That's a courageous man. I'm not sure I could swim that far towing that load behind me," Lieutenant Collins said quietly.

"Not surprising. He comes from a family known for its bravery and service to the United States," McDougal mused. "His grandfather was rumored to have been an orphan boy raised by a French missionary in Canada, and went on to help the U.S. win the War of Independence."

"Really? I hadn't heard that story before, is there more to it?"

"Apparently, his great-grandfather was an Irish trapper somewhere in the wilds of Canada who fell in love with a Mohican woman in a village he had been trading with. They married and had a son. When the son was twelve, his village was attacked by a warring tribe and the entire village was killed except the boy, who was off checking his trapline. The boy wandered into a village almost two hundred miles away where he was found by a missionary priest. The priest raised the lad until he was seventeen. When the War started, he joined an American militia. He used the skills he'd learned from his trapper father and Indian uncles to conduct many surprise attacks against the British and the Huron tribes during the war."

Collins shifted uneasily. "You mean the half-Indian boy fought against other Indians?"

The commodore turned and faced his lieutenant. "Some say the boy wanted revenge against the Huron for wiping out his village. Some say that's why he volunteered to fight in every skirmish."

"Well, let's hope his skills have been passed on to the commander, because he's going to need them tonight."

"If Commander Callaghan's past performances are any indication, his skills are top notch, and our lives may depend on his success. I suggest you have the men ready the ship and get some sleep. I want two men with lanterns on the bow on watch for Callaghan's return."

"Aye aye, sir. I'll assemble a team to ready the ship for Commander Callaghan's return."

As Callaghan began his arduous three-mile swim, the cargo net and gunpowder felt like an anchor. A small school of fish swam past and his thoughts turned to sharks. Sunup and sundown are the best times to fish, for sharks as well as men. Mike ducked underwater to get a look around. The salt water stung his eyes as he searched the darkening waters. Sure enough, he saw a shark following the school. There was only one, but one was enough. "Damn it, why did there have to be sharks? This will slow things down a little." He stopped kicking and began a breaststroke to reduce splashing, hoping the shark would ignore him. Luckily for him, the shark continued to follow the fish. It would have been difficult for Callaghan to fight off the ten-foot monster while towing the gunpowder.

As he kicked his way past the tip of the island and into the open strait, he could feel the ocean current moving with the tide. Just as he'd planned, the current was pulling him into the strait. Callaghan pulled the net close and used it to float with the current. "First-class transportation, just as I intended."

As the commander floated into the quay, he could see the enemy's defenses laid out on the hills. There were three well-lit batteries on each side of the harbor, with cannons set on palisades and aimed toward the strait. The three ships were two sailing boats and a steamer. A bark and a brig were anchored on the east side of the harbor and the steamer protected the west side. All of the ships had cannons mounted on the bow, starboard, and port sides. The strait was a narrow, measuring only three hundred yards from one side to the other. Unless Callaghan was successful, the Japanese would be shooting fish in a barrel. An American fish called the U.S.S. *Wyoming.*

The brig was closest to shore and was therefore his target. He could see men moving about the ship and lights from various portholes.

Callaghan drifted around the port side until he found the anchor chain. He secured the cargo net to the chain and climbed up the massive steel links. Once on deck, he searched until he found a portside stern docking rope and lowered it over the side so he could haul up the cargo net and gunpowder. After climbing down the rope, securing his cargo, and climbing back up, he hoisted the gunpowder onto the ship. So far, he had been hidden by the shadows on the stern. Now he would have to carry his load nearly two hundred feet to the cannons on the bow.

He stayed close to the railing, inching forward. At the halfway point, he heard footfalls from a stairwell on his right. He slid against the cabin wall and waited. It didn't take long for someone to appear. The man was dressed in traditional Japanese samurai garb, complete with a sword and helmet. He walked to the railing, lit a cigarette and began to urinate into the sea. Callaghan glanced into the stairwell and found it empty. The rest of the deck looked clear. He crossed the deck in two silent strides, slipped his arm around the samurai's neck and choked the life out of him. Not wanting a splash to attract attention, he stuffed the body into a lifeboat under the tarp. Returning to his cargo, Callaghan crept to the bow cannons and planted his gunpowder. The lack of security was undoubtedly related to the laughter and revelry from below deck.

Commander Callaghan slipped back into the water with his empty cargo net and vanished into the dark waters. After a quick three-mile swim, he climbed the starboard side anchor chain and joined the forward lookout post. "See anything yet, sailor?"

Startled, the sailor dropped the driftwood he'd been whittling and jumped to attention. "Commander Callaghan... I—I didn't see you coming, how did you, how—"

"Take it easy, sailor. I swam underwater for the last five minutes." The commander patted him on the shoulder. "Notify the commodore that I would like to assemble the officers in his quarters in twenty minutes. I'm going to change and have a drink before the meeting."

Twenty minutes later Commander Callaghan was providing a detailed layout of the enemy's positions. "One thing we can use to our advantage is that the shore cannons are mounted on palisades and aimed toward the middle of the strait at the harbor mouth. If we go in at high tide and stay close to the eastern shoreline, the cannons will be shooting over our heads and the cannons opposite will fall short." Commander Callaghan took a long pull from his rum. "If we sail in without colors flying, we should be able to get close enough to the bark to take out her forward cannons. Once we open fire, the brig will fire *her* forward cannons, and the gunpowder I set will hull the bow of the ship."

Commodore McDougal straightened up with a crooked smile. "Good work. Commander. Any difficulties in to report?"

"Just one casualty, sir. I hid him under a canvas tarp on a lifeboat."

Before first light, and at high tide, the U.S.S. *Wyoming* steamed toward America's first battle with Japan.

The *Wyoming* succeeded in taking out the forward cannons on the bark. Commander Callaghan and his sharpshooters concentrated their rifle fire on the few crewmembers on the bridge. The expert marksmen quickly dispatched the bridge crew, and with no hands on deck, the fight was all but over. The surprise attack came together as the early morning sun appeared.

The bow of the brig did blow and sunk several hours later. The men aboard abandoned ship.

With several well-placed volleys from their cannons, the U.S.S. *Wyoming* set the bark on fire. With less than ninety feet separating the *Wyoming* and the bark, the rate of fire became a matter of life and death. Callaghan left his men to the care of Lieutenant Collins and raced to his cannons.

"Concentrate your fire on their cannons. They can't sink us if we take out their cannons." Callaghan helped his men. The *Wyoming* took multiple hits before silencing the barrage.

Callaghan directed his men to turn their fire on the steamer anchored on the opposite shoreline. After climbing the bow rigging, he was able to coordinate their attack from atop the mast. As anticipated, the *Wyoming*'s upper rigging and mast beams took a pounding.

The Japanese steamer, severely damaged and burning, was still letting loose her cannons on the U.S.S. *Wyoming*. When the *Wyoming* rounded the brig and began to head toward open waters, she continued her assault on the Japanese steamer. The U.S.S. *Wyoming,* whose cannon fire consisted of one sixty-pounder cannon and three thirty-two pounders, made every shot count against the Japanese steamship. The steamship took a direct hit to her boiler room and a massive explosion caused the ship to sink at anchor. Although the U.S.S. *Wyoming* was outgunned thirty-two cannons to her four and took eleven direct shots to the hull, the mighty warship sailed away under her own power. With but five dead and six wounded, the battle was a success.

Later that night, celebratory drinks were flowing, and a few of the men were toasting their commander, whose strategy and bravery saved them from certain death and led them to victory. Those gathered at the table were Callaghan's best. They had fought side by side with the commander in many battles. These sailors followed Callaghan's orders without question, and trusted him with their lives.

"Here's to Commander Callaghan, long may he live, his bravery and cunning have saved us again." Lieutenant Collins was happy to be alive and was consuming large amounts of alcohol.

Commander Callaghan stood up. "Now lads, while I appreciate your accolades, it took many good men to win this, and you, my fellow Men from Bray"—all the men had ancestors from Bray, Ireland—"are among the finest sailors on all the Seven Seas."

"Men from Bray… The MFB. I like that, Commander. It has a nice ring to it," Collins said.

Callaghan raised his glass. "Then so be it, from this day forth, these men and all of the brave men whom we select to join us shall be called the Men from Bray or the MFB." The clanking of raised mugs ushered in a new era… the era of the MFB.

After the war, Callaghan received a special Medal of Honor for bravery and became a trusted confidant of the president. He would be called upon many times to perform special missions for the

President of the United States. His greatest wish was that his descendants would carry on the MFB with the same courage and cunning as he had.

When he was finished reading, Michael reflected on his life. Mitch's death had hit him hard and he was beginning to rethink having a family. Life was short and he did want a loving wife and children. Now that he'd met Amanda, maybe it was time begin a family of his own.

CHAPTER 14

Over the next two weeks, Michael Callaghan and Amanda Kane were virtually inseparable in their off hours. During the day, Michael worked out of MFB HQ, monitoring the situation with the Black Blade of Allah and the Taliban. Amanda was busy integrating Caulkins Lumber into the Kane Empire.

When they were together, they spent time golfing, shopping, horseback riding, and rollerblading. Regardless if it was a weeknight or a weekend, Michael and Amanda always went to their own homes at the end of the night. They hadn't slept together. Their romantic kisses were getting steamier, and their passion was building with every touch.

Amanda knew she'd find herself in a situation with Michael that would lead to lovemaking, and she wouldn't be able to resist. She wanted to make love to Michael, she even dreamed about it.

But her mother's voice haunted her. "Never trust a man. You don't have to. You're pretty, intelligent, and you have lots of money." Those sage words had saved Amanda on two occasions. Now it was time for her to test Michael.

The phone rang twice before a young, sexy voice answered. "Good morning, this is Gina, how can I be of service to you today?"

"Hi, Gina, this is Amanda Kane." Amanda tried to sound upbeat, but she couldn't pull it off.

"Hey, Amanda, it's been a long time. How are you doing?" Gina had attended the same prep school as Amanda and they'd stayed in touch over the years, mostly on a professional basis.

"I have a job for you." Amanda's voice was weak and shaky, and there was no hiding her hesitation.

"Amanda, honey, are you sure you want to go through this again?" Gina asked.

Gina was gorgeous. She could have graced the cover of the Sports Illustrated Swimsuit Edition. Five feet nine inches tall with rich, mahogany red hair. Her size D breasts were firm, her legs were long and slender, and she had an irresistibly sexy voice. Her sex appeal was as natural as walking or talking. Gina was the most popular girl in school with the boys and her professors. Moreover, most of the girls wanted to be her best friend.

"Yes, I have to know." Amanda's voice sounded defeated.

"I don't know. I always feel really bad after I do it, and they take me home." Gina's indecision was apparent in her tone.

"I'll make it worth your while. Let's say ten thousand if he says no and twenty thousand if he says yes. That way I'll know you really tried." Amanda sounded desperate as she sat at her desk staring at her mother's picture.

"Are you at the office now?" Gina was all business. Twenty grand was still twenty grand.

"Yes, and I'll have everything ready for you to pick up at 2:00 this afternoon, including the ten thousand up front."

"Okay, I'll see you then. I hope that you know what you're doing. Bye."

After Amanda hung up the phone, a tear crept down her cheek. "You better pass this test, or I'll hate you forever, Michael Callaghan. But if you pass, I'll love you forever."

Amanda picked up the phone and called him. She thought about hanging up, but the voice in her head kept telling her she was doing the right thing.

"Hello." Michael was looking at a live satellite feed of the Black Blade of Allah conducting training exercises in Syria. The Black

Blade of Allah had been expanding and recruiting new members at an alarming rate. He suspected they were moving new cells into the United States and South America.

"Hi, it's me, how are you doing?"

"Good, how are you doing? You sound like something's wrong." Michael dropped his pencil and leaned back in his chair.

"No, everything's fine. I'm just loaded down with work, and my mind was somewhere else, but I'm back." Amanda tried to inject some cheer in her voice.

"Yes, I know the feeling. It's a crazy, hectic world out there."

"How would you like to meet me at Woody's Friday night, say around eight?" Woody's was a local pub that was home to many after-work revelers.

"That sounds great." Michael wrote *eight o'clock/Friday/Amanda* on his desktop calendar.

"I have a meeting with some advertising people, but I should be done by eight." Amanda set up the possibility of being late.

"What do you say about dinner tomorrow night?" he asked cheerfully.

"You want to have dinner, tomorrow night?" Amanda was unsure of what to say.

"Yes, you know, the day before Friday. Are you sure you're okay?"

"I'm sorry, I just got a note about a meeting in ten minutes," Amanda said, attempting to cover her hesitation. "I can't tomorrow, I've got a late meeting on the Minnesota thing that may run into extra innings, but I'll be looking forward to Friday." She sounded tired and worn down.

"I suppose tonight is out of the question?" Michael's brow furrowed in frustration. A bomb exploded on the satellite monitor in front of him, temporarily distracting him.

"Oh, Michael, I'd really like to, but I just can't. If you just give me a couple of days to get this acquisition straightened out, then I'll have the whole weekend to spend with you, and we can do whatever you want."

"It's a deal. You take the next couple of days, and I promise I won't bug you except for maybe an occasional phone call. I'll plan a great weekend for us."

"Thank you for being so understanding," she said gratefully. "I've got to go now, but I'll call you later." She felt horrible for lying, but it had to be done.

"Okay, take care." Michael tuned in to the satellite feed. It appeared the Black Blade of Allah had just blown up some of their men in a training exercise. Dumbasses.

"You take care too, Michael. Bye." Amanda hung up the phone and felt like crying.

The next several hours were like a never-ending bad dream for Amanda. She left her office and decided to go for a long walk. For nearly two hours, she walked through the heart of the city, past skyscrapers, sidewalk vendors, and homeless people lying on the street.

Amanda looked at the time and temperature board outside one of the downtown banks. It was 1:53 p.m. and she knew that if she was late for her two o'clock meeting, Gina would leave. She was six blocks from her building. There were no cabs in sight. The clock ticked to 1:54 p.m. and Amanda had no choice but to run.

Amanda weaved in and out of traffic, jumping over people lying on the sidewalk, and dodging cars on side streets. When she crossed the bridge over the Genesee River, just half a block from home, she saw Gina walk through the revolving doors of her building.

Amanda's heart was racing when she reached the revolving door.

"Hold that car," Amanda yelled, bursting out of the spinning glass cage and running toward the elevator on the right. Luckily, the elevator only stopped twice on the way. Amanda stepped out on the top floor to see Gina at the reception desk.

"Hello, Gina." Amanda smoothed back her hair and attempted to regain her composure.

Gina turned around with a smile on her face. "Hello, Amanda, how are you?"

"I'm fine, thanks. I see you look as great as ever. I hope you're doing as well as you look." Amanda smiled.

"Better," Gina whispered, happy knowing that her bank account was growing, as was her high-profile client list.

"Let's go to my office."

Gina's leather miniskirt, sheer white blouse, and sky-high heels turned every head in the office. Coffee cups spilled, pencils dropped, papers fluttered to the floor, and conversations stopped in mid-sentence. She stopped outside Amanda's office and bent over to brush an imaginary speck of dust off her shoe. Heads popped up everywhere to stare at her gorgeous bottom.

"Gina, would you please come in here and have a seat? You're disrupting the entire office." Amanda gestured at a visitor's chair.

"Boys will be boys, and we just love them." Gina sauntered over and sat in the chair across from Amanda.

"Let's just hope they're not *all* the same," Amanda said grimly as she handed Gina a large manila envelope. "Inside is a picture of Michael Callaghan, and ten thousand. If you succeed and take him home, I'll send you the rest of the money Saturday."

"How will you know if I succeed?" Gina put the money in her purse.

Amanda ignored her. "He expects me to meet him at eight o'clock on Friday. By nine, he'll be wondering if I'm going to make it. By ten, he'll decide I couldn't make it, and he'll either leave with you, or tell you to get lost. I'll be outside watching from my car. If he tells you to get lost, leave the bar immediately and I'll go in and apologize for being late. If he leaves with you, then you'll get your money, and you'll have saved me from a lifetime of heartache." Amanda's eyes went to the picture of her mother on her desk.

"Amanda, honey, we've been friends for a long time. I hope that you're not offended at what I'm about to say. I'm a professional escort. I've made a career of studying men. I've learned what they like in and out of bed. I know what they want, and I know how to give it to them. No one has ever turned me down." Gina's face was serious.

"That's why you've got to do it for me, Gina. If he can resist you, then he'll never cheat on me, with anyone. And that's why you have to give it your best." Amanda was determined.

"You do love him, don't you?" Gina shook her head.

"I'll answer that question on Friday night."

"No, you'll find out if he's faithful to you on Friday night." Gina realized there was nothing she could say to change Amanda's mind. She picked up the envelope and her purse and rose to leave. When she got to the door, she said, "I admire your loyalty to your mother. I just hope you don't end up living in loneliness, like I do."

She didn't strut on her way out. Instead, she was thinking over what she'd told Amanda about her lonely life. Someday, she would have to settle down and retire, but only if he was handsome and rich.

The men in the office didn't notice Gina's distraction, only her gorgeous body. It wasn't until she reached the end of the hall that she remembered where she was. She turned around and smiled when she saw three men peeking out of their offices. Gina gave them a little extra wiggle as she left.

CHAPTER 15

It was Friday evening and Cathy Kane was talking on the phone with a childhood friend Claire Pulaski. "Oh, he'll be playing *poker* all right, but not with a deck of cards. He'll be playing that slut, Ann."

"How can you be so sure?" Claire knew Cathy was in pain.

"I called Jeff's office while he was in St. Paul to see if they knew when he would be coming home, and they had a temporary receptionist filling in. This girl didn't know anything, so she transferred me to Joshua, who was taking Jeff's calls while he was out of the office."

"I thought Joshua always went with Jeff when they did takeovers?" Claire questioned.

"So did I, and so did Joshua. He sounded more pissed off about it than I was." Cathy was fuming.

"Well, why don't you come down tonight? I'll get a babysitter, and we can go out and pick up a couple of guys. That'll teach the bastard a lesson." Claire had three failed marriages and two kids. She knew a lot about teaching bastards a lesson.

Cathy thought about the proposition for a moment and finally said, "That sounds like an excellent idea." Cathy smiled at herself in the bedroom mirror. "It's been so long since I've had sex that I'm getting wet just thinking about it."

Claire laughed. "Yes, now you're talking. I'll see you when you get here."

Cathy dug through her walk-in closet and found the sexiest dress she owned, grabbed a pair of high heel shoes, her makeup and purse, and then headed for the kids.

She left Jeff a note on his dresser saying that she was taking the kids out to dinner, and then dropping them off at her parent's house in Mount Morris before going out with Claire. Cathy intended to spend the night at her parents' house.

She would call her mother on the way to Mount Morris. She needed to leave the house and have some fun.

Cathy pulled out of her driveway with her kids in the back and pushed the accelerator on her pink Cadillac like a woman on the run. She never noticed the dark green Dodge Dart parked several hundred yards down the road, or its occupant. All Cathy knew was that tonight, she was going to get very drunk and have sex, and not necessarily in that order.

With Cathy out of sight and the house empty, the man in the dark green Dodge Dart got out of his car and started jogging toward the house. He looked like any other health conscious man in dark-maroon sweats with the hood pulled up. He jogged into the driveway and strolled up to the house.

He inserted two lockpicks into the deadbolt and within seconds it was open. The entry door lock was just as easy. He opened the door and said, "Now, time to see what secrets you're hiding."

The stranger crept through the house, listening for noises. Confident he was alone, he began his search. He started in Jeff's study. There was typical paperwork overflow from work—not why he was here. He continued his search, looking behind every painting and picture for a concealed wall safe. Failing to find a wall safe, he moved up to the second floor. He peered into the children's rooms—typical boy and girl.

He clenched his fists, pulling his leather gloves taut over his knuckles. He was growing impatient. As he entered the master bedroom, he sneered at the loving family pictures on both dressers. The pictures were a lie. They would never know real love, the kind of love he'd had stripped from him by Jeff Kane.

He picked up the note on Jeff's dresser and read it. "Mount Morris, that's interesting." He replaced the note on the dresser.

The closet was next in his search. On a shelf above the clothes, he found a shoebox, and in the box was where he found it. He retrieved a handkerchief from his pocket, picked up his prize, and placed it in a two-gallon Ziploc plastic bag.

The sound of a car door closing startled him. He ran to the window and saw Jeff Kane walking toward the house. The stranger replaced the box on the top shelf and went to the boy's room. He went in and pulled the door far enough to slip behind it. There he waited with his silenced Kahr 9mm semi-automatic weapon drawn.

Jeff wasted no time entering the house. He shouted several times but no one answered. The stranger could hear Jeff as he walked up the stairs and down the plushly carpeted hallway.

He tensed and waited for the door to swing open.

Jeff Kane walked past the room without stopping and went into the master bedroom.

The stranger stepped out into the hallway. Jeff's back was to him, reading the note that Cathy had left. The stranger leveled his gun and aimed it at the back of Jeff's head. The gun trembled, and he tightened his grip. Sweat formed on his brow as thoughts raced through his mind. He pictured his lover dangling from the rope. He tightened his finger on the trigger and began to squeeze. His vision narrowed into a tunnel.

"What the fuck is this?" Jeff said once he read the note. "You take the kids out to dinner and to hell with me. To hell with you too." He reached into his jacket pocket, pulled out his monogrammed gold pen, and wrote down the words he had just spoken aloud. He folded the note and tossed it on top of Cathy's jewelry box.

Jeff's outburst snapped him back to reality. Vengeance would be his. This was the promise he had made. But not like this. He took his finger from the trigger. It would be too easy to kill him now, but that wasn't enough pain and suffering. No, he intended a life of torment for Jeff Kane. Jeff Kane would have to live his life knowing that he was responsible for the deaths of so many people that he loved. He lowered the gun, turned, and slipped down the stairs and out the door, happy that he had so easily re-mastered his skills. He returned to his vehicle and waited for Jeff. Jeff would lead him to his next target. Then he would begin taking apart Jeff's life, piece by piece.

After a quick change of clothes, Jeff Kane left his mansion, jumped into his yellow Ferrari Testarossa and left for Ann's apartment.

The stranger started his car and smiled.

CHAPTER 16

It was 7:00 p.m. when Cathy Kane arrived at Claire Pulaski's house in Mount Morris. The front yard was an island of overgrown grass surrounded by dirt with a broken and heaved up sidewalk out front. The house had cracked and peeling paint, a broken handrail on the porch, and the screen door was so damaged it wouldn't close. Claire's house was a reminder to Cathy what it was like to live in poverty.

The air was dead calm and the temperature was 86 degrees, the forecast calling for rain.

After a visit with Cathy's mom and dad, the two women headed out for a night on the town. Their first stop was the Genesee River Hotel. It was a nice place to shoot pool, have a few beers, and drink a couple of shots. It was 10:00 p.m. when Claire and Cathy left and headed for the Yankee Loft.

The rain finally came, some relief from the humidity. The sound of the windshield wipers, the splash of water under the tires, and the faint murmur of the radio filled the car.

"Well, Cathy, I think it's time we found us a couple of Italian studs to screw our brains out," Claire said.

They laughed the rest of the short drive to the Yankee Loft. Cathy was glad to see it hadn't changed. The same wood floor, brass bar stools and hardwood bar she knew and loved as a regular here.

At the far end of the bar, closest to the pool table, Gino Torchia saw them come in. Gino and Cathy both had had secret crushes on each other. And each of them thought the other was out of their league.

Claire made a beeline for Gino's table. She and Gino had hooked up a few times in the back of Gino's van. It was just a physical thing that didn't mean anything to either of them.

"Hey, how's my buddy?" Claire leaned over and gave Gino a kiss on the lips.

"Great! How are you doing tonight, sweetheart?" Gino looked past Claire to Cathy.

"Good. Hey, do you remember Cathy? This is Cathy Kane. She was Cathy Potter in high school."

"Hi, it's nice to see you." Gino reached out and shook hands with Cathy.

"It's nice to see you again too." Cathy beamed. "I don't think we knew each other very well in high school, did we?"

"No, we never did get to know each other." Gino noticed the huge diamond on Cathy's finger. "Are you married now?"

"Well, let's just say that I got married to a guy with a lot of money and a roving eye. So I came to Mount Morris to rediscover myself and have some fun." Cathy gave Claire a wink.

"It sounds like this ought to be a real exciting night." Gino cocked an eyebrow and gave Claire a half smile. "Here's some money, Claire. Why don't you buy us a round of drinks while I visit the little boy's room?" Gino slid a roll of money into Claire's hand and headed to the restroom.

"Sure, sounds great." Claire turned to Cathy and whispered, "What do you think of Gino?"

"Do you and Gino have something going?" Cathy inquired.

"No, not really. We've gotten together once or twice but it's not a *thing*, you know? I mean, who wouldn't want to have sex with him? He's ripped, and did you see his butt? Besides, you know what they say about Italian lovers, once is definitely not enough… especially in Gino's case."

"Well, I might just have to see if he's as good as you say." Cathy laughed.

Ann Chantel grew up in a big city, in a lower income family. As a result, she knew the ins and outs of inner-city life. Ann had always believed that her difficult childhood motivated her to achieve a better life. She currently lived at Colonial Manor, an apartment complex in Gates, a suburb of Rochester.

Jeff had left a note on Ann's desk telling her that he would stop by around seven. He offered to bring champagne, and suggested she wear something sexy. The note had cheered her up. She was excited her relationship with Jeff seemed to be progressing nicely.

When Jeff arrived, Ann opened the door wearing a satin robe and a smile that could have lit up all of Rochester.

"Hi." Ann reached out and pulled him into the apartment, kissing him passionately, reminding Jeff why he was there.

"Do you always open the door for strangers?"

"I saw you coming." Ann closed the door. "Welcome to my humble abode." Ann led Jeff up the stairs to her living room.

"Would you like a tour of my apartment?" Ann offered in a cheerful voice. Even though it wasn't much, she was proud of it.

"I'd love a tour, and since I can see the living room and the kitchen from here, why don't we start with your bedroom?" Jeff picked her up and carried her to the bedroom.

Ann wrapped her legs around Jeff's waist and he slid his hands under her satin robe. By the time they reached Ann's bed, with its giant sheer canopy, Jeff's right hand had begun to prepare Ann for what was next.

Jeff gently laid Ann down on the bed so he could kneel down before her, and he untied her satin robe, and found her body even hotter than he remembered.

He undressed quickly and reached for her legs. He wrapped them around his waist and pulled her into the most unusual position she had ever experienced. Her legs still wrapped around his waist—her shoulders and head were the only part of her body touching the bed when he penetrated her and began his relentless incursion.

When Jeff was finished, Ann pulled herself up and put her arms around him. She started rocking her hips, grinding against him. He could feel his legs weakening, so he turned around and sat on the bed, leaving her straddling him. He lay back on the bed with his hands behind his head. The sight of Ann's breasts heaving up and down kept him hard.

When the second wave of ecstasy ebbed, she leaned over and kissed Jeff several times.

Ann got up and asked, "Why don't you open up the champagne while I get dressed?"

She slipped on her robe and went to freshen up.

"Honey, we have one small problem. I forgot to pick up the champagne on my way here," Jeff admitted sheepishly.

"I've got some wine in the refrigerator. Why don't you open it and pour us each a glass?" Ann suggested then turned on the shower.

"Now that's a great idea." Jeff wiped a trickle of sweat from his brow.

When Jeff opened the refrigerator, he couldn't help but see the plate of leftovers sitting on the second shelf. Knowing that this could be his only meal of the night, he picked up a hamburger and started to eat it while he looked for the wine.

"Here." Jeff found the wine on the bottom shelf. "Premiat, hmm, I've never heard of it. Well, it has a cork, it can't be too bad." Jeff started looking for a corkscrew as he munched on the hamburger. He was so busy eating that he didn't hear the water shut off.

"Is there something I can help you find?" Ann asked, walking into the kitchen with a towel wrapped around her.

"I was looking for a corkscrew to open the wine with," Jeff said, with a hamburger in one hand and a knife in the other.

"Why are you eating a hamburger?" Ann was dripping water onto the floor.

"Because Cathy stiffed me on dinner tonight, and I'm going over to a friend's house to play poker a little later. I don't like to drink on an empty stomach. If I do, I'll get really drunk and lose a lot of money."

"I thought we were going out to dinner." Ann's voice was sharp.

"My note didn't say that. It said that I'd stop by at seven, and I did." Jeff could tell Ann was upset. "I'm sorry if you misunderstood."

"I understand completely. You came here for a quick lay so you could brag to your friends about what a big stud you are. You've got some nerve coming here, screwing me, eating my food and drinking my wine."

"Ann, you've got it all wrong." Jeff tried to explain but Ann wouldn't have it.

"No, Jeff, *you've* got it all wrong. I'm not a slut, and I'm not going to be a sex toy for you. I must be really stupid to think that you'd leave your wife for me."

"Who said anything about me leaving my wife?" Jeff asked in disbelief.

"Nobody did. Now please leave." Ann had tears in her eyes.

"Did I miss something here?" Jeff shoved the last bite into his mouth.

"Yes." Ann snapped. "I asked you to leave."

"Look, Ann, I think there's some kind of misunderstanding here."

"Don't worry, Jeff, it's all very clear to me now." She crossed her arms and glared.

Jeff decided that retreat was the better part of valor and slunk back to the bedroom to get dressed. When he returned, he said, "Look, I'll stop back later tonight, say around two or so, to straighten everything out," and stepped outside.

Mrs. Cooper from Apartment 3 was coming in and she saw the tears streaking down Ann's cheeks. "Is everything okay, Ann?"

"Yes, Mrs. Cooper. He's just leaving."

"I'll stop back later." Jeff backed away from the unpleasant scene.

"Don't bother, Jeff." Ann wiped tears from her eyes and straightened.

"Ann, honey, you have to be careful. Did he hurt you? Are you okay?" Mrs. Cooper put her arm around Ann's waist. "Who was that man?"

"He's my boss. I'm okay, Mrs. Cooper, thank you for your help," Ann said.

Mrs. Cooper was a short, robust black woman with a heart of gold, always keeping an eye on the neighborhood. If anyone ever needed anything, somehow, Mrs. Cooper was there.

"It's like I was saying, honey, you've got to be careful. Why, on my way in, I saw a strange-looking fellow with an out-of-town license plate, just sitting in front of our building. God knows who he could be. For all I know, he's some murderer."

"Mrs. Cooper, thank you so much for your help, but I've got to get back into my apartment and get some clothes on," Ann said.

"Okay, dear, but if you need anything or if you just want to talk, I'll be home. Just knock." Mrs. Cooper's sympathy knew no bounds.

"I'll do that. Thank you again." With that, Ann closed the door behind her.

After a long hot shower and plenty of tears, Ann decided that she needed to go out and have a good time. She knew just the place to go and find a friend, or so she hoped.

CHAPTER 17

It was eight o'clock when Michael walked into Woody's Bar and Grille, dressed in jeans, and a navy blue golf shirt. He scanned the bar for Amanda. When he didn't see her, he found an open spot at the crowded bar and ordered a Molson Golden. The time dragged but the happy hour crowd started to thin and bar seats opened up.

It was eight thirty when a man in his late twenties asked if he could sit next to Michael. He introduced himself as Carl. Michael, not realizing that Carl had already taken full advantage of happy hour prices, agreed. After thirty minutes of Carl's non-stop chatter, Michael began to wonder about Amanda being so late.

A gorgeous brunette wearing a miniskirt and a silk blouse that revealed a tantalizing view of her low-cut lace bra was staring at Michael. There was the hint of a smile on her ruby red lips, her six-inch heels accentuated her legs, and she was oozing sex from every pore of her body.

She asked, "Do you mind if I join you?"

"No, help yourself. Sit down and let me buy you a drink." Carl's voice was slurred.

Michael rolled his eyes. "Thanks, Carl."

"Hi, I'm Gina." She sat down on the stool to Michael's right and extended her hand.

"How ya doin', Gina, I'm Carl, and this here is my friend, Michael." Carl reached across Michael and shook Gina's hand.

"Hi, Gina, it's nice to meet you," Michael said, giving Carl a look.

"You look like I feel." Gina flagged down the bartender.

"You mean kind of disgusted?" Michael noticed how translucent Gina's blouse was and his brow creased.

"That would be one way of putting it," she agreed and ordered a glass of white wine from the bartender.

"Take it out of this," Carl offered, as he pushed his pile of money toward the bartender.

"Thank you, Carl," Gina purred.

"My pleasure, Gina." Gina's long slender legs grabbed Carl's attention. This was a fox, and Carl would do anything to sleep with her.

"I'm so upset. I just don't know what to do. I really need someone to talk to. Could you be that someone, please?" Gina leaned over, exposing a large amount of cleavage.

"Well, actually, I'm waiting—" Michael began, wondering how to get away without being a jerk.

Carl interrupted, "Sure, we'd love to help you out. You just relax, take it easy, drink some wine, and when you're ready, we'll be here for you. Michael, could you please move your stool back so I can talk a little bit with Gina?" Carl was practically salivating.

"Sure." Michael pushed his stool back, taking the opportunity to look for Amanda.

Gina started out by telling Carl and Michael that she felt betrayed and hurt because she'd just found her boyfriend in bed with one of her girlfriends.

"I went to my boyfriend's apartment wanting to celebrate his new promotion. I snuck in to surprise him. On the way to his bedroom, I unbuttoned my blouse." She pouted. "I also took off my panties and tossed them on a living room chair. When I got to his bedroom, he was too busy screwing my best friend to notice I was there. Humiliated, I was so upset that I left without my panties and came straight here to get drunk."

Carl's jaw dropped. In an attempt to recover, he motioned to the bartender for another round for Michael and himself. "You poor thing."

"I just want to get drunk and forget the whole thing." Gina uncrossed and re-crossed her legs, leaving Carl with an overpowering desire to peek up her short skirt.

"Now do you understand why I needed a friend?" Gina asked Michael leaning closer, resting her hand on his thigh.

Michael gently moved Gina's hand and said, "Yes I do, and what I generally do at times like that is get very drunk."

Gina was poured on the charm. "That sounds like a great idea. Can you believe that after a long day at work, I spent my evenings making him chocolate chip cookies? Every night when that man came home, he wanted me to give him a blowjob while he ate those damn chocolate chip cookies. I'm such a fool for trusting him." A single artful tear fell from Gina's eye.

Carl could feel his pants growing tighter. "You deserve better than that, better than him. You need a man who will appreciate your skills and take care of you."

"Will you have some drinks with me?" Gina implored Michael. "Help me forget that jerk."

Michael sighed. "Well, like I was saying, I'm waiting for someone, and when she gets here, I'll be leaving with her."

"I'll get drunk with you," Carl offered.

"Have another drink. Just until she gets here?" Gina went from victim to seductress without missing a beat.

"Sure." Michael waved to the bartender for another round and checked his watch again.

Nearly two hours and fifteen minutes had passed, and Gina's spirits seemed to be lifting. The trio were doing shots of peppermint schnapps and drinking beer. Gina's soft, gentle hand started to feel familiar on Michael's leg and back. Every time she placed her hand on him, he gently pulled it off. Once, she took his left hand in both of hers and put it on the inside of her thigh. Michael excused himself to go to the men's room. In spite of that, the time passed quickly, and to his surprise, Michael realized he was enjoying himself.

Carl wondered how he could get rid of Michael so he could hit on Gina.

Michael wondered what happened to Amanda. She was three hours late, his cell calls all went straight to voicemail, and she hadn't called to offer an explanation as to why she was so late. He briefly entertained the idea that something could have happened to her, but he dismissed it the thought. She wasn't far away and he was feeling the effects of the alcohol.

Gina wondered what she was doing trying to seduce the first guy she'd ever met who looked at her like a person instead of some sex object. She wondered how her life would be different if she had met Michael in college. Could she give up her profession for a man as genuine and caring as Michael?

Gina shook her head to clear it and got back to work. "Michael, your friend seems awfully late. Are you sure she's not in bed with one of your buddies?" Guilt washed over her as the words came out of her mouth.

"That's not possible." Michael's friends were all dedicated, loyal members of the MFB Black Ops team.

"How can you be so sure?" Gina put her right hand on his leg, just above his knee.

"You don't know my friends," Michael joked, which got the three of them laughing.

Realizing she was getting nowhere with Michael, Gina went for the jugular. "Could you please take me home and stay with me for a while, Michael?" When Gina sensed his hesitation, she pressed him, "I'm a little buzzed, a little horny, and vulnerable right now, but I promise I won't try to give you any wild sexual pleasure. *Please* take me home, Michael."

"Gina, if I wasn't involved with someone right now, I'd take you home in a heartbeat, but I just can't do it. Maybe Carl can take you."

"Sure, I'll take you home, and I'd love to stay. Even all night, if that's what you want," Carl jumped on the chance.

"Are you sure, Michael? I really would love for you to spend the night with me." Gina couldn't believe he was turning down her offer.

"I'm really sorry, but I should go and try to call my girlfriend again."

Michael went toward the door to get a stronger signal, and Carl made his play. But Gina wasn't listening to him. After a quick check to make sure she had everything, she bolted toward the back door. Once outside, she scanned the street for Amanda. It wasn't until Amanda flashed her lights that Gina saw Amanda's British racing-green Jaguar XK convertible across the street and down about a block.

"I didn't recognize the Jag with the top up," Gina said as she climbed into the Jag.

"I don't usually drive the convertible in the rain," Amanda replied. Getting right to the point, she asked, "How did it go?"

"Honey, you've got the strongest willed man I've ever met. He just passed up a night of heaven in the hope that you'd be here." Gina smiled wistfully.

Amanda's eyes widened. There was an expression on Gina's face which Amanda had never seen before. A muffled ring broke the silence. Amanda slowly picked up the phone.

"Amanda, are you okay?" It was Michael.

"Yes, Michael, I'm fine. My meeting's over—I'm almost there." Amanda was smiling and Michael could hear it in her voice.

"Great. I can't wait to see you." Michael breathed a sigh of relief.

Since Gina looked and smelled as if she had consumed a large amount of alcohol, Amanda suspected that Michael had been drinking heavily too, but his voice sounded like it always did. He could hold his liquor. "I can't wait to see you too," she said.

As she hung up the phone, it finally sunk in that Michael had passed the test. Relief crashed over Amanda like a breaker, and she smiled so hard it hurt. "Thanks for your help, Gina. I don't know what I'd do without you."

"Don't thank me. Michael is a very nice man. I had a lot of fun. I wish you two the very best." Gina's voice sounded sad but sincere, and as she walked away, for the first time in a long time, she felt that she was more than a pretty woman and a good lover. Maybe she could find happiness.

Amanda hurried into the bar, hugged Michael, and ordered a drink—the first of many.

CHAPTER 18

It was eleven p.m. when Ann Chantel stepped out of her silver BMW 228i coupe into the misty rain, creating prisms around the security lights in the parking lot of the California Brew Haus. Ann wasn't sure how she was going to tell Joshua she was sorry for acting like a naïve fool. She was hoping to convince him to give her a second chance. She didn't know that her life depended on it.

The California Brew Haus was practically a landmark in Rochester. The dark interior, secluded parking lot, and the fact that its next-door neighbor was a strip joint, attracted some seedy characters from the city's gritty north side. On the plus side, beer was cheap, the clientele was lively, and the many pool tables resulted a fast-paced and recession-proof bar.

When Ann walked through the front doors, she saw Joshua in the game room playing pool. She looked for an open barstool. Better to watch Joshua from afar and build up some confidence first.

Sipping on her second beer, Ann was enjoying Joshua's winning streak. He played pool as if he owned the table. His bank shots, combination shots, and long shots all seemed to fall where he wanted them to. Nearly forty minutes had passed when Ann noticed the losing players kept handing Joshua drinks, probably as part of a bet.

After her third beer, feeling a buzz and some courage, Ann decided it was time.

When she got to his table, he looked up and said, "Look what the cat dragged in." He straightened and watched her warily.

"Hello, Joshua." Ann put on her sexiest smile. Her shorts were sinfully short and her top was tight. She had just the right amount of cleavage to miss looking slutty, or at least she hoped so. She leaned forward slightly to show off the twins.

"What are you doing here? Is Jeff busy?" Joshua pretended not to notice how sexy Ann looked as he watched his opponent make a perfect combination shot.

Shit, he didn't look twice at my cleavage, she thought. "Oh, that. Well, let's just say I've learned my lesson. So I thought I'd stop by and see how you're doing," Ann replied cheerfully.

Joshua stood up to take his next shot. He missed what looked like an easy shot, and his frustration was obvious. "So, you thought you would just stop by and see if good ol' Joshua could cheer you up. Is that it?" He picked up the chalk and went to work on the end of his stick.

"I was wrong about Jeff, and I realized my mistake. I felt guilty about the way I treated you. I thought I would apologize and buy you a couple of beers." Ann looked like a puppy dog, practically begging Joshua for forgiveness. "I was hoping that *maaaybe* we could start over."

Joshua turned his attention back to the pool table. It was his turn to shoot, and he was losing... badly. He got up from his stool and shot his worst shot in years. He pulled a twenty out of his pocket and laid it on the table.

"So, you thought a quick 'I'm sorry,' a couple of beers, and presto, we'd be back together again?" Joshua asked.

"Not quite, but I'm willing to try." He sounded edgy. This wasn't going the way she's hoped.

He said, "Let's see if I got this right. Jeff Kane, the rich and powerful scion of the Kane Empire, dumps you, and you suddenly find out what it feels like to be walked on. And that's supposed to somehow make me forgive you for treating me like dirt?" He held up his wrist. "You gave me this watch on our second date. You wanted me to remember that anytime was a good time to call you."

Ann's face flushed.

"The inscription reads, 'Remember me, Ann.' I thought we had something going. Right up until you tried to steal my job and jumped in the sack with the boss," he said harshly.

"I came here tonight because I wanted us to be friends, at least. It looks like that was a mistake." She couldn't hide her frustration.

"Friends don't steal jobs from each other." He was furious now. "You knew exactly what you were doing when you went to Minnesota. You should have said something to me."

"You don't want to talk to me. You wanted to talk to Jeff. If you ever cool off and feel like talking, give me a call." Ann got up and made a beeline for the door before Joshua could see her tears. So much for trying to be sexy and irresistible.

Her relationship with Joshua was over, but that was the least of her problems.

CHAPTER 19

The skills he acquired as a part-time locksmith and in the Marine Corps were paying off. The main entry door deadbolt and entry lock were as easy to open as the locks on the apartment itself. Ann Chantel had been kind enough to leave a light on, making it easy to move around her apartment. He took it all in. Very middle class, he decided. The vase with silk flowers added a feminine touch to the living room. And of course, the large screen TV so typical of the younger generation.

In the bathroom he could smell the moisture of her shower, and the vanilla lotion she favored. Perfume bottles and makeup were scattered across the counter. All of the tricks of her craft were laid out for him to see. "Pretentious little bitch, nothing about you is real," he murmured absently.

The bedroom door was ajar and inside he could smell the sex. He breathed in deeply and closed his eyes. He could see them in his mind's eye. Jeff had ravished her body and she gave into his every demand. He moaned and gave his attention to her dresser, inspecting everything and touching nothing. He left the room with a final deep breath, enjoying their scent. There was a platter of meat and a half-empty bottle of wine on the kitchen counter. A long knife with a black handle was sticking up from the meat.

He was drawn to the knife. Its slick black handle was smooth and he could see fibers of meat still clinging to its long, sharp, blade.

"This will work just fine." He retrieved a handkerchief from his pocket and carefully picked up the knife and dropped it into a plastic bag that he'd helped himself to. "Time to go to Mount Morris, but I'll be back soon enough, and then we'll have our fun."

The ex-Marine had spent two years in special ops as a sniper and his training gave him certain specialized skills. To be stealthy and sneak up on the enemy, to blend in to the surroundings, and to kill with a pistol, rifle, or knife with equal facility were all part of the training. Even though he had been dishonorably discharged, the skills had been mastered, and now he would put them to use to exact his revenge.

It was midnight and Cathy Kane was in the women's room at the Yankee Loft, preparing for the moment she had fantasized about years before. After having spent the better part of the evening reminiscing about the good old days with Gino Torchia, the two of them had decided to act on their secret desires in the back of Gino's van. As the lipstick glided across her lips, Cathy could feel the butterflies in her stomach growing stronger. There was no guilt or remorse for her husband. Instead, Cathy was pleased that she could finally start to get even with him. It was a bonus that Gino could just be ten times the lover that Jeff was.

As Cathy headed toward the door, Claire gave her a thumbs up.

The night was dark and the rain had caused a light fog and a muddy parking lot. Crossing the lot to Gino's van, she heard what sounded like a car backfiring.

"I hope that thing runs. We may want to have some AC on," Cathy said nervously to herself.

Cathy's left heel caught in the mud and stuck. When she bent over to retrieve it, a dark green sedan sped by and sprayed her with mud as it tore out of the parking lot.

"I don't believe this." She examined her muddy clothes. "What kind of drunken idiot would do such a thing? He practically hit me, for crying out loud."

When she reached the van, no sign of Gino, just fogged windows. "Hey, stud, you're fogging up the windows without me. Don't tell me you couldn't wait."

She wrapped her knuckles on it and circled around to the back doors. When she opened them, she was greeted by a smoky haze and a disgusting coppery stench that made her wince.

"Gino, I don't know if I can do this…" Then she realized blood was seeping into the carpet from Gino's head.

She turned from the horror and the stench and began to vomit.

After an eternity, Cathy slowly turned and looked again. The dawning realization that she must never be connected to this terrible thing filled her with panic.

Before she closed the van door, she noticed a pistol lying on Gino's stomach. *It can't be suicide because the gun wasn't in his hand. How could I explain being here?* These thoughts raced through Cathy's mind and the solution was the same every time. Run, run, run.

And she ran for the Yankee Loft, slipping and sliding in the mud and rain. Claire was talking to an old girlfriend at the far end of the bar.

"Well, that didn't take long." Claire tilted her head and raised her eyebrows.

"Claire, I've got to talk to you right now." Cathy pulled her from the barstool.

"Cathy, what's wrong? You're hurting my arm."

Cathy didn't speak until they were safely ensconced in the woman's room. She confirmed they were alone.

"We've got to leave. Gino's been murdered, and I can't be connected to this, or Jeff will kill me. We have to leave before someone finds the body."

"Cathy, calm down." Claire shook her shoulders. It was then that she realized that Cathy's clothes were soaked. "Is that blood?"

"No, it's mud. Claire, are you listening to me? Gino is dead and we have to get out of here."

"Did you and Gino get into a fight?" Claire's face turned white. "What do you mean dead? Did *you* kill him?" Disbelief and horror were starting to set in.

"No. I told you, this is mud. Someone killed him before I got there. My heel got stuck in the mud. When I bent over to get it, a car drove by and splashed mud all over me. I walked over to the van, and that's when I saw blood all over the place and Gino's eyes were wide open. It was terrible." Cathy started to tremble.

"Oh my God, he really is dead." The reality of what Cathy was saying had finally hit Claire full blast. "Cathy, we've got to get out of here... You go get the car, and I'll be right out."

"Claire, don't say a word to anyone. If anyone finds out, I'll be ruined." Tears streamed down her cheeks.

"Don't worry. I don't want to be involved any more than you do." Claire was in full panic mode now.

Claire quickly and quietly retrieved her purse from the bar and raced outside. Cathy pulled up the pink Cadillac next to the bar and Claire jumped in. On the way to Claire's house, the two friends devised a plan. Cathy dropped Claire off and went home.

Claire called Cathy's mother and explained that Cathy had gone home at ten o'clock with a bad headache, and she would be back the next day to pick up the children.

CHAPTER 20

Michael and Amanda were enjoying themselves at Woody's Bar and Grille. Amanda was thrilled that Michael had passed the test, and for the first time in her life, she was with a man that she knew she could trust.

Michael's cell phone rang shortly after Amanda had excused herself to use the restroom. "Hello, this is Callaghan."

It was Johnson at HQ. "Commander Callaghan, I'm sorry to call you at this hour, but I have an important update on the Black Blade of Allah."

"What have you got, Johnson?" Michael scanned the bar and cupped the phone so no one could hear his conversation.

"We just picked up two operatives entering Montreal. Our facial recognition program is running them right now. We verified the tattoo on one of the men and both are wearing the signature black suits."

"Understood. Monitor all their activities. Tap into all traffic cams and airport security cameras. See how long you can stay with them." Michael thanked Johnson for the update and hung up.

Amanda returned from the ladies' room to find a fresh drink and a shot of peppermint schnapps waiting for her. "You're so thoughtful, aren't you? If I didn't know better, I'd say you were trying to get me drunk."

"I would never do such a thing. Besides, you need to be on your game tomorrow at the cottage when you meet my friends," he teased.

"Oh yes, I did promise that we could do whatever you wanted this weekend. So, what are we doing?" Amanda sipped her drink and waited for the big news.

Michael let the warmth of his bourbon caress his throat before answering. "We're going to my cottage in Bayshore Estates. It's up in the Thousand Islands area. My friends are dying to meet you."

"Your friends are dying to meet me? What did you tell them about me?" Amanda was happy that Michael was talking about her to his friends.

"I didn't tell them anything. Greg Connors told them that I was seeing you and they all want to meet you."

"I see. Well, here's to going to your cottage and meeting your friends." Amanda lifted her shot glass.

When Michael clinked his shot glass with hers, he said, "Cheers to meeting my friends and a relaxing weekend at Bayshore Estates."

CHAPTER 21

There was a knock on the door at two forty-five and when she opened it, Cathy Kane was surprised to see Joshua Stein. He was five feet eleven, had medium-length curly brown hair, and reeked of booze.

Joshua had switched to bourbon after his heated discussion with Ann Chantel. He was ready to confront Jeff and quit his job. Trying to keep his cool, he managed a tight smile and said, "Hi, Cathy, I'm sorry to bother you so late, but I really need to speak with Jeff. Is he home?"

"No, but why don't you come in for a while, so we can talk?" Cathy asked, thinking that Joshua could be useful as an alibi.

"Talk? Talk about what?" Joshua realized Cathy was dressed in a sheer peignoir. She was beautiful and Jeff didn't deserve her.

"Oh, I think we have an awful lot to talk about." Cathy gently pulled him inside and closed the door behind him.

Cathy led Joshua to the recreation room. He admired her shapely derriere.

Joshua was alone with Cathy Kane, and she was in a very sexy gown. Cathy was five feet four with a body that wouldn't quit. Her shoulder-length brown hair glistened in the lamplight. Her blue eyes were the color of the Caribbean Sea. Joshua couldn't take his eyes off her perfectly shaped breasts.

He could smell jasmine in her damp hair as he admired the outline of her beautiful body. His mood was changing from anger to something else.

"Why don't you've a seat, and I'll pour us some wine," Cathy offered, pulling a bottle of French wine from a wine rack.

Joshua sat at the corner of the bar closest to Cathy. He could feel his mood begin to lighten.

"Why don't you sit on the couch, where we can be more comfortable?" Cathy suggested as she poured the wine into Mikasa crystal wineglasses.

"Sure." Joshua got up from the bar. "I've always liked this room."

"I hope that's not all you've admired," Cathy said in a husky voice, handing Joshua a glass of wine.

Cathy slid onto the couch next to Joshua. Cathy started out by telling Joshua that she had known that Jeff was cheating on her for some time. She also guessed that Joshua was there to confront Jeff and quit the company.

The wine was excellent. Joshua wasn't much of a wine man, but with wine this good, he could make a change. "You're right on all counts." Joshua smiled. Things were definitely looking up.

Cathy took a sip of wine and licked her lips suggestively. "That would make it too easy on Jeff. He's had it too easy his whole life."

"What do you suggest?" Joshua swirled the wine in his glass.

"Not you, us." Cathy set her glass down.

He searched her eyes. "What do you mean?"

"This," she whispered. She leaned over and kissed him passionately, and began to unbutton his shirt.

Joshua pulled away. "One question."

"Make it quick." Her lips brushed against his neck.

"Will Jeff be home tonight?"

"No. Do you feel better?" She stood up and pulled Joshua to his feet, her hand finding the bulge in his pants.

"Not yet, but I think that's about to change."

After another long sensual kiss, Cathy led Joshua up the stairs to the master bedroom. As they began to undress each other, Joshua could feel his passion throbbing. He didn't notice his wristwatch falling to the floor.

Once they were naked, Cathy sat Joshua down on the edge of the bed, knelt down in front of him and began to pleasure him with her mouth. Before he could reach climax, she kissed her way up his strong torso and positioned herself for the moment she had been waiting for since she first learned that Jeff had cheated on her. Joshua lay back as she engulfed his manhood.

It had been a long time since she'd had sex and even longer since it felt this good. They made love for what seemed like hours before they finally collapsed in each other's arms.

"Do you know what I think?" Cathy was gulping air.

"No." Joshua tried to catch his breath while admiring her sexy body.

Cathy was feeling young, sexy and wanted again, a feeling she hadn't had in many years. The wheels were starting to turn. "I think we should get rid of Jeff so you and I can get married and take over the company."

Joshua chuckled. "I'd like to get rid of Jeff, but I need to rest for a while first." Joshua was still breathing hard and the alcohol he'd had that evening was taking its toll.

His intention was to rest for a while before leaving. The soft mattress, the silk sheets, and the fluffy pillows made that impossible. What seemed like minutes quickly turned into hours, and this would turn out to be a very big mistake.

CHAPTER 22

Ann Chantel walked into her apartment just before three after spending two hours at a local tavern. She ordered two extra beers at last call and spent the rest of her evening talking with some locals. She had locked up and was headed for her bedroom, when someone knocked on the door.

Her heart sank. Jeff said he'd be back after his poker game ended, so she went the door.

Feeling too drunk, used, and abused to deal with Jeff's ego, she said, "I don't know how you got into the building, Mr. Jeff Kane," and unlocked the deadbolt. "But when I said not to bother coming back, I meant it."

She opened the door, ready to confront the two-timing, womanizing, loser Jeff Kane.

"Hey. You aren't…" Ann realized she didn't check the peephole. And then she saw the knife.

She tried to scream, but the terror was too much. The dark-handled knife with meat still clinging to it plunged into her throat, penetrating her vocal cord but missing the jugular.

She staggered back with her hands on her throat and tried to retreat up the steps to her living room. He caught her easily and yanked her back down the steps.

The intruder's face was twisted into a murderous mask. He kicked the door shut and raised his arm again.

Ann kicked at him but was too weak to slow him down. With a strange feeling of inevitability, she lay there helpless as the blade buried itself in her chest with a dull crunch. The pain came next, followed by her own blood spraying her face.

The knife stayed in Ann's chest for a moment or two, giving her hope. Her mind seemed to clear. Hanging on to her throat with one hand and clutching the knife in her chest with the hand, she shook her head, pleading with her eyes.

Ann's hopes vanished when the man licked her blood from his face and smiled down at her. He jerked the knife from her chest and raised it back over his head. Blood flowed out of her chest and the pain became unbearable. She closed her eyes and blackness consumed her.

He was happy with his work. He'd wondered if he still had the stealth and speed to perform an assassination with a knife.

He'd been sloppy earlier—he missed his target and it was small consolation that he had caused some collateral damage. Maybe the gun would be enough. Only time would tell.

He knew he needed to keep honing his skills. He had to be at peak performance in the very near future. There would be no escaping his wrath.

He watched Ann bleed out, placed the murder weapon next to the body, cleaned up in her bathroom and left, closing the door quietly behind him.

Ann was his second victim and he was getting better.

CHAPTER 23

Cathy and Joshua woke up to a loud banging. It was full daylight outside and as they both tried to figure out what they had heard, the pounding resumed. Reality hit them like a slap on the face—someone was knocking on the front door.

"Who could that be?" Cathy bolted from the bed and went to the front window.

Joshua was frantically searching for his clothes. "I don't know, but I've got to get out of here before someone finds out about us."

"It's the cops." Panic washed through Cathy's body.

Joshua looked up with his mouth agape. "What the hell do they want? We can't be arrested for adultery, can we?"

"I don't know." Cathy raced into the walk-in closet in search of clothes. She knew she needed an alibi, and Joshua was it.

An amplified voice shattered the morning. "This is the Monroe County Sheriff's Department. You have ten seconds to open the door, or we will break it down."

Blouse in hand, Cathy said, "Holy shit, we better hurry."

"I'm right behind you." Joshua slipped on his sneakers and grabbed his shirt.

Cathy stopped on the stairs and yelled, "I'll be right there, please wait just one more second." Then she turned to Joshua and said, "Listen, Joshua, we've got to have a good reason for you to be here so early. I'm going to tell the sheriff that you stopped by last night to talk with Jeff and he wasn't here. I told you I thought I saw a prowler so I asked you to spend the night, and you did, as a favor to me." Cathy was out of breath and brushing her hair out of her face. Panic was creeping back in.

"Okay, but where did I sleep?" Joshua frantically tucked in his shirt.

"You slept on the couch in the billiards room. We'll say you fell asleep there." Cathy wiped the sleep from her eyes and ran her fingers through her hair.

Taking a deep breath, Cathy opened the door to three police officers. A Mount Morris Village officer, along with the Mount Morris chief of police, and a Monroe County sheriff's deputy with a warrant to search her home. The police were asking questions regarding Jeff's whereabouts.

Cathy began to tell the story that she and Joshua had agreed on to one of the officers. The other two searched her house.

Cathy was jolted back to reality when she heard the chief of police say, "There was a murder last night in Mount Morris, and your husband's gun was found at the scene." Cathy's mind went back to the scene of the murder. She could see the gun, but this time she recognized it as Jeff's .38 caliber Smith and Wesson. Her head was swimming and she felt dizzy.

"Mrs. Kane, I'm afraid your husband has a lot of explaining to do. Where can we reach him?"

Cathy regained her composure. "Like I said, he goes out on the first Friday night of each month to play poker with his buddies. I really don't where the game was last night, or who the players are, for that matter. He's usually home by ten the next morning." Cathy's voice was shaking and her face was white.

Time dragged as the police conducted their search. After what seemed like hours to Cathy, someone yelled for the chief from the master bedroom. The chief came out of the kitchen and headed for the stairs.

"I'll get it," Joshua said.

The chief and Cathy waited while Joshua opened the door.

"Mr. Kane, I'm Detective Hill, with the Gates Police Department, and this is Officer Barnes, from the Monroe County Sheriff's Office." Detective Hill was nearing fifty years old, had a potbelly, and wore a blue blazer missing the middle button.

"Oh, uh, I'm not Jeff Kane. My name is Joshua Stein, and I'm just a friend of the family, actually an employee, but Mrs. Kane is here. Would you like to speak with her?" *Damn it, more cops. From the city this time?* He wondered what was going on.

The thought that something might have happened to Jeff sent her to the door. "I'm Cathy Kane."

"Is your husband Jeff Kane?" Detective Hill asked in a raspy voice.

"Yes." Sweat was dripping down Cathy's back.

"Is he home?" His voice was irritating.

"No, he's been away since yesterday evening." The detective drew a folded paper from his coat.

"I have a warrant to search your home, Mrs. Kane." Detective Hill handed Cathy the paper. "If he arrives while we're here, I also have a warrant for his arrest."

"You have a warrant for his arrest? What are you going to arrest him for?" Cathy was stunned.

"He's wanted for the murder of Ann Chantel." The detective handed Cathy the warrant for Jeff's arrest.

The world suddenly became hazy for Joshua Stein. "What? Are you sure? Jeff murdered Ann last night?" he asked. "How... why would he? What happened?"

"We have a witness who saw Mr. Kane and Ms. Chantel arguing earlier in the evening, and our witness heard Mr. Kane threaten to return later to, and I quote, 'straighten her out.' We also have his fingerprints on the murder weapon." The detective studied Cathy and Joshua with an air of suspicion.

Joshua and Cathy stared at each other, wide-eyed. Both of them had flashbacks of their conversation from the night before. *'How great it would be if we could get rid of Jeff, take over the company, and live out our sexual fantasies.'* Then, like an explosion, it hit them. Ann Chantel was dead.

"May we come in now?" Detective Hill asked.

"Yes," Cathy replied, still staring at Joshua.

After a brief discussion between police agencies as to protocol, they all proceeded upstairs to the master bedroom.

The officer that had summoned the chief was standing in the hallway. He led them to the note that Jeff had left Cathy, on top of Cathy's jewelry box. Detective Hill picked up the note with gloved hands and read it aloud.

"From the heavy indentation on the paper, and the language, it looks as though Mr. Kane was quite upset." Detective Hill asked Cathy, "Had you and Mr. Kane been fighting?"

"No."

Holding a family picture, the chief asked, "Are your kids home, Mrs. Kane?"

"No, they're at my mother's." Cathy had forgotten all about her kids.

"If you and your husband weren't fighting, why do you suppose he would leave you a note like this?" Detective Hill jumped in.

"I don't know." Cathy began to sob. The reality of her husband being wanted for two murders was too much for her to bear.

Detective Hill gently ushered Cathy to the bed, so she could sit and try to gather her composure. As he turned away, Detective Hill's foot bumped something concealed by the bedskirt. When he pushed the fabric back, his eyebrows lifted and he reached down and picked up a watch. It was inscribed. "Remember me, Ann." He studied the watch carefully, and then asked Cathy, "Is this your husband's watch?"

"I don't know. I don't think so. It doesn't look familiar."

"Does the inscription on the back mean anything to you? Remember me, Ann?" The detective waited for a reaction.

"No, it doesn't mean anything to me." Cathy looked at Joshua and he shrugged.

"Could I see that, please?" The chief slipped the watch into an evidence bag.

Detective Hill and the chief began to argue about who was going to take the watch into evidence. The rest continued to search the house. Cathy got up and went out into the hallway with Joshua.

"Let's go," he said urgently. "I could use a drink to settle my nerves."

Cathy sighed. "That sounds good to me. I can't believe what's going on here. It feels like a bad dream." He followed her to the second-floor study for a dose of courage.

CHAPTER 24

Amanda Kane slowly opened her eyes. She could see the second hand on Michael's alarm clock pounding off the time. Amanda moaned as she rolled over to face Michael Callaghan.

When she realized that he wasn't in bed, she quickly rolled back over to check the clock again. It was 8:30 a.m., and the large amount of alcohol she consumed on an empty stomach the night before felt like a vice on her temples.

Despite her hangover, she managed to crack a smile as she wandered down the long second floor hallway. She went down the stairs and headed into the kitchen.

Amanda Kane was five feet eight inches and weighed less than one hundred and twenty pounds. Her long, flowing blonde hair had a wavy bounce to it and her brown eyes shimmered like stars. Amanda had learned many years ago that most men only wanted her for her money. Sure, she was good looking, some would even say "hot," but in the end, it always came down to money and not love. Amanda had decided two years ago that she had endured enough heartache and pain. She decided to stop dating, which ended when she met Michael Callaghan.

The note was leaning up against Amanda's coffee cup. She sipped her mocha coffee and read, "Good morning, sweetheart. I'm out loading the SUV for our weekend in the Thousand Islands. You did say we could do whatever I wanted for the whole weekend, remember?"

Amanda raised her eyes from the note, then slowly moved her arms away from her body and looked down to see what she was wearing. She couldn't remember putting on Michael's flannel shirt, or taking off her bra, but that didn't matter right now. What mattered was the fact that she needed a cold shower and a touch of makeup to cover the dark circles under her eyes.

After a quick shower, Amanda wrapped herself in a towel and darted from the marble and tiled master bathroom into the master bedroom to get dressed. As she was dressing, she surveyed Michael's room. The expensively decorated room had original paintings of both oil and chalk that hung in what appeared to be very old gilded frames. There were two cedar walk-in closets in the room. One held expensive suits, ties of every color, shoes for work and play, and shelves of boxes. The second cedar walk-in closet contained casual clothes, sneakers and work boots.

An oak dressing table had a large antique framed mirror attached, and a thin state-of-the-art laptop computer. A moderately-sized high definition flat-screen TV hung on the wall opposite the bed. She could see the downtown Rochester skyline and a view of the Genesee River from his second-floor bedroom window.

When she was finished dressing, she headed to the kitchen to refill her coffee. She found Michael sitting at the kitchen table drinking hazelnut coffee and reading the paper. "Good morning, dear," Amanda said as she walked over and kissed him on the cheek.

Michael was a shade over six feet tall with dirty blond hair, golden brown eyes, and an athletic build. Michael was good-looking, but not in the pretty boy type of way, more of the rugged outdoor look, and he wore it well.

Michael pulled out a chair for Amanda. "Good morning, sweetheart. How are you feeling today?" Michael responded in a bright cheery voice as he refilled her coffee cup from a second coffee maker.

"I feel like I drank more than I should have last night. Maybe that's because I didn't eat before I started drinking." Amanda picked up her coffee and took a sip.

"We sure had a good time. We got home..." Michael shook his head in disbelief.

"What did we do when we got home?" Amanda softly asked, fearing what the answer might be.

"We were so intoxicated that we raided the fridge and the cupboards. I'm not sure exactly what we ate, but we ate it all." Amanda and Michael laughed.

Amanda sipped her coffee trying to clear the cobwebs. "This coffee is really good, what kind is it?"

"An Italian coffee. I got it while I was in Sicily a year or so ago. It's one of my personal favorites." Michael got up to clean the kitchen.

After Michael and Amanda finished their coffees, they went to Woody's Bar and Grille to pick up Amanda's car, and then on to Amanda's house to drop her car off, and pick up a few of her clothes. Then they would begin their three-hour ride to Michael's cottage.

The cottage was located at Bayshore Estates, which was on Pillar Point, an area of upstate New York in the Thousand Islands region. Michael had lived at Bayshore Estates with his cousins Greg and Mitch Connors and their family after his mother died.

Michael moved back to Rochester to live near his father after he finished an eight-year stint in the Navy (four of those years were with the Navy SEALS) and then four years in the intelligence community working for the CIA. The relationship between Michael and his father had grown stronger over the years because of the weekend visits and the extended stays during leave. After Michael left the Navy SEALS, his father shared how Michael had become the eighth generation of Callaghans to serve honorably in the U.S. Military, and about the existence of the MFB Black Ops (Men from Bray).

He learned that other Callaghan businesses were started as covers to keep their black ops work a secret. Their missions and their lives depended upon the secrecy of their membership in JSOC. Michael also learned that his father ran all the businesses including the MFB, but that one day Michael would be expected to take over the mantle.

After Michael left the CIA, he joined his father in running the MFB Black Ops team, and continued the tradition of running the other family businesses as cover. Today, Michael was the head of the MFB and all of the other legitimate businesses.

It wasn't until Michael was living in Rochester and carrying out black ops missions for the MFB that he realized how much he missed having a place at Bayshore Estates. Then one year ago, when a cottage came up for sale in Bayshore, Michael paid the asking price in cash and bought the cottage three doors down from his cousin.

When they reached Amanda's house, Amanda went upstairs to pack and Michael went into the kitchen to get a couple of sodas.

He discreetly checked in with HQ, and after an intel briefing, he gave the go ahead for one of his black ops teams to continue surveillance of a high-ranking Taliban leader who was meeting with the Black Blade of Allah in the Philippines. Due to the fragile relationship between the U.S. and the Philippines, POTUS had asked the MFB to conduct a deep black ops surveillance operation to determine what these two terrorist organizations were looking to do.

The MFB team stationed on a nearby island was monitoring the secret meeting that was taking place inside a mosque on Jolo Island. By attaching hi-tech listening devices to mini-drones that circled above the clandestine meeting, they could hear everything being said. Infrared and X-ray technology from MFB satellites provided imaging of the people in attendance. So far, they were discussing mutual problems and the possibility of working together.

When Michael was done talking with Johnson at HQ, he returned a call to Greg Connors who wanted to check in on Michael's progress.

Amanda came down the stairs with two suitcases in her hands.

"We're only going for two days, honey." Michael reminded Amanda as he walked over to take the two bulging suitcases from her.

"I know, but I wasn't sure what to bring. Besides, I wanted to make sure that I have enough clothes for each occasion." Amanda stressed her last two words.

Michael could see his plans falling apart. "Each occasion, what each occasion are you referring to?" He wasn't used to having someone else alter his plans.

"You're going to take me out to dinner, aren't you?" Amanda questioned.

"Yes," Michael replied firmly.

"Plus, I was hoping you would take me sightseeing on my first trip to the islands?" Amanda had her trip all planned out, and it didn't include working on the cottage.

"Yes," Michael muttered.

"And you still go to church on Sundays when you're there, don't you?" Amanda questioned.

"Yes, I do." Michael resigned himself to the fact that he wouldn't be getting any work done.

"And, of course, I need special clothes for when we're alone. So every item is necessary," Amanda finished.

"Now I understand." Michael curled his lips in to prevent himself from smiling.

"Michael, you're the best. I just knew you wouldn't be upset by not having time to do your home repairs this weekend." Amanda flashed a big smile, and gave Michael a big hug.

"No problem, honey. Most of the cottage is done, except for one room and the porch. I can always work on the porch next weekend." Michael half-hugged Amanda, with the suitcases in his hands. "Besides, we have the rest of the summer to fix the room, and then everything will be done."

When Amanda reached Michael's SUV, Michael had put her suitcases on top of four large white pails. "What's in those large pails?"

"Two are full of joint compound," Michael said, pointing to the pails on the left. "And two have different types of nails and screws in them." Michael opened one pail and showed its contents to Amanda.

"Why do you keep screws and nails in those pails, when they already come in a box?"

"These pails are airtight, and they keep my hardware from rusting." Michael explained as he replaced the lid. "Of course, they won't get much use *this* weekend, but I'll leave them at the cottage until next weekend, when I can do a little work on the steps."

CHAPTER 25

The ride home for Jeff Kane was grueling. His canary-yellow Ferrari Testarossa swerved all over the road as he reached for the bottle of ibuprofen that had fallen from the glove box to the floor. "Piece of shit car." He muttered to himself. "If you pay one hundred and eighty thousand dollars for a car, it should be able to hand you the damn ibuprofen on a silver platter."

Jeff Kane was an above average–looking man with black hair. His sideburns were slightly longer than they should have been, and he had a soul patch under his lower lip. When he walked, his one-hundred-and-sixty-pound, five-foot-ten-inch frame had the swagger of a wealthy man.

The short ride was only twenty miles from Poncho's house to Jeff's home.

Poncho was a mid-level drug dealer who had been distributing drugs since he was thirteen years old. Poncho was wanted by the police for a plethora of charges including drugs, promoting prostitution, and suspicion of murder. He had owned a house in Rochester's inner city that the police had raided for drugs two years before. The police believed that Poncho had left town, and that's the way Poncho liked it.

As Jeff turned onto his long winding driveway, the tall oak trees blocked the view of his house. Panic came over him as he drove out into the clearing that accented his multimillion-dollar home and he saw the police cars.

"Holy shit, what is going on?" Jeff mumbled as he got out of the car and started toward his house.

Jeff recognized Joshua Stein's car, but seeing the Mount Morris Village police, the Gates Police, and the Monroe County Sheriff cars caused him to be concerned about the welfare of his family.

As Jeff opened the front door, he yelled, "Cathy, Joshua?"

"We're up here," Joshua responded, looking down from the second floor.

Jeff started up the stairs at a full sprint, and when he reached the top, two police officers greeted him. "Are you Jeff Kane?"

"Yes, now what is going on?" Jeff demanded in his arrogant tone.

"I'm Detective Hill from the Gates Police Department and this is Chief Alice with the Mount Morris Police Department, and you are under arrest for the murder of Ann Chantel."

Chief Alice cut off Detective Hill and added, "And Gino Torchia."

Both Detective Hill and the chief noticed that Jeff looked a mess and reeked of booze.

"This is a warrant for your arrest." The chief showed Jeff the warrant.

Jeff stood in silence as Detective Hill began to read him his rights. He couldn't believe that Ann was dead. He looked at Cathy and Joshua. "Call my father and have him call our corporate attorney and get me the hell out of jail," Jeff demanded as the police handcuffed him.

The tears rained down Cathy's face. It seemed like a bad storm had rolled in, and Cathy's life took a turn for the surreal.

"We'll get you out, Jeff!" Joshua shouted as the police escorted Jeff out of the house.

Detective Hill called for the other officers and discussed the results of their searches. Several plastic bags with evidence were produced, and the entire brigade of police slowly began to leave the house.

Turning to Cathy, Detective Hill said, "That will be all for now, Mrs. Kane." The detective headed for the door, then stopped and turned around. "Please stay in the Rochester area in case we have any further questions."

After Detective Hill closed the door, Cathy hugged Joshua and started to cry. "How could he have killed Ann?" Cathy sobbed.

"I don't know, but you should call George before he hears about it from someone else." Joshua's mind wandered through the conversation he'd had with Ann the night before. If Ann would have told Joshua about her fight with Jeff and the threats he made, perhaps Joshua could have done something to stop her murder.

Cathy slowly pulled away from Joshua. "You're right, I should call George now."

The phone began to ring at George Kane's residence, and as usual, on the third ring James answered it. James was George Kane's personal assistant. He took care of running the mansion and chauffeured George six days a week, around the clock. Thursdays were James's days off. It seemed like the worst job in the world to the rest of the Kane family, even if it did pay two hundred fifty thousand a year, with room and board.

"Hello, this is the Kane residence."

"Hello, James, please get me George—it's an emergency." Cathy's tone suggested she was upset.

"I'll get him straightaway, please hold."

James ran up the stairs and headed toward the master suite. "Mr. Kane, you have an urgent phone call." James spoke into the intercom system from the hallway.

"James, I'm taking a bath. Please take a message," George responded as Sylvia Brown, his personal attendant, continued to wash George's back.

"I'm afraid it's your daughter-in-law, and she says it's an emergency. She sounds quite upset, sir."

"Why didn't you say so in the first place, James? I'll take it right away." After George released the intercom button, he switched the intercom over to phone mode.

"Cathy, what's the problem?" George wasted no time getting to the point.

"Hello, Father, Jeff has been arrested and needs your help." Cathy's voice was shaky.

"Arrested... arrested for what, gambling with the boys?" George laughed at the thought of Jeff being arrested for gambling when he prided himself on being so smart and such a good card player.

"No, Father, he was arrested for murder."

"What? Hang on." George got up out of the tub and turned the intercom from speaker to receiver mode. Sylvia tried to hand George a towel, but George stepped out of the tub, walked over to the dressing table, and picked up the phone.

"Give me the details." George took several notes as Cathy told him about the police searching the house and arresting Jeff.

"I see." After a short pause, George requested the names of the police officers who made the arrest, and where they took Jeff.

"Don't you worry, I'll get our boy out of this terrible mess. You just stay there and I'll get him back to you and the kids in a few hours." George hung up the phone, reached for the towel still in Sylvia's hand, and turned back to the intercom. "James, are you still in the hallway?"

"Yes, Mr. Kane, I'm here."

"Get me the district attorney and our corporate attorney right away, and patch the calls to the master bedroom."

"Yes sir, very good, sir," James responded.

CHAPTER 26

When Michael and Amanda pulled up to the end of her driveway, he noticed a man who seemed out of place. His disheveled appearance and his dark-colored, older model car were atypical for this neighborhood. The stranger appeared to be finishing up with changing a flat tire. Between the glare of the sun and the distance from the car, Michael wasn't able to get a good look at the man or the car.

"Boy, I'll tell ya. In these rundown neighborhoods, people are always getting flat tires. I'd better be careful where I drive." Michael laughed, trying to hide his concern. His years of running black ops missions for the CIA and the MFB had taught him to notice everything and discount nothing. Someday, if he married Amanda, he'd have to tell her about the contract work he did for POTUS and his country… but not today.

Amanda looked at the multimillion-dollar homes that dotted the countryside. "Rundown neighborhood? That beater probably picked up a nail miles ago. Just look at that weirdo with his greasy hair and scruffy face. He looks like he hasn't shaved in a week," she protested. "I'm sure he doesn't live anywhere near here."

"You're probably right." He made a mental note of the man's appearance and headed toward the Thousand Islands.

The ride went by quickly. Michael enjoyed the views of Lake Ontario while Amanda slept.

Michael turned onto Moffit Road and the bright afternoon sun shone through the passenger window.

Amanda woke up with a yawn and stretched. "Are we there yet?"

"Not quite. We have about two miles to go." Michael glanced over, trying to read her.

"Good, because I'm hungry. Do you think we can stop for an ice cream cone on the way?" Amanda smiled and rubbed her hands together.

"Sure, I could go for a cone myself." Michael smiled and continued past the turn to the cottage and went toward Chaumont.

As they entered Chaumont, Michael described various points of interest to Amanda.

"Now right up here past the cement mixing truck is the Chaumont Bridge." A construction crew was pouring cement through a basement window into a house.

"How come there's no one inside that cement truck?" Amanda was shocked that it was running and there was no one behind the wheel.

"What do you mean?"

"The truck is turned on, and the cement mixer is turning in the back, but no one is *in* the truck. Isn't that kind of dangerous?" Amanda stared at the empty cab of the cement truck as Michael's SUV passed.

"No, it's not really dangerous at all. They can control the cement mixer from the rear of the truck, and as long as it's in park and the emergency brake is on, the truck won't roll forward," Michael explained as the bridge came into view.

Several cars behind Michael, a black Cadillac Seville with two passengers dressed in black suits, black shirts, and black wing-tipped shoes noticed Michael in his SUV.

"The Chaumont Bridge has a very slight incline due to the natural drop-off of the land as it meets the water," Michael said, continuing his description of the village. "But as you can see, there's a forty-foot drop from the center of the bridge to the water."

"What's the name of this river?" Amanda was absorbing the sights and becoming more enthusiastic.

"It's not really a river, it's a bay. It's part of Chaumont Bay, which connects to Guffins Bay and Lake Ontario. My cottage is in Guffins Bay," Michael said. "We can come down here on the boat sometime."

When Michael's SUV got to the other side of the bridge, he flicked on his turn signal and turned left into the Bay Side Ice Cream Parlor's parking lot.

A moment later, the black Cadillac cruised slowly by the ice cream parlor, drove a short distance up the road and made a U-turn. Two cars behind the black Cadillac was a dark green Dodge Dart. The Dodge Dart drove another half a mile before turning around.

"I'm so hungry, I might just get two scoops instead of one." Amanda unbuckled her seat belt.

"You might have to wait in line if those people get to the counter first." Michael pointed to a car that had pulled right behind him.

"Quick, meet me there." Amanda opened her door without waiting for the SUV to come to a complete stop.

By the time Amanda got halfway to the counter, she realized that she was racing an eight-year-old boy who was determined to get there first. Amanda's pace quickened, but the little boy took the lead and got there first.

"Nice try, I really thought you had him for a second." Michael chuckled as he joined her.

"Ha ha, very funny, but I bet he could've beaten you too." Amanda groaned as three little boys piled in line behind their big brother.

Between the four children and their parents, Amanda and Michael's wait lasted ten minutes. When it was over, Amanda got her two scoops of chocolate and Michael got a soft strawberry ice cream cone.

"Now this is what I have been craving." Amanda's tongue swirled around the chocolate ice cream.

"I'm glad I could make you happy."

They walked back toward the SUV, looking at the boaters and water-skiers out on the water.

When Amanda reached for her door handle, she realized that the door was unlatched and slightly ajar. "Michael, my door is open. Someone's been in the car."

"Are you sure you didn't leave the door open when you jumped out to race that little boy?" Michael raised his eyebrows and scanned the lot, but nothing looked suspicious.

"I'm pretty sure that I closed it," Amanda replied in a thoughtful voice. Still licking his ice cream cone, Michael got into the SUV and closed the door behind him. "Well, your purse is still here and nothing seems tampered with." Michael made a mental note to keep an eye out for possible threats. Michael tried hard to keep his secret life from this corner of the world and he wanted it to stay that way.

He surveyed the interior with a careful eye. There were receipts from building materials delivered to his cottage, pens, scribbled notes, and some blueprints. Everything seemed to be untouched.

"You're right. I'm just used to the big city, and always looking over my shoulder," Amanda conceded, and Michael started the car. "Don't forget to buckle your seatbelt."

"Yes, dear," he said with a mouthful of ice cream.

As the SUV started over the bridge, Amanda was watching a teenage girl water-skiing just up the shoreline.

"What's that... *watch out!*" Amanda yelled when she saw the cement mixing truck cross over the double yellow line and come straight at them.

"Hold on." Michael kept his cool and honked his horn at the oncoming truck.

There was no room on the two-lane bridge. The mixing truck was weaving all over the road, and the distance between them was closing fast.

With a quick glance, Michael looked over the steel guardrails and saw no one in the water directly below. If he stopped, they would be trapped by the cars behind him, and crushed by the oncoming cement mixer. There was no way to avoid the thirty-ton truck.

"It's going to run us over." Amanda was terrified.

Michael calculated their best odds for survival. "Brace yourself for impact."

At the last possible second, Michael pulled hard to the right in order to avoid a head-on collision. As he scraped the guardrail, the cement truck plowed into the SUV and pushed it through the steel guardrail and off the bridge. The forty-foot drop from the center of the bridge seemed like an eternity to Michael and Amanda. When the SUV finally hit the water, a huge splash shrouded the SUV like a waterfall.

The SUV quickly began to sink. Water seemed to be pouring in from every crack and crevice. "Are you okay?" Michael asked Amanda as he assessed the situation.

Amanda's face was red, she had some slight burns from the airbag. "Holy crap, we almost died. My face hurts but my seatbelt and the airbag stopped me from hitting the windshield." Amanda rubbed her forehead with one hand and reached for her seatbelt. "You were right to avoid a head-on collision. That thing hit us so hard, it rattled my teeth."

"Quick... unbuckle. We need to get out of here before we sink. This water is about thirty-five feet deep." Michael reached for his seat belt.

"I can't get it unbuckled," Amanda said, panic in her voice. "I can't get the button to push in."

"Mine's jammed too," Michael replied.

"Michael, the water is almost up to my knees. What do we do? We're sinking. *What do we do?*" Amanda was terrified.

Michael's military training kicked in. "Try to wiggle out from behind your seat belt, and try to keep calm."

Within a dozen seconds, both Michael and Amanda realized their efforts were useless. Their seat belts had locked and there was no way to get their legs free. With every second, the SUV sank deeper into the water.

"Michael, the water is up to my waist. We're going to drown if we don't get out of here. What are we going to do?" Amanda's face was a mask of terror.

"Hang on and don't panic. I've got an idea." Michael slid out from behind his shoulder harness, took a deep breath, leaned over his lap, and went face first into the water. Michael's waist strap was still locked in place, and kept Michael in his seat.

He was underwater for a long time, searching for something under his seat, and it looked like he was having a hard time finding it.

"What are you doing?" Amanda was still trying to wiggle out from behind her shoulder strap.

Several seconds later, Michael emerged from the water with a hunting knife in his hand. "Move toward the door, I'm going to cut you out," Michael told her calmly.

Without a word Amanda moved as close to her door as possible. Michael started cutting her seat belt, but because the belt was wet, it took longer than Michael had expected.

When Amanda was finally free of her seatbelt, the water was up to their necks. The SUV was completely submerged, and it was getting dark as the vehicle sank toward the bottom of the channel.

"Quick, take a deep breath and get out." Michael looked into Amanda's eyes and could see her apprehension.

"If I open that door, you'll drown."

The water level was up to Amanda's chin.

"If you don't open that door, then *you'll drown*. I'll cut myself out, and meet you on shore… Now go."

They both took a deep breath before Amanda opened the door. It was hard to get the door open, but finally, she was able to squeeze through. She found herself fifteen feet from the surface of the water.

Amanda pushed off the SUV and swam as hard as she could. It felt like forever before she broke the surface. Gasping for air, she looked down into the murky water, searching for the SUV in the dark channel of Chaumont Bay.

She started toward shore, yelling for help. Before she could get halfway there, two men in a rowboat pulled her into their small but welcome craft.

Amanda cried as she pointed toward the spot where the SUV went down. "Please, you've got to help. My boyfriend is still trapped in the SUV."

"Don't you worry, miss. We'll go after him as soon as we get you back to shore..." said a man wearing a baseball cap with fishing hooks and lures hanging from the sides.

"No, don't take me to shore. I've got to help Michael." Amanda reached for an oar, trying to turn the boat around.

The men stopped her.

Amanda tried to jump out of the boat, but the second man grabbed her and held her back. "She must be in shock, get us back to shore fast."

"I'm not in shock! My boyfriend is still in the SUV and he's drowning," Amanda pleaded. "Please, you've got to help him!"

"Miss, I'm sorry, but your boyfriend has been down there for over ten minutes. We didn't think either of you were going to make it."

"You aren't listening to me," Amanda sobbed.

The men docked the rowboat and helped Amanda onto the dock. There were several hundred onlookers standing on the bridge and both sides of the water. They were all waiting for some sign of the remaining victim.

Time moved in slow motion for Amanda. She ran toward the end of the dock, where two men stopped her from jumping back in.

Seagulls circled and cried out without an answer.

The floodgates opened and Amanda's emotions poured out.

Two middle-aged women and their teenage daughters tried to comfort her. A third woman came and put a blanket around her.

The cement mixing truck, which had struck Michael's SUV, had stalled out in a tangle of guardrails. It was hanging over the edge of the bridge, threatening to topple on top of the place where Michael's SUV had splashed into the water.

Bubbles came to the surface of the water near where the SUV had sunk, and there was still no sign of Michael. As the bubbles broke the surface, and the lifeless ripples of water dissipated from their spot of origin, all hope seemed lost.

"Michael… Michael…" Amanda screamed toward the water. "He cut me free from my seat belt and told me to escape while there was still time." Amanda sobbed uncontrollably.

Two dark-skinned men stood on the opposite shoreline of Chaumont Bay looking across the water at Amanda and scanning the water for signs of life. The men wore matching black suits, black shirts, black wingtip shoes, and both men had a tattoo. Two daggers with black blades crossed under a waning crescent moon.

"The infidel Callaghan is finished. Let us go celebrate with a meal," Abu said to his companion.

The terrorist cell was setting up in Montreal, Canada, less than an hour away. The men had only recently received intelligence reports of the man called Callaghan. Al Qaeda had obtained the information from a captured clandestine CIA operative. Rumor was, Callaghan's name was the last name the operative spoke before he died.

"He must have loved you very much." One of the women wept quietly as she attempted to comfort Amanda.

"He gave his life to save you, *he* made the decision, and you can't blame yourself," the second woman said.

Several boats were circling the area where the SUV went down, their motors turned off, paddling and looking for signs of life.

Suddenly there was a giant splash and a loud wheeze as Michael burst out of the water and gasped for air.

The whole shoreline erupted in applause and cheers.

Amanda sprang to her feet. "Thank you, God—thank you for bringing back my Michael."

Michael saw Amanda at the end of the dock on the west bank of the channel, and he began to swim toward her. One of the nearby boats paddled over and took Michael aboard.

When he made it to shore, Amanda and Michael hugged and kissed as hundreds of well-wishers clapped and shouted approval.

"How did you do it, young fella?" An old man wearing a fishing vest had moved up close to Michael. "How on earth did you stay under water for seven or eight minutes?"

Without letting go of Amanda, Michael said, "Well, our seat belts were jammed. I had to cut us loose with a hunting knife that I had under my seat. When Amanda opened the door, I took a big deep breath and started cutting mine. By the time I finished, I had very little air left, so I got to the back of the SUV. I have a couple of buckets in the cargo space I keep nails in. They're airtight. So I cut a small hole and sucked the air out of both buckets and headed for the surface."

"That was some pretty quick thinking," the old angler exclaimed.

"Yes, it worked out." Michael kissed Amanda's forehead. "Let's call one of my friends from Bayshore and get a ride to the cottage."

"That sounds great." Amanda wiped the last tear from her eye.

Michael put his arm around Amanda and they started toward the ice cream parlor. He surreptitiously observed everyone, absorbing every detail. Nothing looked out of place except the cement truck still hanging perilously off the bridge. Something was not quite right, but Michael couldn't put his finger on it. Things like this nagged him, until he figured them out.

In Michael's line of work, there was no such thing as coincidence. Something wasn't right and he needed to find out what was going on.

On the other side of RT 12, the dark green Dodge Dart was parked behind another vehicle in a public parking lot. Its owner sat on the hood of the car, using binoculars, watching Michael place a call from a phone booth.

CHAPTER 27

George Kane slid into the back of his silver-gray stretch limousine. James waited until George settled in, then closed the door and proceeded to resume his responsibilities as chauffeur. As George thumbed through the Democrat and Chronicle looking for any mention of Jeff having been arrested, James continued trying to reach the corporate attorney and the district attorney by phone.

Satisfied that the local rags had not discovered Jeff's predicament, George turned his attention to the business section. "Any luck yet, James?" George's patience was wearing thin.

"Yes, sir. Mr. Walsch from corporate will be on the line shortly."

"Very good, put him on speakerphone and I'll take it when he picks up." He settled in with market reports.

"Yes, sir."

A few moments later, "Hello, Mr. Kane, this is Jack Walsch."

"Jack, we have a problem. I need you to meet me at the Gates Police Department right away. Jeff has been arrested for murder and we need to get this cleared up before the local newspapers get ahold of this."

"I'll meet you at the Gates Police Department. Since the courthouse is in the same building, I'll find out who the judge is, and give you an update." After a moment of thought, Jack asked, "Did you bring money for bail?"

"I brought a million."

"Let's hope it's enough. Jeff is a wealthy man charged with murder and the bail, if we can get it, will be high." Jack sounded concerned.

"Let's hope you earn your retainer this week," George snapped.

"I'll meet you there in forty minutes," Jack replied, understanding the implications of George's statement.

When George and James arrived at the police department, Jack Walsch was waiting for them at the door.

"What have you got?"

Jack held the door for George. "Judge Aberdien is on this morning. He's tough, but fair. I'm still waiting for a copy of the police report. As soon as the report is ready, the judge will give us an arraignment."

"Have you seen Jeff?" George started toward the front desk.

"When I got here, Detectives Hill and Trout were attempting to interrogate Jeff. He refused to give a statement until he met with me," Walsch replied.

"What did you find out?"

"I got a copy of the preliminary police reports that were used to get the warrants..." Jack stopped talking until George looked him in the eye again.

"Well?" George snapped.

"It doesn't look good. The police here *and* in Mount Morris have a lot of evidence against Jeff. They have his fingerprints all over both of the murder weapons." Jack raised his eyebrows.

"What do you mean, the police here *and* in Mount Morris? What do the police in Mount Morris have to do with a murder that took place here, in Gates?" George asked.

"A man by the name of Gino Torchia was found shot to death in his van late last night in the parking lot of a bar in Mount Morris. The police found Jeff's revolver at the scene," Jack said carefully. "Also, Jeff has no alibi."

"How could he be in two places at the same time? Do you know how far Mount Morris is from Gates?" George's face was reddening. "I'll tell you. Mount Morris is about an hour away. That would be at least a two-hour round trip *without* taking the time to commit a murder. This whole thing is crazy." George threw his hands in the air.

Walsch waited for George to settle down.

"Well, did you talk to my son? What the hell is going on?" George demanded.

"When I got here, I sat with Jeff while the police interrogated him. We refused to answer any questions." Jack paused to collect his thoughts. The whole thing was happening very fast. "When the police left, I cautioned Jeff to watch what he said, and that our conversation was probably being listened to via an intercom. He claims he was playing poker at a friend's house and he didn't commit any murder."

"Well, there you go. He has an alibi. His friend can back him up!" George barked.

"It's not that easy. Jeff refused to name his friend, or any of the individuals that were there. Apparently, none of them cares to talk with the police."

"What? Who cares what they want? My son is in jail and they can get him out!"

"Apparently Jeff cares. He won't give us their names."

An officer returned to the desk. "Mr. Walsh, Mr. Kane, Jeff is on his way to the courtroom to be arraigned."

"Thank you, Officer Robinson, we'll wait here for Jeff to come by." George turned and looked for Jeff. "Let's get this over with."

Detective Hill and his partner Detective Trout led Jeff from a hallway in the back. Jeff was handcuffed and looked like he had been up all night.

"Jeff, are you all right?" George asked his son.

"I'll be okay, Father, just get me out of this terrible mess." Jeff sounded so deflated, you could practically hear the air escaping and running for cover.

In the courtroom, George Kane recognized the man sitting behind the prosecutor's desk. It was the district attorney himself. Without drawing attention to it, George and the DA, Roger Reilin, exchanged nods. At six feet two inches and one hundred seventy pounds, the DA looked like a former track star.

Jeff Kane down sat with Jack Walsh. George Kane took a seat in the first row behind the defense table.

The court officer announced, "All rise." Everyone stood and Judge Aberdien entered the courtroom.

The judge told everyone to be seated, then the clerk read Jeff's name, the case number, and the charges into the record. Judge Aberdien looked solemn.

"Does the defendant understand the charges against him?" The judge looked at Jeff and then at George.

"Yes, your Honor," Jack Walsh replied.

"How do you plead?"

"Not guilty. Your Honor, we ask that the defendant be released on his own recognizance. He has strong community ties and is not a flight risk." Jack straightened his suit.

"What do the people say about this?" The judge looked the DA.

The tension was so thick that it was like a fog in the courtroom, making their vision blurry.

The DA replied, "Your Honor, the people ask that bail be denied. The defendant is charged with two murders, one here and one in Mount Morris, and the evidence is overwhelming."

"Objection noted. However, the defendant and his father are upstanding members of our community. Bail is set at two hundred and fifty thousand dollars, cash or bond."

The judge looked at George Kane. "This court is adjourned."

George flashed a wink at the judge. He'd been a major campaign contributor for many years.

Everyone stood up and the judge left the courtroom. As the DA and his assistant collected their papers, Jack and George left the courtroom, followed by Jeff and the two detectives.

James had been waiting in the hallway outside the courtroom, with a briefcase handcuffed to his wrist.

George turned to Jack and said, "Take the money and post bail. I'll meet you and Jeff back at the house."

After James gave Jack the briefcase and the handcuffs, George patted Jeff on the shoulder, then said, "Let's go, James."

Jeff's days were numbered, and he knew it. It was only a matter of time before the police checked Ann and found his DNA.

CHAPTER 28

The car was cherry red with white leather seats, and it was a classic. The dual carb, 350 horsepower motor pushed the needle past the limit on several occasions. Billy Bernard was driving the mint condition 1972 Oldsmobile Cutlass Supreme convertible. Everyone called Billy "Ace" because he could fly, drive, or operate anything that moved with natural ease that few could match. He had an easy-to-like air about him.

"So, both of your seat belts just locked up when you hit the bridge and you couldn't get out?" Ace asked as he turned off North Shore Road onto the Bayshore Estates' private road.

"Yes, and that was really strange. I thought we were going to drown until Michael got out his hunting knife. I was so scared. I thought he would never get out of the SUV." She tensed up just saying it.

"Yes... it *was* strange the way the seat belts froze up." Michael gave Ace an almost imperceptible nod.

"What's even stranger is the cement truck just popped into gear all by itself and almost ran us over," Amanda added.

"How did that happen?" Not liking coincidences, Ace turned his gaze to Michael and compressed his lips.

Amanda was staring out the window, unaware of their silent conversation. "Supposedly a wrench or something dropped off the seat, hit the shifter, and fell onto the accelerator after the truck

124

popped into gear. Then the truck just drove itself halfway across the bridge and stalled out when it hit us." Amanda was rambling, and both Michael and Ace pretended not to notice.

"What do you make of that, Michael?" Ace pulled up in front of Michael's cottage.

Michael didn't want Amanda to be alarmed. "I'll wait until the police take a better look before I reach any conclusions." Michael opened his door to get out. "Well, honey, we finally made it. This is the place you've heard so much about."

"Yes, we're here, and my clothes are on the bottom of Chaumont Bay. I have nothing to wear, I'm still soaking wet, and my cell phone doesn't work," Amanda laughed.

"I've already taken care of that." Ace gave a crooked smile. "I took the liberty of having my wife round up some clothes and toiletries at Michael's."

Amanda didn't know what to say. "Thank you, I appreciate that, Ace."

Michael and Amanda thanked Ace for the ride and watched him pull away.

Michael said, "There are two things left to do here. One is to finish repairing the front steps, and the other is to finish the spare room."

"I see you've roped off the left side of the steps," Amanda replied.

"Correct. So please remember to use the steps on the side closest to the house. I only tied off the bottom because I ran out of rope," Michael explained with a sheepish smile.

Michael had insisted on doing all the renovations to the cottage himself. Since he frequently left without a moment's notice if POTUS called in a field operation, it was taking longer than expected.

"I think I can remember that." Amanda followed Michael into the house.

He took her on a tour of the cottage, explaining, "The cottage has three bedrooms, one bath, a kitchen and living room. The front window looks out over the bay and Cherry Island. I liked the naval theme because this window," he pointed, "is an actual nineteenth century porthole from a wooden sloop. Most of the paintings are from the sixteenth century, sailing ships—naval mostly."

"Why do you have this room sealed off with plastic?" Amanda asked.

"Because if you'll notice..." Michael gently removed the plastic over the door, "I have a lot of work left to do in here and I didn't want dust to get all over the house." Michael opened the door so Amanda could look into the room.

"Let's go down to the shore," Michael suggested.

She smiled. "That sounds like a great idea."

They left the cottage and navigated twenty feet of winding stairs to a concrete sidewalk that led down to the water. When Amanda reached the sidewalk, she gently took Michael's hand.

Michael pointed directly across the bay. "We got our ice cream in the village of Chaumont, directly across the bay."

"Are those islands out there?" Amanda shaded her eyes and looked across the water.

"Yes. The two small islands really don't have names, but the big one is Cherry Island," he said.

Michael continued his tour of the grounds, showing Amanda the boat slip, garage, and the layout of his property behind the cottage on the other side of the road.

"What's that dark spot in the grass up there on the top of the hill?" Amanda pointed to a small hill that rose up fifteen feet and leveled off.

"That, my dear, is where we have our bonfires." Michael smiled.

"We? Who is we, and when do these bonfires take place?" Amanda was intrigued. She had never been to a bonfire before.

"Just a bunch of friends from Bayshore Estates, most of whom you haven't met—yet, and we have them pretty often. I know you'll love the bonfires as much as I do," he said confidently.

Michael and Amanda started back toward the cottage when someone called for Michael. Michael's friends were strolling up the private road, coming to welcome Michael and his new guest to Bayshore.

Michael said, "Looks like the welcoming committee is here!"

Michael and Amanda walked over to meet them. Amanda could see the excitement on everyone's face. Her apprehension was replaced with anticipation that was brought on by the warm smiles and outstretched arms.

The four young women took turns hugging Amanda while men grabbed, hugged, and shook hands with Michael.

The sisters, Karen and Sue Miller, Teresa Bernard and Mary Cormine wasted no time in introducing themselves to Amanda.

"We've heard so much about you, Amanda. I feel like I know you already," Mary gushed.

"You have? I wonder *who* could have told you so much about me." Amanda smiled at Michael.

"Yes, and Greg told us all about you too. You remember Greg, don't you?" Mary asked.

Amanda realized Greg Connors, Michael's cousin, was part of the crowd. She met him in Chicago at the trade show.

Greg stood next to Billy "Ace" Bernard (Teresa's husband and childhood boyfriend).

Jimmy Ryan "JR," who was dating Mary Cormine, was an ex-Navy SEAL. His good looks opened a lot of doors for him... very helpful in covert ops.

Lou Petrone, the strong silent type. When he was a kid, his nickname was Cool Hand Lou.

They were childhood friends, all from Bayshore Estates. They all joined the military at the same time, and went on to join Michael at MFB.

As everyone chatted, Michael pulled Greg aside and described the incident on the Chaumont Bridge. "I don't believe in coincidences like that," Michael whispered. "It feels like a Black Blade of Allah move."

"Do you think they're on to our location up here?" Connors scanned the neighborhood.

"No, I think we were targets of opportunity. There's no way they could have planned a mission like that. There were too many variables involved like the cement truck being there, and us deciding to get ice cream was a last-minute thing. Johnson told me last night that HQ identified two Black Blade of Allah operatives landing in a Montreal airport. My guess is they've opened up a new cell somewhere in Canada, maybe Toronto or Montreal. Have HQ start looking for this new cell, see what they can find."

"I'll let them know as soon as we leave. You realize that we're looking for a needle in a haystack." Greg was less than enthusiastic.

Michael ran a hand through his hair. "I know, but it still needs to be done." He nodded at Greg and they rejoined the party.

"Hey, let's head into the cottage and make plans for the weekend." Michael hoped Amanda would get to know them better.
***

After everyone left, Amanda turned to Michael and said, "What do you want to do for dinner?"

He realized that all of their weekend food had sunk to the bottom of the Chaumont Channel. "What do you say we borrow someone's car and go down to Foote's and get some pizza?"

With a chuckle and a half a hug, Amanda and Michael headed out the door and up the road to borrow Ace's car. Foote's, a local restaurant and bar, served a brisk summer clientele and a regular winter snowmobile crowd. Foote's was the kind of place where everyone knew everyone. From the very old to the very young, everyone was welcome, and you felt it within minutes of entering the door.

The stranger in the dark green Dodge Dart didn't see Ace turn off the North Shore Road. He had been all the way around Pillar Point and was now on his return trip. That's when he saw the cherry red Oldsmobile pull into Foote's.

CHAPTER 29

George sat quietly in the study of his mansion, sipping on a Hennessy Cognac. The study, lined with built-in mahogany bookshelves, contained books on almost any topic. George hired a librarian to fill his library shortly after he built the house, and then he contracted her to update it four times a year. At the far end under a picture window was a large mahogany bar, which he stocked with top-of-the-line liquor.

The private line rang and George answered solemnly, "George Kane."

"George, you called. How can I help you?" DA Roger Reilin asked.

"Roger, thanks for getting back to me." George paused, took a deep breath and said, "As you know, I've got a little problem and I hope you can help me."

"Well, George, strictly speaking, I'm not supposed to discuss the case with you now that Jeff has been arrested." There was an awkward silence. "I appreciate everything that you've done for me. The contributions that you've made to my campaigns have been very generous, but there's too much evidence against Jeff for me to do much good for you."

"Are you sure there is nothing you can do?" George was grasping at straws.

"I would suggest that you get a private investigator involved. Maybe they can dig up something to cast a shadow of doubt on the evidence."

"Thanks for the advice," George replied and hung up the phone.

George was pondering his next move when Jack Walsch and Jeff arrived. "Come on in, Jack, put the briefcase next to the wet bar. You and Jeff can pull up a chair."

Jack Walsch put the briefcase with seven hundred fifty thousand dollars in it on the floor next to the wet bar and then sat down next to Jeff.

"Either of you care for a drink?" George took a sip of his cognac.

"No thank you," Jeff and Jack both replied.

"Jeff, could you please explain to me why none of your poker buddies are willing to corroborate your whereabouts last night?" George's tone was very serious and his sharp eyes could have cut glass.

"It's a long story. Besides, I didn't kill anyone and the evidence will prove that," Jeff said in his usual arrogant manner.

"Well, I've got the rest of my life to hear your long story," George snapped.

Jeff wondered how he could explain that he associated with drug dealers, and he was indulging in drugs with those people. His mind raced to find an explanation. "I'm not sure how to say this...."

"Just say it," George ordered.

"When I was in high school, I knew some guys who came from poor families. You and Mother always taught us to befriend people who are less fortunate, so I became friends with them." Jeff picked at the arm of his chair, trying to decide what to say next.

"These poor friends of yours, did they go to that very expensive private high school with you?" George queried.

"No, I didn't meet them at my high school, but that's another story," Jeff replied. "Anyway, I became friends with these guys and as we got older some of them got into trouble with the law. As a result, they don't want anything to do with the police."

"What kind of trouble?" George took another sip from his drink.

"They were using drugs." Jeff cringed and his fist clenched around the chair's arm.

"How many of your poker buddies are wanted for using drugs?" George swirled his cognac, already knowing the answer.

"All of them." Jeff lowered his head in shame and tried to ignore his body sweating out the alcohol from the previous night.

"I know life has been different since your mother died, but haven't I provided you with a good home, and a good job?" George growled.

"Yes, Father." Jeff wished he had taken that drink. His head was still pounding and his mouth was drier than cotton.

George examined his son. "Then why do you take drugs and associate with criminals?"

"I wasn't doing drugs, I was just playing poker." Jeff's response was quick and insincere.

"Don't insult my intelligence," George snapped. "Of course you use drugs, which is why you hang out with drug dealers."

"I'm sorry, Father. I'll never lie to you again." Jeff's tone was chastened and seemed genuine, but deep down he knew he was lying to his father.

"Jack, I'm going to hire a private investigator. I want you and Jeff to cooperate completely." George was stern.

"Yes, sir," Jack replied.

"Jeff, I want you to consider whether your friendship with these criminals is worth your freedom." George looked at Jack and Jeff and shook his head. "Now, both of you leave me, I need to do some thinking."

CHAPTER 30

Michael and Amanda were drinking beer and shooting pool while they waited for their pizza.

Amanda, who grew up playing pool on her father's eight-foot billiards table, was on a roll. She effortlessly made bank shots and combination shots on the six-foot pool table at Foote's.

Amanda stalked the table like a leopardess eyeing her next meal. Circling the table, chalking her stick, calculating angles, analyzing shot sequences, Amanda operated in the zone.

Once she decided her strategy, she began knocking down shot after shot, moving with the ease and confidence of a skilled predator. She was methodically clearing the table of her balls while skillfully avoiding the rest.

When she was down to her last ball and the eight ball, disaster struck. The eight ball was wedged behind one of Michael's balls, making it impossible to sink without dropping the eight ball and losing the game. Amanda hit a slow roller and left her ball hanging on the lip of a corner pocket.

Michael surveyed the table. "Impressive shooting, Amanda. It looks like your father gave you a few lessons—and you were an excellent student."

Amanda smiled and bowed her head in acknowledgment.

Michael circled the table like a shark, calculating shot angles, and making shot after shot. Clearing the green-felted table was simple for Michael since he didn't have to contend with Amanda's balls. When Michael was down to his last ball, the eight ball, and Amanda's last ball, he scrutinized the table.

Michael was too busy looking at the pool table to see the stranger walk in. He had parked his dark green Dodge Dart in front of Foote's, down by the water, where it couldn't be seen. He took a seat at the far end of the bar and ordered a beer. He'd changed his shirt, slicked his hair straight back, and after adding a pair of black-rimmed glasses, he barely recognized himself.

Michael called for a jump shot that would send his ball into a corner pocket, followed by the eight ball, leaving the table with Amanda's ball. It was a high-risk shot, but he made it look easy.

Amanda clapped her hands. "Bravo, Michael. Nice shooting. You were lucky that I didn't clear the table. Good game. But next time, the game is mine," Amanda promised as their pizza arrived.

Michael looked at Amanda and smiled. "Why don't you give us each another slice and I'll get us another pitcher of beer?" He put his pool stick in the rack and headed toward the bar.

He stopped at the end of the bar closest to his table and waited for Carol, the bartender.

Michael was idly watching the horse race that was on the television when he caught the reflection of a man wearing dark glasses—and he could have sworn the man was looking at him.

"Hi, Michael, what can I get for you?" Carol was Foote's daughter, and knew all the regulars.

"Who's the new guy with the dark-rimmed glasses and his hair slicked back?" Michael nodded toward the other end of the bar.

"He's new around here. He said he was renting a cottage up the road for a week." Carol tipped her head. "Did you want me to refill that pitcher of beer?"

Michael handed Carol the empty pitcher. "That would be wonderful."

When Michael and Amanda finished eating, Amanda wrapped up the leftover pizza while Michael paid the bill.

Michael gave the parking lot a hard look, but didn't see the dark-colored car that had been at Amanda's house. They hopped into the Olds and Michael said, "Let's see what this baby can do." He punched the accelerator to the floor, and the three hundred and fifty horses with dual carburetors roared. He wanted to make sure no one could follow him.

A short time later, the stranger got into his dark green Dodge Dart and retrieved his laptop. With the press of a button, the cherry red Oldsmobile appeared on the screen.

"You can run but you can't hide." The stranger started his car and headed toward Bayshore Estates.

When the cherry red Cutlass Supreme was close his cottage, Michael and Amanda could see his friends getting ready for the bonfire. The Miller sisters were gathering lawn chairs. JR joined Greg in filling coolers with alcoholic beverages, while Ace and Teresa were carrying firewood from their back lot. Several ice-laden storms had come off the lake during the winter months. They knocked down a few trees, that were now firewood, courtesy of Ace's chainsaw.

"We better hurry and get ready for the bonfire," Michael said.

"What do we need to do?"

"We need to get gasoline to start the fire, our lawn chairs, and two five-gallon buckets of water and bring them out back. We have some wine and beer in the cottage that needs to be put on ice in a cooler, and lug that up to the fire as well." Michael ran through his mental to-do list before he and Amanda got out of the car and headed into the cottage.

By 8:30 p.m., everyone had gathered for the "official" lighting of the summer's first bonfire.

Michael was finishing some last-minute things and Amanda was pouring herself some wine and talking to the Miller sisters, when Greg walked over to Michael and whispered, "I need to talk with you for a minute, Commander."

If one of his team referred to Michael as commander, he knew it involved MFB business. Michael looked at his other men, and he could see that something had happened. "You know what… I forgot to get some extra ice." Michael made sure everyone could hear him. "Amanda honey, I'll be right back. Greg, can you give me a hand?"

"Okay." Amanda and Karen kept talking together.

In Michael's garage, Greg said, "Commander, I didn't have a chance to tell you earlier, but when we were at Mickey's Bar and Grille in Chicago, I had a run-in with a Black Blade of Allah operative when you went over to meet Amanda. His name was Jamaal Aziaya and he jumped me in the men's room. He knew I was with you… Commander Callaghan." Greg let the reality of their exposure sink in. "And that we were part of the group that took El Karazim. He pulled a dagger and I had to dispatch him. I put his body in a dumpster behind the bar and cleaned the men's room." Greg's lips tightened, he felt guilty for not reporting it sooner. "I scanned the bar when it was over and he appeared to be alone. I didn't want to tell you that night because I thought you seemed genuinely interested in Amanda. I'm sorry, sir."

Michael considered that and replied, "After this business of being run off the road and the seatbelts being jammed, I don't want to take any more risks with Amanda's life. Contact HQ in Rochester and tell them I want a surveillance team on Amanda when she's in Rochester." Michael was deep in thought. He had the feeling that someone was following him. "Here at Bayshore, there's only one road into Bayshore Estates. Set up a surveillance post at the top of our road so we can watch every vehicle that comes into Bayshore. Have Lou take the first watch tomorrow morning and figure shifts for everyone until we get additional support from HQ."

"Yes, sir, I'm on it. I'll notify HQ before I go back to the bonfire." Connors could see the wheels turning in Michael's brilliant mind. "Will there be anything else, Commander?"

"Yes, I want to get some men down here and set up surveillance cameras. Have HQ send an additional team here first thing tomorrow morning to put up cameras on all the major roads leading onto and off of Pillar Point."

"Good idea. If we see something suspicious, we'll be able to act quickly."

HQ, a two and a half hour drive from Bayshore Estates, is located in Rochester, New York, in a cave overlooking the High Falls of the Genesee River. In 1956, the MFB received 122 million dollars from the president's black budget to build a secret facility in the high cliffs on the west side of the Genesee River, just south of the waterfalls. The cave was three hundred feet above the riverbed. Over the years, it was re-shored and outfitted with the latest in technologies including military satellite access, ground sensors that detected motion within five hundred feet of the secret entrances, high-grade weapons, and state-of-the-art defensive systems.

The commander could see LT's distress over holding back the information for so long. Commander Callaghan's facial expression softened a bit. "Good work with the Black Blade of Allah operative. I appreciate your consideration of my feelings. See what you can find in our database about this Jamaal Aziaya character and why he was in Chicago." He gave a curt nod and headed back to the bonfire with several bags of ice as Greg pulled his phone and called HQ.

Shortly after Michael put the extra ice in the coolers, Greg reappeared and said, "Let's get this party started."

After a few short words toasting the commencement of the season, Michael lit a match and tossed it into the meticulously stacked wood. When the match met the gasoline-soaked woodpile, the fire roared to life and flames, fifteen feet high, danced below the outstretched limbs of the giant oak trees.

The darkness settled over Bayshore Estates like a blanket. For the next several hours, the women talked about their winter experiences, while the men recounted adventures from their childhood. The evening was sprinkled with laughter and good spirits.

The stranger in the dark green Dodge Dart waited until it was dark before he ventured onto the private road of Bayshore Estates. He slowly followed the flashing dot on his computer screen that represented the Olds. When he was getting close, he pulled his car into the driveway of an empty cottage. There were no other cars and all the lights were out inside. After a quick recon to verify the place was empty, he opened the trunk of his car and retrieved a backpack and a Remington model 700 in .300 caliber with a night vision scope. There were very few streetlights on the private road and he slipped across the road and into the pasture that backed up against all of the cottages. He used the stone fence that separated the cottages from the cow pasture for cover as he moved closer to his target. When he saw the bonfire and recognized the Kane woman and her boyfriend, he backed off fifty yards and found a maple tree to climb to get a better vantage point.

Amanda began feeling the buzz from her fourth glass of wine when Mary asked her if she'd like to join the girls for a walk to the cottage for a potty break.

The walk from the bonfire to the cottage was close to seventy-five yards, and between the darkness and the alcohol, Amanda had to focus on walking straight. Amanda looked up and for the first time, she saw the brilliance of the star-studded sky of Bayshore Estates. The stars seemed closer, brighter and more abundant than Amanda had ever seen before. "Wow, look at the stars, they seem so big and close." Amanda was enraptured.

"Yes, it's great, I love the summers up here. We have great weather and we're surrounded by magnificent views," Karen agreed. All of the girls looked up at the starlit sky.

"Look—there goes a falling star, look how bright it is." Teresa pointed.

"I see it! It has a huge tail behind it."

"Your first one of the summer, don't forget to make a wish." Sue Miller was searching for more falling stars and making her own wishes.

"How many falling stars do you guys see in the summer?" Amanda was searching the sky. She felt like she could see a million galaxies.

"Tons, maybe fifteen a night when we're looking," Mary replied.

"I can tell I'm going to like it up here." Amanda smiled and the others could hear it in her voice.

On the walk back to the bonfire, Amanda realized how lucky she was to have Michael in her life. His friends treated her like one of their own and couldn't care less how much money she had.

As the night wore on, they sat contentedly around the fire sharing stories, telling jokes and drinking steadily. Bouts of gut-wrenching laughter could be heard several cottages away. Amanda wasn't used to drinking so much, but the s'mores and the munchies made her white wine taste even better.

At two a.m., the women converged on Michael's cottage to use the facilities. Amanda could hardly believe how fast the night was passing. Her buzz had taken on a new form.

He was perched between two limbs fifteen feet off the ground, and he had good shooting lanes. He could see that most of the men were carrying pistols tucked in the small of their backs. They probably knew this cow pasture inside out. If he shot, his escape options would be limited. He took out a bottle of water and sipped it slowly, trying to decide his next move, when he saw a snake slither past the tree he was perched in.

The women finished up and headed outside. When they started down the stairs, Mary and Amanda were walking side by side, with Mary next to the house.

The conversation was in full swing and no one heard the cracking of the steps under Amanda's feet. Just before they reached the bottom stair, it gave way. Amanda's leg dropped through the step as momentum carried her forward. Amanda grabbed for the outside railing and Mary's arm. Luckily, she found both.

Mary's quick reflexes and a sturdy railing saved Amanda from breaking her leg.

When the girls helped pull Amanda's leg out of the broken stair, they realized that she had probably suffered a sprained ankle. Mary and Teresa helped her back to the bonfire where she found relief in Michael's arms and another glass of wine.

Through his night vision scope, he could see that the Kane woman had fallen and was now limping along. He was beginning to formulate a plan, and he knew where to go to get the materials he needed. He'd had enough of this recon mission; it was time to set the trap. He climbed down from the tree and headed toward his car.

Within the hour, the bonfire had dwindled down to glowing embers and Michael and the guys extinguished the remnants with five-gallon buckets of water. After saying their goodbyes, everyone headed home to the sanctuary of their own beds.

After propping up Amanda's ankle and putting ice on it, Michael lay in the darkness that had become so familiar to him over his years performing black ops missions. He began to think about how his life might be with Amanda. A smile crept onto his face as he pictured them together at the cottage, swimming, boating, fishing, and enjoying bonfires with star filled nights.

The smile on Michael's face faded as his thoughts turned to the accident in Chaumont. The sticking seat belts, the open door, the runaway cement truck and the stranger at Foote's... all of these needed investigating, but not tonight. Michael was too tired and decided it could wait until morning, if his mind would shut down and allow him to sleep.

Tomorrow was a new day. A day of danger, and Michael would need his wits if they were going to survive the trap that had already been set.

CHAPTER 31

As the morning light peeked through the curtains, Amanda could hear bottles and cans clanging together. She rolled over and found that Michael was gone. The clock read 9:12 a.m. Her ankle and her hangover were painful.

"I've got to learn to watch how much I drink. These hangovers are a killer," Amanda groaned as she lifted up the covers to assess the damage to her ankle. "That doesn't look good."

Amanda slid out of bed and hopped to the window to see what Michael was doing.

He'd finished his five-mile run and was now at the bonfire site, picking up the bottles and cans from the night before.

Michael came in and sat next to Amanda. "How's my girl doing on this fine morning?"

"Not too good. My ankle hurts worse today than it did last night."

"You better let a doctor take a look at it." Michael pulled off the covers and looked it over. Years of field triage on wounded men had taught Michael basic medical care.

"I didn't know that you were a part-time doctor. What an added bonus for me," she joked.

Michael lowered the blankets. "I'm not. I was referring to the doctor in Watertown. That's about twenty minutes from here."

"Do you really think I need to see a doctor?" She sighed in frustration.

"When it comes to your health and well-being, it's better safe than sorry. You have a severe sprain or a break. Either way, you need to see a doctor and get an X-ray." The cottage phone rang, and Michael left to answer it while Amanda took a closer look at her ankle.

After a brief conversation on the phone, Michael returned to the bedroom. "That was Ace. He and Teresa wanted an update on how you're feeling."

"Did you tell them I feel like an ignorant fool for not paying attention last night and falling through the stairs?" Amanda pulled a pillow over her head in embarrassment.

"No, I didn't. I asked Ace for a ride to the city so you could see a doctor and then we can get a rental car to go home with." He pulled the pillow away. "You don't need to be embarrassed. I should have fixed the steps when we first got here. Come on, I'll help you get ready to go."

Ace and Teresa picked them up in the Olds. The morning was cool and dew clung to the grass, coating their shoes with moisture with every step. Michael eased Amanda into the back seat next to Teresa, and she lay her head against the headrest and closed her eyes.

Ace turned on the radio. During a news break, it was reported that the Thompson Park Zoo in Watertown had been broken into. The police called it malicious vandalism. Nothing of value had been taken, but some animals had been released, several of which were still unaccounted for, including several poisonous snakes.

"Damn kids, I don't get them sometimes. Why break into the zoo and let a bunch of animals go free?" Ace was shaking his head.

"Yes, I know what you mean."

Michael felt something rub up against his leg. He looked down and saw a pygmy rattlesnake slithering out from under his seat and coiling next to his ankle.

Michael knew that snakes were lethargic in cold weather and this poisonous killer was looking for warmth. "Ace, we have a situation. Look at my feet." Michael pointed at the snake.

Ace glanced over, his eyes going wide when he recognized the snake beginning to coil. "Those things aren't indigenous to this area. How in the hell did it get in my car?"

"Maybe we can revisit that question once we get rid of it." Michael wanted to get rid of the snake before it warmed up and became alarmed enough to strike him.

"If you've got a plan, then I'm all ears, let's hear it," Ace said with one eye on the road and one eye on the snake.

Both Amanda and Teresa were sleeping in the back seat. Teresa was snoring lightly with her mouth open, and Amanda was breathing heavily.

"Okay, here's the plan. I want you to turn the heat on high, the airflow to low, and switch the vents to the floor. The snake will feel the heat, and start to move toward it. When it's moving its head toward the heater and away from me, you pull a hard left, I'll open my door and the momentum should send the snake flying out of the car."

Ace positioned the heater as Michael had directed and slowed the car down. There was left hand turn coming up. The snake lifted its head and flicked its tongue at the new source of heat. It started to move toward the heat. Thankfully, Michael's seat had been pushed back as far as it could go to accommodate his long legs, allowing enough room for the snake to move forward.

Ace calculated the distance to turn off. "Michael, I can make this turn, but it's coming up fast, are you ready with the door?" Ace gripped the wheel tighter as the snake began to recoil itself closer to the heater vent.

Michael grabbed the door handle with his right hand. "I'm ready when you are. Make sure you've enough momentum to get this snake out of here."

Ace reached the turn in the road, slammed the accelerator to the floor of the car, pulled hard on the wheel, and executed a perfect three hundred sixty-degree spin. Michael had pushed his door open as the car began to spin and everything in the car began to slide toward the right. The snake launched out of the open door and landed on the road. As the car continued its slide, the squealing rear tires flattened the snake when they passed over it. They came to a stop and Michael closed his door.

"What happened?" Amanda startled awake in the back seat.

"Oh, nothing, it was just a raccoon crossing the road. Ace swerved a little to avoid hitting it," Michael reassured Amanda. "Are you all right back there?"

"Yes, we're fine." Teresa was still snoring.

A half hour later, they were at the House of the Good Samaritan Emergency Room, and by 11:30 that morning, Amanda was diagnosed with a severe ankle sprain. Doctor Heaply put her in a walking cast for six weeks so her ankle would have a chance to heal.

Ace and Teresa left to get a rental car for Michael; he stayed with Amanda and waited for the cast.

Michael and Amanda said their goodbyes to Ace and Teresa, and prepared for their ride back to Rochester. Less than a half hour into the two-and-a-half-hour trip, Amanda was sound asleep, and Michael was still thinking about the stranger at Foote's and who could have planted the snake in Ace's car.

Michael and Amanda had been there for less than an hour, when Amanda got the call that she was to report to the Rochester DA's office. Michael volunteered to go with her.

CHAPTER 32

By 4:30 p.m. Monroe County Sheriff Tom Mahoney, Monroe County Deputy Sheriff Barnes, Gates Police Detectives Hill and Trout, Monroe County District Attorney Roger Reilin, Livingston County District Attorney Paul Morgan, Mount Morris Police Chief Gordon Alice, and his deputy, John Popper, were gathered in Roger Reilin's conference room and had been reviewing evidence for three hours.

"Something is missing." Reilin shook his head.

"How can you say that?" Chief Gordon Alice was rubbing his temples. "On the Torchia case, we have *Kane*'s fingerprints on the bullet casings that were in *his* gun, which was left at the scene of the crime. We have a bartender that puts *his* wife going hot and heavy at the bar with the victim." The chief reviewed his notes.

He found the page he was looking for and continued. "He probably saw his wife and Torchia and he blew a fuse. When he goes back to his car to get his gun, he sees Torchia heading for his van. Kane decides to confront him outside instead of in the bar. They argue, and things get carried away. Torchia reaches for a tire iron, and Kane pulls his gun. They struggle and Kane shoots Torchia. In the heat of the moment, he panics and drops his gun. Then he drives an hour back to Rochester. Panicked, enraged, whatever you call it, Kane goes back to Chantel's place and carries out his threat against her. We also have *his* fingerprints on the knife, and semen on

Chantel's bed. I'll bet that when the autopsy comes back, she's loaded with his semen. On top of that, we have an eyewitness that says Kane was arguing with Chantel and threatening to come back to her apartment to straighten her out. What could possibly be missing except a confession?" The chief closed his notebook and shrugged.

Detective Hill was tired of beating the same dead horse. "Everything fits. We even found a watch that Chantel gave Kane in his bedroom. Kane goes to Chantel's apartment, they have sex, she tells him to leave the wife or she'll tell her about the affair. They get into a fight, and he takes off for Mount Morris to do damage control with the wife. When he gets there, he finds Cathy with Torchia, and in a jealous rage, he shoots Torchia. Then he returns to Rochester to settle the score with Chantel."

Detective Trout disagreed with his partner. "I don't see it. Doesn't make sense. Kane is college educated and has all of the disposable income he could want, so why throw it all away for a piece of ass? The wife probably wouldn't divorce him anyway, she just wanted to get even and have some fun. Even if Kane was that outraged, why wouldn't he hire the job out?"

DA Reilin set his pencil on the table and spoke up. "We need to get some answers. For example, was Cathy Kane at the scene of the murder, did she know Jeff had a gun, and did she have access to it? Did she leave the gun at the scene or did someone else? And why was Joshua Stein at the Kane residence at 8:30 on Saturday morning?" Reilin knew there was more to the story and he wanted answers.

"Either Kane is the dumbest guy out there, or someone did a great frame-up." Sheriff Tom Mahoney saw holes in the case, but couldn't refute the evidence they already had.

"Let's get some people in here for questioning. I want Jeff and Cathy Kane, his sister Amanda, the bartender from the Yankee Loft in Mount Morris, Mrs. Cooper from Colonial Manor and Joshua Stein," DA Reilin said. "I want everyone questioned separately. I want this to be a marathon interrogation. Let's get everyone here and keep them as long as possible. Maybe once fatigue sets in, we'll be able to trip someone up."

DA Reilin assigned specific tasks to everyone in the room. The game plan was to start the questioning that evening. No one would have a chance to rest, or conjure up alibis. DA Morgan chimed in and directed everyone to get prints from the person they interviewed as discreetly as possible.

Sheriff's deputies, police officers, and detectives were dispatched, and subpoenas were prepared. The process was started and it would be a long time before anyone would get any rest.

CHAPTER 33

The time was 6:00 p.m. on Sunday and due to the high-profile investigation, everyone was brought into District Attorney Reilin's offices to keep exposure to the press at a minimum.

Everyone brought in for questioning was separated, mirandized, and put in different rooms. Just to soften them up, they didn't start the questioning for forty-five minutes. DA Reilin's strategy of allowing fatigue and anxiety to work on those who had something to hide was starting to work.

Cathy Kane startled when Sheriff Mahoney and Deputy Sheriff Barnes entered the room.

Sheriff Mahoney wanted to set Cathy at ease. "Before we get started, is there anything we can get you, maybe a soda or some water?"

"No thank you, I'm fine." Cathy sounded nervous.

Sheriff Mahoney turned on the video recorder. "I know you were mirandized, are you sure you don't want an attorney?"

"I won't need an attorney." Cathy didn't want to raise suspicions.

Deputy Barnes began the questioning.

"Where were you on Friday night between the hours of 6:00 p.m. and 3:00 a.m.?" Deputy Barnes was leaning against the gray cinder block wall behind the table.

"At six o'clock I took my kids down to my parents' home in Mount Morris. The kids decided they wanted to stay the night, so around 9:30 I left and came home." Cathy hoped the bartender at the Yankee Loft would cover for her.

Sheriff Mahoney shifted uneasily in his chair. "I see. And what time did Joshua Stein come to your home in Mendon?"

"Joshua came to see Jeff around eleven or so. He said that he had some business to discuss with him." Cathy was starting to perspire.

"Why was Josh there the next morning at 8:30 when the police arrived?" Sheriff Mahoney watched Cathy's eyes dart back and forth.

"Earlier that evening, I heard some noises, and I thought it might have been a burglar, so I asked him to stay and sleep on the rec room couch." It sounded rehearsed.

Deputy Barnes examined his notes. "Do you know a Claire Pulaski?"

"Yes, I know Claire, we grew up together." Cathy's face turned pale and her voice dropped to a murmur.

"We talked to Claire and your parents yesterday. They both have a different story about what you did on Friday night. We have a statement from a bartender named Paul Scordo, who corroborates their stories." Sheriff Mahoney watched Cathy lower her head and saw her eyes fill with tears.

"This is going to be a long night, unless you start telling the truth." The deputy was getting impatient and didn't like Cathy lying.

"Okay, I wasn't truthful about what time I went home. Jeff and I got into a fight, kind of, and I wanted to go out with Claire and have some fun." Cathy pulled herself together and tried to hold back the tears.

The sheriff folded his arms across his chest and sat back in his chair. "Let's get to the crux of the matter. Tell us what happened at the Yankee Loft."

Cathy and stared at the wood grain on the glossy oak table. "When we got to the Yankee Loft, an old classmate named Gino Torchia was there. Gino was the first man in eons to pay any attention to me. He gave me so many compliments, I was swept off my feet."

She sighed. "We were drinking and laughing and after a couple of hours, he asked me if I wanted to go out to his van to listen to some music. I knew he was talking about having sex, and I didn't care. Jeff has been cheating on me for years and I wanted to even the score. I told him I'd meet him in the van, because I had to go to the women's room first. When I went outside, the parking lot was muddy from the rain, and I had a hard time getting to his van. When I got there, the windows were all steamed up so I went around to the back and opened the door."

There was a long silence as Cathy remembered the horror, and her eyes filled. "The stench hit me first, and I started vomiting. When I was finished, I saw Gino lying in all that blood, and there was a gun on top of him. I was scared, and I ran back to the Loft, slipping and sliding in the mud all the way. I had been splashed with mud on the way to Gino's van, so after I got Claire, we headed straight for the bathroom so I could clean up. That's when I told Claire that Gino had been murdered. After I scrubbed the mud off, we hightailed it out of there, and I came home."

Mahoney finished his notes, leaned forward and said, "Do you know if your husband owns a gun?"

Cathy was surprised by the question. "Yes. I know he owns a pistol and some hunting rifles, but I think he's got a permit for his guns."

"Do you know where he stores his guns, are they kept locked up?" The sheriff was fishing.

"He keeps his rifles in a locked gun cabinet and he keeps his pistol in a shoe box in the master bedroom closet."

"Do you have any idea what time you left the Yankee Loft and headed home?" Deputy Barnes ran a hand through his short brown hair.

"It must have been a little after midnight, I'm not really sure. I was pretty upset at the time."

"Your mother said you went home at ten o'clock and she tried calling you at home but got your voicemail. Which is it ten, or midnight?" The sheriff double-checked his notes.

"It was midnight. I had Claire call my mom and lie to her about what time I went home." Cathy swiped more tears from her cheeks.

"You said you got splashed with mud on your way to Gino's van. What kind of car was it that splashed you?" Deputy Barnes sat down beside the sheriff.

Cathy closed her eyes, trying to remember. "I don't know, it was raining out, and I had gotten the heel of my shoe stuck in the mud. I was bent over when it went by, but it looked like a dark sedan."

The sheriff leaned closer to Cathy. "Did you hear anything when you went outside—people fighting, yelling, or a gunshot, anything?"

"I heard a car backfire. It must have been that junker that splashed me with mud." Cathy was frustrated.

"How many times did the car backfire?" Deputy Barnes scribbled some notes.

"Just once, I think. That's all I heard was one."

"We'll be right back, sit tight." The sheriff and his deputy got up and left.

The questioning of Joshua Stein had been underway in another room with Chief Gordon Alice and his deputy, John Popper. The chief read Joshua his rights, and he declined counsel.

Chief Alice was sitting across from Joshua. "How long were you in the Marines?"

"Three years. I was discharged for striking an officer. After that, I got my bachelors and masters degrees from RIT and went to work for Kane." Joshua seemed composed. "I'm sure you could get a copy of my military records if you wanted to."

"How about Friday night? You said you went to the California Brew Haus at ten o'clock. You had a few drinks and played some pool. Is that what you were doing when Ann Chantel came in at eleven?" The chief read from his notes.

Joshua tried to be careful; he didn't want to misrepresent anything. "That sounds about right."

"What time did you leave?" The chief was taking notes.

"Around two a.m."

"Why did Ann come to talk to you?" Deputy Popper narrowed his eyes.

"I don't know." Joshua shifted in his chair.

"What do you mean?" Chief Alice leaned up onto his elbows.

"Ann and I were fighting over some work stuff, and we were barely on speaking terms," Joshua explained. "I was always the one to work with Jeff on acquisitions, and I was the one who carried the ball for Jeff when we traveled... until Ann started sleeping her way to the top." His resentment was obvious.

"Isn't it true that you and Ann used to date?" Deputy Popper inquired.

"Yes, Jeff put an end to that." Joshua spit out the words as if they tasted bad.

"How did he do that?" The chief started scribbling notes again.

"We had a product show in Chicago a while ago. On the first night of the show, I mentioned to Jeff that I was dating Ann, and he ordered me to stop," Joshua's said angrily. Deputy Popper and the chief made a note of it.

"I guess you were pretty mad at *both* of them, weren't you?" The chief egged him on.

"Not really. I got over it a long time ago." He sat back in his seat and sighed.

"What did Ann say to you that night at the bar?"

"She wanted to know if I was still interested in dating. I said no, and she left."

"I thought she was sleeping with Jeff Kane?" The chief was looking over his notes.

"She said she lived and learned. I guess Jeff dumped her and it was over between them."

Deputy Popper took a swig from his bottle of water. "Did she say that she and Jeff Kane had gotten into a fight?"

"No."

"That's all you and Ann talked about?" The chief didn't believe it.

"Yes, that was it. She just left and said if I change my mind to call her."

"Why did you go to Kane's house that night?" Deputy Popper asked.

"I went there to quit. Cathy told me she thought she heard an intruder shortly before I arrived and asked me to stay." It sounded rehearsed, but Joshua didn't care.

Chief Alice was not buying into Joshua's story. "Why did you want to quit?"

Joshua rolled his eyes and shook his head. "I was tired of dealing with Jeff Kane. The man is so arrogant and demanding. He has no loyalty to his employees." Joshua rubbed his forehead. "I deserve better."

The chief said, "Let me get this straight. You and Ann were fighting because she was sleeping her way into your job. You were tired of Jeff's shenanigans and wanted to quit. You deserved better than Ann and Jeff. Sounds like they both betrayed you."

Joshua sighed and said, "Look, I know it doesn't sound too good when you put it like that, but I didn't kill anyone."

The chief shot back, "It sounds like motive to me."

Joshua shook his head and wondered if he should get a lawyer.

"Sit tight, we'll be back in a little while." The chief motioned to his deputy and they left.

Detectives Hill and Trout had already gone over some of the information with Amanda, such as where she was on Friday night and Saturday morning during the times of the murders. Then the pressure started. Detective Hill went fishing.

"Amanda, do you know how much your father is worth?" He was reading a financial printout.

"No I don't, not exactly." Amanda hated when people brought up the money issue. "I thought I was here in regards to the murders of Ann Chantel and some guy I don't even know."

"Does twelve and a half billion dollars sound about right?" Trout ignored Amanda's reply.

"I'm not sure, but yes, that sounds close." Amanda just wanted to get it over with and get out of there.

"Do you and your brother fight much?" Detective Hill never looked up from his pad.

"No, actually we get along pretty good."

Detective Trout tilted his head and raised his eyebrows in question. "Do you know if your brother owns any guns?"

"Yes, I'm aware that he owns some guns." Amanda narrowed her eyes.

Detective Hill looked at Trout and then Amanda. "Do you know where your brother keeps his weapons stored?"

"What are you getting at? Are you trying to say I'm a suspect?" Amanda looked astonished.

"Everyone is a suspect, until we say otherwise," Trout snapped. "Jeff claims he didn't do it. The murderer used *his* gun. You knew he had one, and may have had access to it."

"Why would I want to kill those two people? What possible reason would I have?" she demanded.

Hill furrowed his brow and said, "I can think of twelve and a half billion reasons, Ms. Kane, why you'd want your brother to take the fall for a murder."

Amanda's face reddened. "I have absolutely nothing to gain by any of this. If Jeff goes to jail, then his stock in the company will be held in a trust for his children." Amanda was outraged and all but shouted, "Cathy would be the trustee of share of the estate until the kids turn twenty-one. *She* would control Jeff's share of the company, not me."

The detectives exchanged a look. Amanda realized that she had just given the police a motive for Cathy to frame Jeff.

"Cathy could never murder anyone. She's not like that, no way," Amanda backpedaled.

Detective Trout raised his right hand in an attempt to calm Amanda down. "How much would you guess Jeff's stock is worth today? Just your best guess, please."

Amanda shook her head, regretting what she had said.

"Ms. Kane, answer my question." Trout was getting angry.

"Over a billion dollars. Jeff and I both own stock worth over a billion dollars. But Cathy wouldn't—"

Detective Hill interrupted her. "We'll be back. Make yourself comfortable." Detectives Hill and Trout stood up and walked out of the room.

Detectives Hill and Trout led Michael into a small empty office. They confirmed that Amanda was with Michael on Friday night, and that they had spent the weekend together. Michael left out the part about his SUV being forced off the bridge.

Detective Hill started on Michael. "We have reason to believe that Amanda had two people murdered in order to frame her brother. What can you tell us about her demeanor this past weekend, was she nervous, on edge—did she seem distracted in any way?"

"That's insane," Michael blurted. "She would never kill anyone, let alone do it to frame her brother." He glared. He knew they were fishing.

"Maybe *she* wouldn't, Michael, but you could. We did a background check on you. Your records are classified. It seems you don't have any history beyond your stint in the Navy. Amanda stands to inherit billions of dollars if Jeff is in prison." Hill closed his folder. "Amanda meets an ex-Navy SEAL just before these murders take place. Strange timing, don't you think?"

Michael responded curtly, "As far as my military experience is concerned, my record of service to this country speaks for itself. As to the Kane fortune, I don't need it. I do quite well on my own."

Detectives Hill and Trout knew they were going nowhere with Michael.

"We'll find out soon enough. You stay here. We'll be back in a little while."

Michael pulled out his cell phone and texted a secure message to Greg Connors. Michael wanted Phillip Anzio and his MFB team to start investigating Jeff Kane, both murders, and both victims. Michael didn't mention in his text that he suspected Amanda's life was in grave danger.

District Attorney Roger Reilin and District Attorney Paul Morgan were questioning Jeff Kane. Attorney Jack Walsh was there, and as a courtesy, George Kane was allowed to sit in.

"Look, Jeff, if you didn't do it, we're here to help you clear this up, so start telling the truth." DA Reilin didn't like wasting time. "We know you went to Ann Chantel's apartment on Friday night, and that you left at eight. We know you got into a fight with her. We have a witness just down the hall that is putting that in a sworn statement as we speak. You claim you didn't go back to her apartment later that night, but you won't tell us where you were. We also have the murder weapon with your prints on it. In Mount Morris, Gino Torchia is murdered, and the gun found at the murder scene not only has your prints on it, but it's registered to you. So why don't you stop the bullshit and tell me what you did Friday night."

"I went to Ann's house and told her I was going to a friend's house to play poker and couldn't take her out. She got mad, we had a few words, and I left... that was it. As for Gino Torchia, I've never seen him before." Jeff dodged the question of where he actually was.

DA Morgan folded his arms across his chest. "How did your gun end up in Mount Morris?"

"I have no clue how my gun got down there. It could have been stolen months ago for all I know." Jeff had been coached on what to say.

"Whose house did you play poker at, and who was there?" inquired DA Reilin.

"I'd rather not say."

George Kane tried to convince Jeff what he needed to do. "Listen to me, son. If your buddy was such a good friend, he'd come forward and testify that you were with him, and get you out of this. You've got to think about yourself now."

"You don't understand, Father. He won't, he's wanted by the police," Jeff replied.

"Stay here. We'll be back in a few minutes." DA Reilin signaled to DA Morgan and they left.

The interviewing teams met in Roger Reilin's office to share what they learned. After exchanging notes, they began to piece the puzzle together.

DA Reilin wrote notes on a large dry-erase board as everyone pitched in to fill in the blanks.

There were pictures and photographs connected by strings, phone records, and bank accounts. When an ex-Navy SEAL with classified files and a former Marine are added, it's anyone's guess as to who committed the murders. Murder, wealth, betrayal, and a spy, what could happen next?

CHAPTER 34

The dark green Dodge Dart slowly approached Willey's bar and Grille, a local hangout on the edge of Shamrock that attracted a mixed crowd of bikers, locals and drug dealers.

The black Cadillac parked outside had the same Canadian plates as the car whose occupants had tampered with the SUV that the Kane woman and her boyfriend were riding in when the vehicle was forced off the bridge just a few days ago.

After parking around the corner from the Cadillac, he lit a cigarette and inhaled deeply. "Enemy of my enemy is my friend," he reminded himself, tucking his Smith and Wesson revolver into his belt at the small of his back and exiting his car.

He sat at the far end of the bar, where he could see the two men in black suits talking to two men dressed in blue jeans and T-shirts. The suits were of dark complexion with short-cropped hair, smoking short cigarettes without filters.

He had watched the suits talk to several different groups of young men over the last few hours. Most of the young men were happy to take advantage of the free drinks, but didn't seem interested in what the two men were selling. It was obvious to the trained eye that these two suits were recruiting.

One of the suits got up from the table, grabbed the empty pitcher of beer and went to the bar for a refill. When he paid the bartender, a flash of a tattoo was visible on the inside of his wrist. His Middle Eastern accent was unmistakable when he spoke to the bartender.

Two Middle Eastern men dressed in matching suits, driving a car with Canadian plates, recruiting men in America, sounded a lot like a terrorist cell looking for new members. Maybe it was time he made some new friends.

He waited patiently for the suits to run out of prospective candidates, and then he made his move. He sent of round of drinks over to their table—two White Russians. The suits asked what type of drink was being served and who ordered it. When the server told them, they waved him over.

After both parties expressed a mutual interest in a relationship, he was handed a burner phone with a preprogrammed phoned number. He was instructed never to use it unless they called him.

It would take several more meetings before he joined their terrorist organization, and a plan was devised for the Kane woman.

CHAPTER 35

There was a soft knock on the six-panel oak door. Assistant District Attorney Tim Roth walked in to a meeting was in progress. "We just got back some of the lab results you ordered from the medical examiner's office, and the crime tech's reports from the murder scenes, sir." Tim began reading the results to DA Reilin and his guests.

"Ann Chantel's autopsy reveals that she had sex several hours before she was murdered. There were no signs of vaginal tearing or other signs of rape. The medical examiner believes she engaged in consensual sex. He was able to match semen found on her bedspread to semen found in the victim. The stab wounds appear to have been made by a right-handed individual with an approximate height between five feet eight and six feet three, depending on whether the perpetrator was standing on the inner step or down on the outside landing." Tim passed the folder to his boss.

Tim pulled open a second folder with another report, and began to read from it. "As far as Gino Torchia's report, there were no signs of a struggle, no defensive wounds or any other physical signs that lead us to believe that Gino Torchia fought with the killer." He handed the folder to the DA.

ADA Roth opened a third folder and began reading. "According to the crime tech's report, there was no evidence of semen at that crime scene or on Gino Torchia. The gun found on the body was a thirty-eight caliber Smith and Wesson registered to Jeff Kane. The prints on the gun and bullet casing belong to Jeff Kane. The watch found at Jeff Kane's house has two prints on it and neither matches the prints on Jeff Kane's pistol permit." Roth slid it across the table to the DA. "There's a note in the file. They're still in the process of comparing the bullet that killed Torchia with the gun found at the murder scene."

DA Reilin looked around the room. "Does anyone have any thoughts they would care to share?"

The room was silent.

Reilin said, "It's too early for speculation—we need more information. Detective Hill, I want you to tell Joshua Stein that we found semen in Ann Chantel's body and ask if he would be willing to give us a blood sample so we can exclude him."

He looked at Mahoney and said, "Sheriff Mahoney, you and your deputy can tell Cathy Kane that we found vaginal fluid belonging to an unknown woman at the crime scene in Mount Morris and ask if she would consent to a vaginal smear to confirm it's not hers."

Without waiting for comment, he said, "DA Morgan and I will tell Jeff Kane that we found blood in Chantel's apartment that does not belong to her, and ask him for a sample to rule him out. If everyone consents to the tests, we'll find out who is sleeping with whom, and where a motive might come into play." Reilin was on a roll, and his excitement showed.

"Hold on a second," Chief Alice countered. "Why do we need to get a vaginal smear from Cathy Kane? Won't a blood test work?"

"A vaginal smear will tell us if she's had sex in the last day or two. If she has, then maybe we'll be able to identify her partner." DA Reilin rubbed his stubble.

All of the interviewees, in an attempt to show they were cooperating fully, consented to the tests without hesitation. Within minutes, all of the interview tapes were collected and everyone who had to give a blood test or get a vaginal smear was escorted to the Genesee Hospital Emergency Room for their procedures, courtesy of the Monroe County District Attorney's Office.

Thursday morning, DA Reilin, who had the samples shipped to the Monroe County Forensic labs for testing, was receiving a fax at his office that would detail the results of the tests.

"Okay, Roger, now we find out who's lying." Morgan pulled the first page from the fax machine. "The DNA in Jeff Kane's blood matches the DNA in the semen found in Ann Chantel's body. This means Jeff Kane slept with Ann within twenty-four hours of her death."

"Well, this is interesting." Morgan was still reading the reports. "The vaginal smear taken from Cathy Kane reveals there was semen and fluids present, and the DNA of that semen is Joshua Stein's."

"So, Jeff Kane is doing Ann Chantel, and his wife Cathy is humping Joshua Stein. This is a screwed-up mess." Reilin shook his head

"It gets better," Morgan said. "We got everyone's prints on Sunday night and we tried to come up with a matching print for the watch in Jeff Kane's bedroom. We found our guy, and it's Joshua Stein."

"Joshua and Ann dated for a while." Reilin started to pace. "Joshua is told to back off Ann by Jeff. The more he thinks about it, the angrier he gets. He decides to quit. He wants to get out from under Jeff Kane, so he goes to Kane's house and tells Cathy about Jeff and Ann's affair. Both feel betrayed. They sleep together and one of them suggests they get even with Jeff."

"Okay, do they want revenge bad enough to kill Chantel and Torchia in order to frame Jeff for the murders?" Morgan shrugged.

"With Jeff in jail, Cathy and the kids would have all the money they need and a divorce as well. But Torchia has nothing to do with this mess. What reason would they have to kill him?" Reilin asked.

"And why kill two people? If you're going to frame someone, then one murder would be enough," Morgan suggested.

"What's in it for Joshua Stein? Unless he and Cathy were having an affair, and they wanted to get rid of Jeff before he found out," said Reilin. "That would give them motive, and opportunity.

According to the bartender, Joshua Stein stayed at the California Brew Haus until closing at two a.m., and Mrs. Cooper, Ann Chantel's neighbor, remembers hearing a commotion around two thirty. By the time she got out of bed and checked, Ann Chantel was dead. Except for one problem, we would have a nice case."

"What problem would that be?" Morgan asked.

"We have no witnesses or hard evidence against anyone but Jeff," Reilin replied.

By four o'clock that afternoon Jeff, Cathy, and Joshua were back at Reilin's office in different interrogation rooms.

District Attorneys Morgan and Reilin started by questioning Joshua first.

"Give it up, Joshua. We found semen in Cathy that matched your DNA 99.999%," Reilin accused. "And yours was the only semen we found. She was sleeping with you, and only you."

Morgan chimed in, "And besides that, we have your prints on the watch found under her bed. It looks as though you and Cathy were having an affair. You wanted to be together permanently, and *you* wanted to take control of the company. Maybe you figured the easiest way was to frame Jeff. Put him in jail, take his wife *and* his company."

"It was nothing like that at all. I did go there to quit, and I *was* angry with Jeff, and so was Cathy. She knew that he'd been cheating on her for a long time. She just wanted to have sex to get even with him. After all, if Jeff and Ann were having sex, why couldn't Cathy and I? We had sex, yes, but that was it, that one time, that night." Joshua's mouth dried up and sweat ran down his back.

His mind raced back to Friday night and the conversation he had with Cathy before falling asleep. When Cathy said they should get rid of Jeff, get married and take over the company.

Joshua wondered if he was playing into Cathy's hands. Could Cathy have committed the murders? Did Cathy set up the whole thing to frame Jeff? Was she trying to frame or implicate Joshua, too? It was like a bad dream and. Another bead of sweat dripped down the center of his back.

"We're going to go talk to Cathy for a while, Joshua. You sit here and think about your future." Joshua wiped his sweaty hands on his pants.

Morgan and Reilin walked into the interview room where Cathy was sitting with her attorney, John Marconi. Cathy stopped whispering, sat up straight, and began to rub her hands together. She put them on her lap after a whisper from Marconi.

Marconi was well known in the DA's office as an old-timer who sometimes fell asleep at the table during interviews. He probably should have retired several years ago.

"Tell me about Joshua Stein." Morgan reached for his pencil.

"What do you want to know?"

"Quit the games, Cathy. We know about you and Joshua. What I want to know is how long this affair has been going on," DA Morgan demanded.

"I don't know what you're talking about."

"We found semen in your vaginal smear that belonged to Joshua. We know you two slept together last Friday night. We know that you were the last one to see Gino Torchia alive, and Joshua was one of the last people to see Ann Chantel alive. Now you can either start telling us the truth, or you can tell it to a jury." Morgan was trying to push Cathy over the edge.

"Friday night was the first time." Cathy sighed, feeling as if a huge weight was lifted off her chest and she could breathe again.

"You don't expect us to believe that line of crap, do you?" Morgan snapped. "What a coincidence. Gino and Ann get killed on the same night you and Joshua do it for the first time. What was it, some sort of celebration?"

"What are you saying? Do you think that Joshua or I had something to do with the murders?" Cathy was starting to panic and her face color drained from her face.

"What do you think we should be thinking? We found your husband's gun at the scene of the murder in Mount Morris. You had access to the gun and the victim. Joshua admits to fighting with Ann at the California Brew Haus just hours before she was murdered. You're sleeping with each other, and with Jeff out of the way, what's to stop you two lovebirds from taking over the company and living your life of lust?" Reilin pressed.

"I didn't kill anyone!" Cathy exclaimed in a loud and frightened voice. "You've got to believe me." A tear ran down her cheek.

Reilin shouted, "Did you kill Gino Torchia or Ann Chantel to get even with your husband?"

"No, no, no. I may have been angry with my husband, I may have even hated him at times, but I would never hurt anyone," Cathy denied, pleading with them to believe her.

Cathy elbowed the sleeping Marconi who jumped and said, "I object, your Honor."

Too embarrassed to say anything further, Marconi sat back in his chair and looked at his feet.

Morgan folded his arms across his chest. "Are you ready to stop lying?"

"Yes." Cathy was sniffling.

"How long have you and Joshua been sleeping together?"

"Friday night was the first time... I swear."

Reilin continued, "Why did Joshua go to your house?"

Cathy shrugged. "He said he wanted to see Jeff."

Morgan asked, "When you told him Jeff wasn't there, why did he stay?"

"I invited him in to talk for a while. I thought I would need an alibi, because I knew Gino was dead, but I swear, I didn't kill him. Then after a while, I invited him up to my bedroom." Cathy hung her head in shame as she described how she coaxed Joshua into making love to her.

"Did you notice anything unusual about the way Joshua was dressed when he got there?" DA Reilin stopped pacing.

"No."

"Did he seem nervous or distracted?"

"No..." Cathy tried to remember. "He seemed a little disturbed about something, probably the fact that Ann and Jeff were sleeping together."

"We'll be back." Morgan motioned to DA Reilin to join him.

Morgan and Reilin went back to Reilin's office before questioning Jeff Kane. "What do you think?" Reilin closed the door behind them. "Are they in it together, or are they acting alone?"

"Either they're in it together and she washed their clothes after the murders, or someone else did it. There was no sign of blood at her house or on his clothes. The timeframe is too tight for him to go somewhere else to get cleaned up." Morgan wasn't convinced that Joshua and Cathy had committed the murders. "Besides, I sent our team over to Joshua Stein's house and they performed a top to bottom search that yielded nothing. No fibers, no trace of blood, nothing on his computer... nothing that would indicate his involvement."

"I would have to agree that the timeframe only works if they're in it together. But I'm not sure she has it in her to commit murder," Reilin replied. "What do you say we get a quick cup of coffee and go talk to Jeff Kane?"

CHAPTER 36

The conversation between Jeff Kane and his attorney Jack Walsch ended abruptly when DA Morgan and DA Roger Reilin entered the room.

"Jeff, let's get a few facts out in the open. First, we know you had sex with Ann Chantel because your DNA matches the semen we found in Ann's body and on her bedspread. Second, we found your fingerprints on the murder weapon in Ann's apartment, as well as your fingerprints on *your* gun at the scene of the crime in Mount Morris. So if you want to start telling the truth, maybe we can find something to work with." DA Reilin handed a copy of the DNA report to Jack Walsch.

"Before Jeff answers that question, I want full disclosure of any exculpatory information or evidence about this case that you have," Jack Walsch declared in an angry tone. "You have no right to ask my client any questions about evidence that has not been disclosed to me, and you know that. This is unacceptable. I should report you to the disciplinary board." Jack Walsch was furious.

"Jack... relax, you already know about the gun and fingerprints on the knife. We just got back the DNA results today," DA Reilin replied.

"What else did you get tonight?" Walsch asked. "I want verbal disclosure before my client continues."

"Joshua Stein and Cathy Kane slept together on Friday night." DA Reilin was trying to get a reaction out of Jeff.

"No fucking way." Jeff sat up straight. "You're lying."

"Joshua's DNA matches the semen found in Cathy's vaginal smear, and they both admitted it when confronted with the facts." Morgan couldn't help smiling.

"That cheating bitch, and that backstabbing asshole... I'll kill them both...." Jeff was enraged, his faced flushed bright red and sweat began to bead up on his forehead. There was a brief silence as the three other men realized what Jeff had said, and looked at each other in astonishment.

"It was a figure of speech. I didn't really mean I was going to kill anyone," Jeff continued, realizing how his outburst must have sounded. "You have got to understand—I just found out that my wife is sleeping with one of my employees, a man who I trusted with so much of my company. I was just shocked, you understand that, don't you?" Jeff pleaded.

"I understand that two people are dead, and you have a very short fuse," Reilin countered.

"What do you want to know?" Jeff conceded.

"I want to know if you killed Ann Chantel or Gino Torchia," DA Reilin demanded.

"I didn't kill anyone," Jeff replied emphatically.

"Then who wants to see you framed for murder? Who has a grudge against you? Who has the most to gain if you went to jail for life? Who has a score to settle? Jeff, who do you think could have done this to you?" Morgan queried in an aggravated voice.

Jeff sat staring at the wood-grained table thinking of all the people he had wronged and he inwardly winced. He couldn't begin to count how many times he had cheated on his wife, and how many people must really hate Jeff Kane for being rich and powerful. He knew he abused his position of authority. "I don't know..." Jeff shook his head.

"Perhaps you could tell us who had access to your gun, who could have known about you and Ann? Who else could have done this?" Morgan was not buying Jeff's story.

"I don't know, I just don't know. I can't believe Cathy and Joshua were sleeping together. Maybe it was them. Cathy had access to my gun and Joshua knew where Ann lived. With me out of the way, the two of them would only have Amanda to compete with for control of the company." Jeff was somber and the realization that his wife had betrayed him was clouding his mind.

"What do you mean that Amanda would be their only competition for control of the company? How about your father? He still runs things, doesn't he?" Morgan quizzed.

"He does right now, but he has had Amanda and me handling more of the business over the last few years. My father has not announced this yet, but he plans on a semi-retirement at the end of this year." Jeff sighed and leaned back in his chair.

"Who will run the company, you or Amanda?" DA Reilin was taking notes.

"My father has not decided yet. We are both VPs, and although Amanda is older and has been with the company longer, I have a broader range of duties. We just don't know, and Father won't say until shortly before he announces."

There was a knock on the door, followed by an assistant district attorney announcing that DA Morgan had a call waiting.

George Kane was sipping on a glass of Hennessy cognac in the study of his Mendon estate home. George looked around at the marble statues that his late wife had bought him for various anniversaries, his oversized mahogany desk, the leather furniture, the books that filled out the bookcases, and the wet bar. He began to realize that he had worked too hard at building up his business to let a mess like this disgrace his family name. When the phone rang, George picked it up. "This is George Kane."

"Hello, George, this is Michael Callaghan and I need your help." Michael and his team had spent the last two days investigating Jeff,

169

Joshua and Cathy. Michael had a hunch, but he needed George's help if he was going to track down the murderer.

George rubbed his chin. "What can I do for you, Michael?"

Michael leaned forward onto his desk. "One of the companies that I own does security and investigative work for some private clients. I have taken it upon myself to investigate the murders that Jeff has been charged with." Michael paused for a moment and then continued. "If Jeff is innocent, he is going to need more than an attorney to get him off." Michael was looking to protect Amanda, more than get Jeff off.

George Kane nodded, took a sip of cognac and said, "Michael, don't take this the wrong way, but I have looked into your background. Using some of my connections in congress, I was able to determine that you do some work for the Department of Defense. Is that the private security work that you are referring to?"

Michael sat back and rolled his eyes. "I am not at liberty to discuss my clients, George. I'm offering my help. Now if you would rather rely on the police for a fair and impartial investigation, then I'll be on my way."

George knew Michael was highly respected and didn't want to upset him. "I am sorry, Michael. What can I do to help?"

Michael smiled. "You can start by telling me everything you know or suspect."

"I know my son is a hot head, and he has cheated on his wife in the past. God knows that Cathy had every right to cheat on him. I just wish it were with someone else instead of Joshua Stein. I guess Joshua got caught in a bad mess at a bad time," George said, trying to lay some groundwork for Michael.

"How did you know about Jeff and Ann, and Joshua and Cathy?" Michael inquired.

"I have friends at the DA's office who are keeping me up to date on developments."

"I compliment you on your resourcefulness, George. Is there anything else you can tell me?" Michael pulled out a small pocket notebook.

"I know Jeff is not a murderer, and I think there may be more to this than meets the eye." George picked up his glass and started to swirl the liquid.

"If you have additional information, then please advise me of it, and I'll do everything in my power to clear Jeff." Michael sounded sincere.

"I am not sure what's to be found, if anything. But... possibly a clue or two may turn up." George tried to be as discreet as possible.

"I see, and where would we be looking for these possible new clues?" Michael was in no mood for cloak and dagger conversations.

"I'll have my secretary make copies of some of our corporate files, and I'll include the DNA testing that the DA has completed." George sounded tired and drained. "There could be something of use for you in the files."

"Why would this be a good hunting ground for clues?" Michael wished George would get to the point.

"Well... let's just say that Jeff has on occasion ruffled some feathers, and that perhaps he's been bitten back and doesn't know it." George took another sip.

"Do you know who the bird is?" Michael suspected that George Kane knew more than he was telling him.

"I am not even sure there is a bird at this point. All I know is that my son may have some negative qualities, but committing murder is not one of them. If you would be kind enough as to have one of your people swing by my office tomorrow at eleven a.m., my secretary will have copies of the files in question ready for you." George sighed.

"I'll send a man up to pick up the files, and let's hope for Jeff's sake that a hidden clue can be found amongst all those feathers." Michael wondered if he was being sent on a wild goose chase, or if George knew more than he was letting on.

"Thanks for your help, Michael." As George hung up the phone, he realized how important all those political donations and fund-raising parties really were.

When DA Morgan returned, he informed everyone that he needed to be elsewhere and everyone would be free to leave for the evening.

"I have just one request." Jeff looked at the two DAs. "Would it be possible for me to go up to the Thousand Islands this weekend? My sister has invited me to join her and her boyfriend at his cottage to relax and unwind."

"I think that would be okay. If we need anything, we'll call you on Monday." DA Reilin made a note to check out Michael Callaghan's place in the Thousand Islands.

Jeff was hoping to relax and get away from the stress, but new adventures were just around the corner.

CHAPTER 37

Friday afternoon at the Kane Corporate Headquarters, the news of Ann Chantel's sudden death, and rumors of Jeff's involvement, created a sullen atmosphere. There was no talk of weekend plans, just the quiet shuffling of papers and an occasional *clack*, *clack*, *clack*, as a secretary walked down one of the marble-tiled hallways.

Although Jeff didn't show his emotions, Amanda knew that he was hurting. He wasn't his usual arrogant and condescending self. He'd been quiet and reserved all week. Amanda wasn't sure if Jeff's disposition was due to Ann's death, the police investigation, or both. She knew she loved her brother, and he needed her support.

Amanda walked into Jeff's office to find him staring blindly out his window from atop the Changing Scenes Building. "Hey, little brother, you're still going to join us this weekend at Michael's cottage, aren't you?"

"Yes, but I'll be coming alone." Jeff turned his high-backed leather chair around to face Amanda.

"What about Cathy and the kids, don't they want to come? Michael has plenty of room." Amanda tilted her head.

"Cathy and I haven't spoken all week. Life at home has been… very stressful. I think I need a couple of nights without her so I can figure out what I'm going to do." Jeff didn't want to tell Amanda about the adultery.

"Well, I guess things *have* been stressful around here lately," Amanda consoled him. "Here's the address to Michael's cottage. What time do you think you'll be there?"

"I don't know. I'll try to get there tonight, but it may be first thing tomorrow. That doesn't screw up any of your plans, does it?"

Amanda paused for a moment, somewhat shocked that Jeff had even considered the fact that she might have plans... truly atypical behavior for Jeff. "No, if we're not there, just walk right in. The door is always unlocked when Michael and I are spending the weekend up there. Take the first bedroom on the left and call it home. If we're not having a bonfire, I'll leave a note telling you where we are."

"Sounds good, I'll see you up there." Jeff picked up the paper with the address and directions and Amanda left his office.

Jeff returned his gaze to the view of northeast Rochester, the gritty drug capital of the city.

Michael and Amanda were loading up the back of Amanda's BMW convertible with her clothes.

"Are you sure you want to take the Beamer instead of the Jag? I think we'd have more room in the Jag." Michael eyed Amanda's suitcases taking up most of the trunk, leaving very little room for his clothes, let alone any tools.

"I really want to take the Beamer because I haven't driven it lately and I want to make sure it doesn't sit too long."

"Okay, but I won't have any room for my tools and that means it'll take longer for me to finish up the cottage." Michael hated being without his own vehicle. He made a mental note to buy a second vehicle for emergencies.

"That's okay, honey, with everything else that's been happening around here, you need a break anyway."

"You're right. Besides, my SUV should be ready for me to pick up by now. I wonder how many of my tools were lost." Michael had some semi-automatic weapons hidden in the door panels of his custom built Porsche Cayenne.

174

"I'm sure that most of them are gone." Amanda smiled and winked. Michael knew he wouldn't get any remodeling done this weekend.

The weather on the ride to Bayshore Estates was warm and sunny. Michael put the top down so they could bask in the warm August sun. Amanda made the most of their ride by reclining her seat and soaking up the sun like a flower soaks up a fresh spring rain.

Michael glanced at Amanda and smiled. "You're going to love riding in my boat."

"Are you going to put your boat in the water this weekend?" she asked excitedly.

"That's the game plan, but there could be one minor hitch."

"What?"

"If my SUV isn't ready, then we won't be able to tow the boat to the water." Michael raised one eyebrow.

"Oh yeah, I almost forgot about that, with everything else happening. Michael, you saved my life and I love you so much," Amanda replied. She leaned over and kissed him on the cheek.

When they reached the cottage, there was a message waiting for them on the answering machine from the Jefferson County Sheriff's Office asking Michael to call regarding his SUV.

Michael returned the call and asked for Sheriff Larry Joobsen.

"This is Sheriff Joobsen."

"Sheriff, this is Michael Callaghan. You asked me to call you regarding the accident and my SUV."

"Yes, thank you for calling, Mr. Callaghan."

"Please, call me Michael."

"Fine. Michael, I need talk with you about your SUV," Sheriff Joobsen explained.

"Is everything okay?" Michael looked to see if Amanda was listening.

"We found something very suspicious. It seems as though someone either spilled, or deliberately put some superglue on the buttons that release your seatbelts, and that's the reason you couldn't release them. Do you know anything about this?" The sheriff sounded like he was distracted by something else.

"No, I have no idea what could have caused that. Could you please hold for one second?"

"Sure," the sheriff replied.

Michael put his hand over the phone and yelled to Amanda, "Honey, I'm going to be on the phone another couple of minutes. Do think you could go out to the car and bring in the food so it doesn't get too warm?" He didn't want Amanda to overhear his conversation.

"Sure thing, I can go right now if you want." Amanda put the last of her clothes into the dresser that she'd made her own.

As Amanda walked by, she gave Michael a kiss on the cheek.

"Thank you for holding, Sheriff. I remember Amanda saying that her door was open slightly after we got our ice cream. Up until that point, we buckled and unbuckled our seat belts several times that morning." Michael tried to recall everything that happened that morning.

"Did you see anyone around your car, or anyone that looked suspicious?"

"No, the ice cream stand got real busy, but nothing unusual."

"Can you think of any reason someone would want to hurt you or anyone that might be angry with you?" The sheriff was thumbing through reports.

"No, nothing I can think of." There had been several particularly nasty black ops missions over the past few years that resulted in threats of vengeance against him and his team. He began to wonder if somehow the Black Blade of Allah had tracked him to Bayshore Estates. He hated lying to Amanda, but he didn't want to alarm her.

"If anything comes to mind or anything else happens, call us," the sheriff requested.

"I sure will. Is my SUV ready for me to pick up?"

"I'm sorry, Michael. After we cut out the seat belts, we towed your vehicle to the Coffeen Street Porsche Dealer so they could replace the seat belts and install a new motor and electrical system.

I thought you knew and approved it. You'll have to call them to see if it's ready."

"Thank you for your help." Michael hung up the phone and watched Amanda walk into the house with the cooler containing some of the food.

"Is everything all right?" Amanda asked when Michael hung up the phone.

"Yes, the sheriff thought I might want to know where they towed my SUV to be repaired and asked how we were doing." He began to help unload the groceries.

By the time the groceries and Michael's clothes were unpacked, the phone had rung several times. The whole Bayshore Estates gang had called to make plans for the evening. During one of the calls, Michael told Greg that his seatbelts were tampered with.

"We need to put the team on alert. We could have hostiles in the area."

"I'll see to it, sir." Greg Connors easily switched to black ops mode when they discussed MFB business.

"Do you've any updates on that other issue?" Michael inquired nonchalantly, hoping Amanda wasn't paying attention to his conversation.

Connors scrolled through several encrypted emails taken from the DA's files, courtesy of HQ's hacking. "Jeff Kane has been busy with some buyouts for the company. Ann Chantel and Joshua Stein were involved in a relationship that ended badly. Gino Torchia was a construction worker who had no ties to anyone except Cathy Kane. So far we haven't been able to put together a motive for the murders. It seems unlikely that Jeff Kane had committed the murders, since he was doing some drugs and playing poker with a drug dealer named Poncho Carr in the city on Friday night. We got confirmation of his whereabouts from our tap on the city's closed-circuit traffic cams." LT Connors leaned back in his chair and rubbed his eyes. "We haven't finished tracking Jeff's movements for the whole night yet."

Michael glanced down the hallway. "Okay, tell HQ to keep digging, and keep me updated. Good work, LT. I'll see you later. I can't wait to get a few games of pool in at Foote's."

"Rumor has it that Amanda is pretty good at shooting pool. I think some of the other girls are a little worried, or jealous, or both." Greg laughed.

"I gotta run. Catch you later."

By seven thirty, everyone had gathered at Foote's for beer and pizza. When they were finished eating, the guys shot pool and the girls split up and played shuffleboard or mini-bowling.

In the dusty parking lot, a dark green Dodge Dart slowly backed into a space beneath the low hanging branches of a thirty-year-old oak tree. The stranger sat in his car for thirty minutes, taking in every detail and movement in and around the area. When he got out of the car, he examined the oak tree and its branches, opened the trunk, and retrieved a Remington model 700 in .300 caliber with a night vision scope. After slinging the rifle over his shoulder, he climbed on top of his trunk, reached up, grabbed a limb and climbed into the tree.

Climbing up fifteen feet created the perfect vantage point to see into Foote's and the surrounding area. After using his Ka-Bar knife to trim some branches, he settled on a large limb and rested his back against the trunk. His shooting lanes provided clear views of all of the windows and the doorways.

After cleaning the scope, he lifted the rifle and turned on the night vision. The green hues came to life. He rested the rifle against a branch and looked through the scope and into Foote's. The lighting inside the building was low, which necessitated the night scope. The place was crowded, more so than he would have guessed based on the number of cars in the parking lot.

The crosshairs settled on the Kane woman. She was playing shuffleboard and drinking beer with several other women. From his vantage point a quarter mile down the road, he could see that she and her boyfriend had arrived in a BMW and another shorter, stockier man and a woman had driven the Oldsmobile. Maybe he'd placed the snake in the wrong car—a stupid mistake.

He counted five men, including the boyfriend, playing pool together. They were muscular and fit, maybe ex-military, and maybe they were concealing ankle-holstered pistols. Maybe they were still in the game. He had to be careful and get the Kane woman alone.

Michael finished a game of pool and while he was waiting for Ace to break, he walked over to Amanda and gave her a hug. "How's your game going?" he whispered into Amanda's ear, looked over her shoulder and out into the parking lot.

"Good. The girls are a lot of fun. It's Teresa and me against the Miller sisters." Amanda suddenly felt Michael tense, and she pulled away and looked at him. "What's wrong?"

Michael stepped between Amanda and the window. "Nothing. Would you do me a favor? Would you mind asking Carol if she can turn the music up on the jukebox?"

Amanda could tell something was wrong. Michael was nodding to Greg. "Sure, is there anything else you want me to do?"

Michael smiled and looked into Amanda's eyes. "No, that's all. I really appreciate it."

As soon as Amanda stepped away, Greg joined Michael. "What's up, boss?"

"I just saw a face backlit in green. There's a man in a tree using night vision. Turn off the shuffleboard game and have the women join you on the other side of the pool table. Tell Lou to go turn all of the lights on as bright as possible and have JR meet me out back." Michael reached down and pulled his Glock model 30 .45 caliber from his ankle strap and tucked it into the back of his pants.

"Shit, I've been made." The stranger turned off the scope and dropped down out of the tree. He bent over and slipped into his car, fired it up and took off.

179

Michael and JR came around the back of the building in time to see a dark car with no lights turned on rumble onto the main road. Michael looked up and saw that the streetlight at the beginning of the driveway was out. "Well, JR, it looks like we scared him away. Not a word to the women, I don't want them getting upset."

It was too close for comfort and poorly planned. The stranger cursed at himself as he drove down Pillar Point. He had failed to black out his face and the boyfriend must have seen the green reflection on his cheeks. A stupid mistake and now he had to move quickly. He needed to get the Kane woman soon.

Time passed quickly. Before long, two a.m. was upon them, and it was time to return to Bayshore Estates. They proceeded in a caravan, at a speed that would reduce the risk of being pulled over for a DWI.

When Amanda started to get undressed, her cast began to itch like never before. "Michael, my cast is really itching, do you think the beer that I spilled in it would cause it to itch this bad?"

"Yes, the fabric on the inside probably got wet. I can get a coat hanger and you can use that to help scratch inside the cast," he suggested.

"That would really be a big help." Amanda tried sticking her finger down into the cast to scratch. "Where do you suppose Jeff is? He should have been here by now."

"I guess he got caught up talking with Cathy. They do have a lot to talk about, considering everything that's happened." Michael unfolded the wire coat hanger into one long wire that could slide down into Amanda's cast.

"Thank you, honey." Amanda took the hanger from Michael. "I really thought Jeff would have come tonight. He's not much of a talker when it comes to admitting he's made some mistakes. Besides, the last thing I heard was Cathy really didn't want to talk with Jeff."

"Well, let's not worry about that tonight. I'm sure Jeff will fill you in on what happened, tomorrow." Michael watched Amanda scratch. "You should be careful with that thing, you could cut yourself."

"Every time I scratch one part of my leg, another part starts itching. I don't know if I'm going to be able to sleep."

"Why don't you come over here and I'll take your mind off your leg?"

"I'm not kidding, this thing really itches." As soon as the words came out, Amanda realized Michael was suggesting they end their wait. "Michael, I really want us to make love..." Amanda stopped scratching and looked deep into Michael's eyes. "But this thing is killing me," she moaned and continued to scratch frantically.

"Is there anything else I can do for you?"

"No, I know you're tired, it's been a long night. Why don't you go to bed and if I can get this to stop itching, I'll join you."

"Okay." Michael tried to be understanding. "But if you need any help, let me know."

After a quick kiss and a short hug, Michael got into bed, and Amanda went to the living room to continue scratching.

CHAPTER 38

Jeff Kane left work and went home to find Cathy had taken the kids to her mother's. The note also said Jeff could find a plate of food in the refrigerator. If he wanted to talk, she would be at her mother's house and he could call her there.

"Thanks for the food. I guess we really don't have much to say to each other right now," he muttered under his breath.

After a quick bite to eat and a shower, Jeff was ready to leave for Bayshore Estates. He decided to grab a six pack for the ride.

He slid behind the wheel of his canary yellow Ferrari Testarossa, turned the key and its twelve cylinders roared to life. He unfolded the paper with Michael's address and dropped it on the passenger seat. "Easy enough, only a few turns." Jeff cracked open a beer, and took off.

Jeff consumed his first beer within fifteen minutes of starting his trip. "Ah, that feels better." He tossed the empty out the window and reached for another beer.

"If I keep drinking this fast, I'll have to stop in Oswego for another six pack," Jeff boasted to himself about his high tolerance for alcohol.

The drive was long and monotonous. Every song on the radio seemed to be about falling in love or breaking up. Jeff was not in the mood to hear either. When he reached Oswego, it was nine thirty p.m. and he was down to two beers.

"I guess I should stop and grab that other six pack. After all, it's the weekend and I've had one hell of a week," Jeff grumbled and started looking for a store that sold beer.

As Jeff left Oswego, he looked for some CDs to play instead of listening to the radio. His search kept him so busy that he overshot the turn onto Route 104B that would have taken him to Route 3, and then on toward Pillar Point. Unaware he missed his turn, Jeff kept driving, drinking and changing CDs every time a song remotely hinted about love. He thought about Ann and the good times they had. He couldn't help thinking that if he had gone back to her house the night of the murders she might still be alive. She could have been his alibi. Maybe he wouldn't be in trouble with the law. He could have made up with Ann and they might still be lovers.

The sign on the side of the road read "Mexico 2 miles." "I don't remember reading anything about going through Mexico. I must have missed my turn. What's new. I seem to be missing a lot lately," Jeff complained, reaching for another beer. "If I go straight, I'll eventually hit Route 81 and then head north to Watertown." When he reached Route 81, he took the northbound exit and headed toward Watertown.

Jeff was well into his second six pack when he reached the Watertown exits. "Let's see now, there are three exits... exit 45, 46, and exit 47. Hmm...." Jeff mumbled. "Oh well, I guess if I take the middle exit, I'll eventually get there."

He turned off Route 81 at exit 46 in Watertown and went left. After a short distance, he saw a sign that read "Dexter 12 miles." "Yes! Am I good or what? I needed to go through Dexter, that much I remember. I'll just follow the signs from there and then I'm home free." Jeff's minor good luck was the first thing all day to brighten his mood.

Five miles later Jeff saw another sign, this one for Patti Hill, a hamlet between Watertown and Dexter. Ahead on the right was the Village of Brownville, a quaint little town that was home to the old Brownville Paper Mill and the Cascade Paper Mill. The mills were directly across from each other, separated by the Black River

Waterfalls, the source of power and water for both paper mills. From all outward appearances, Brownville was a quiet place, but being just outside Watertown and the desire of the local kids to be as *cool* as the kids from the city brought the scourge of drugs.

"Well, I'm almost out of beer, and being that I don't have any coke to massage my brain, I guess I should stop in this Podunk place and try to grab some more brews. Maybe one of these hicks knows how to get to Pillar Point." Jeff's arrogant attitude returned along with his brightened spirits.

He made a right, went down a small hill and entered the Village of Brownville. He came to a 'T' in the road and knew he had to turn left to head toward Pillar Point. Next to the stop sign was another sign that read, "No Solicitation within Village Limits." There was a DD sized bra hanging on the edge of the sign.

It was ten thirty when his shiny yellow Testarossa pulled up in front of the Brownville Hotel. The sign in front read Brownville Hotel, but the Miller Beer and Molson signs in the window were speaking Jeff's language. "This looks like a bar and talks like a hotel. Maybe people up here really do have their act together... drink a little, meet a girl, and get a room all in the same place. Not quite as classy as the Strathalen in Rochester, but the same principle." He stepped out of the car and took a deep breath of the warm, humid summer air, definitely feeling buzzed.

He walked into the bar and could feel every eye on him. There was silence as Jeff strutted over to the bar.

"Hello there, stranger, that's a pretty nice car you got." The bartender was a slim brunette. "Hi, I'm Betty, and it's nice to meet you." Betty grabbed a napkin and put it on the bar in front of Jeff.

"Well, actually I wanted to pick up a six pack and some directions to Pillar Point, but I guess a quick drink won't hurt while." Betty was very cute with shoulder-length deep brown hair, large breasts, a tiny waist, and cut off jean shorts that barely covered her shapely bottom.

"Did you get an eyeful?" Betty asked in a playful tone, catching Jeff admiring her derriere.

"Yes... did you?" Jeff jerked his head toward the window and his Testarossa, indicating he noticed Betty's infatuation with his car.

"Okay, we're even now," she laughed. "What will you have?"

He took a shot in the dark. "You can get me a shot of JD and a line of coke."

Betty smiled and turned around to pour his Jack Daniel's. She could feel his eyes on her. "Here's your JD, and if you're a good boy, maybe I can fix you up a little later." She set his drink down.

"Honey, if you can do that, I'll owe you a big favor—and believe me, I'm a good person to have owing you a favor." Jeff was his egotistical self again.

"I liked you better when you weren't being arrogant," Betty replied and turned away.

"Wait, I'm sorry." Jeff tried to get Betty to come back. "I was trying to make conversation and I guess I got carried away."

"I guess I can forgive you this time, but just because you drive a nice car and wear expensive clothes doesn't mean you can talk down to me, got it?" Betty smiled and held her hand out toward Jeff.

"Deal." Jeff shook Betty's hand. "Would you join me for a shot?"

"As long as you're buying, 'cause I'm kind of short on cash." Betty reached for another shot glass and the bottle of Jack Daniels.

The bar had only a few regulars on this muggy summer night. They were mostly paper mill workers in their late fifties that were widowed or unmarried, with no place to go and nothing better to do.

Jeff couldn't help thinking what a lonely job Betty must have if this was her life on a Friday night.

"So what do you do for fun?" He stole a peek at her cleavage while she poured.

"I wait for rich, good-looking guys to buy me shots." Betty's smile was so cute that an involuntary smile flashed across his face. "Here's to you. What's your name, anyway?" Betty lifted her shot glass.

"Jeff." He stuck with just his first name.

"Okay, here's to you, Jeff—may you be as nice as you are good-looking." Betty toasted, threw back her shot, closed her eyes and winced for just a second.

Jeff lifted his shot glass to the toast and slammed it. Jeff sat and watched Betty enjoy the warmth of the whiskey. "You really know how to enjoy life, don't you?" he said.

"Jeff, if you can't enjoy life, I mean every second, every taste, every smell, every smile, and every person every day, then you're losing out on life itself. Sure, everyone has a bad day, or there's someone they just don't click with, but is that reason enough to be mean or miserable to everyone and everything? No way. So live and let live, that's my motto."

Jeff was mesmerized when she talked. Her face was animated, her gestures seemed to compliment her words, and when she looked into Jeff's eyes to see if he was listening, he could feel his heart pound. "You make a lot of sense to me. Live and let live. I like that motto." Jeff reflected on the simplicity of the words, and the enormous meaning they carried.

"You look sad, Jeff. What's wrong?" Betty sounded like she cared.

Jeff pulled his eyes up from the bar and looked into hers. "I've lived so wrong, for so long, that I forgot what it was like to be happy. Live and let live..." he said, amazed.

"Yes. Live and let live. Try it for a while and you'll be happier." Betty's crooked smile looked good on her. She poured Jeff another shot.

"I've been doing a lot of thinking lately—I've had a few problems back in Rochester." Jeff threw back his shot and motioned for another.

"I can give you directions to anywhere on Pillar Point and a six pack of beer. Or, you can hang out here with me, and we can drink a few more shots. Then when my friend comes by, we can do a few lines and you can forget all about those problems back in Rochester. We can have some fun, and maybe you can start being happy." She gave him a flirtatious smile. Jeff's face lit up.

"Deal. I'll stay and you keep pouring the shots." He pulled out a money clip filled with hundred-dollar bills. He put a hundred-dollar bill on the bar and Betty poured another round.

Aside from pouring an occasional beer for one of the *regulars*, Betty spent the next few hours with Jeff, talking, laughing and getting to know him. He seemed to be sincere, and he actually took time to listen to what she was saying. They shared some stories and some drinks, and had a good time.

At one thirty a.m. both Jeff and Betty were pretty buzzed. A tall, thin man with long blond hair walked in. The stranger smiled at Betty and looked around cautiously as he approached the bar.

"Johnny Boy, where have you been? You were supposed to be here at eleven." Betty's familiar half smile appeared.

"Who's the suit?" He ignored her question.

"This is Jeff. He's cool, we can talk." Betty turned to Jeff and said, "Jeff, this is Johnny Boy. Johnny Boy, this is Jeff."

"Did you bring my stuff?" Betty asked Johnny Boy.

"Yes. You want it right now or do you want to go in the back?" His eyes darted nervously around the room.

"That depends on whether you're staying for some," she replied.

"No can do. I have 1 more stops tonight and I'm late as it is." Johnny Boy pulled out a folded one-dollar bill and slid it over the counter to Betty.

Betty picked up the and slipped it in her pocket.

"Thanks, Johnny Boy, maybe next time you'll have time to partake in a *smile* before you leave." Betty grinned.

"Take care till then, Betty Spaghetti. Stay cool, Jeff."

"Nice to meet you too, Johnny Boy." Jeff offered a salute to Johnny Boy as he left.

Betty looked up at the clock and then turned to the few patrons that were still nursing their beers and announced, "Last call, anyone who wants one more, get it now!"

Two patrons looked up at the clock but only one got up for another beer. Betty poured it and cashed the man out.

"It's only one-forty, are you trying to get rid of me?" Jeff raised his eyebrows.

"No, actually, I thought you and I could go up to my place and do a few lines after I close this place up." Betty turned away from Jeff and started cashing out the bar.

"How far away do you live?" Jeff admired Betty's derriere for the hundredth time.

"Just upstairs." Betty continued to count the cash. "I own this place. My mother left it to me when she died." She sighed. "It's a living. Some nights are better than others. I don't get many rooms rented out unless someone gets too drunk to drive, or some horny kids want a place to spend the night."

As the remaining patrons began to leave, Betty came out from behind the bar and said good night to each one by name. When she started picking up the barstools and putting on top of the bar, Jeff got up to help.

"I always wondered why bartenders put stools upside down on the bar."

"It makes it easier to sweep and mop the floor."

"That makes sense. Should I put the chairs on the tables too?" Jeff pointed to tables and chairs.

"Yes, please. Chivalry is still alive. It's nice to see a gentleman."

When they were done, Betty locked the front door, grabbed a bottle of Jack Daniels, a six pack of beer, and motioned for Jeff to follow her up the back stairs.

The paneling on the stair walls was a rich mahogany with a single old-fashioned brass light. At the top of the stairs, Betty unlocked the door to her apartment and Jeff couldn't help but notice the antique skeleton keyed lock and deadbolt.

Once inside, Betty set down the beer and JD on a spider legged cherry kitchen table. "Why don't you open a couple of beers and I'll cut some lines."

Jeff was amazed at how well Betty had put together a collection of antiques. A large leaded glass mirror with a gilded frame hung next to a cherry coatrack that had brass feet and brass hooks. The cherry grandfather clock stood nearly six feet tall and was a perfect complement to the cherry kitchen table.

"I love your apartment, Betty, you've done a great job decorating," Jeff said with approval when Betty returned.

"Thank you. I got a lot of stuff from my mother's house."

Betty sat on the couch and motioned for Jeff to join her. She dumped some of the white powder and spread it across the mirror that she'd set down on the crystal leaded antique coffee table. Using a razor blade, she cut four separate lines, leaving the rest in a little pile on the edge of the mirror.

While Betty worked, Jeff pulled a hundred-dollar bill from his money clip and rolled it into a tube. When Betty finished, Jeff handed her the rolled up bill and she snorted two lines then gave the bill back to Jeff.

When he was done, she licked her finger and gently touched the pile of powder, smiled at Jeff and rubbed her finger across her gums and tongue. When she was done, she did it again, only this time she offered her finger to Jeff, who opened his mouth and licked it.

Betty leaned over and gave Jeff a slow sensual kiss. His sexual desire immediately kicked into high gear and he began his routine of frantic kissing and grabbing at her clothes, as if he was in a hurry to break his former speed record for the quickest sex.

Betty pulled away, "Whoa, slow down, cowboy, what's the rush? Let's enjoy all life has to offer, one piece at a time." Betty stood up from the couch. "Come with me."

Betty led Jeff into her bedroom where she slowly undressed him, kissing and licking every inch of his body.

When Jeff stood before Betty naked and erect, she put her hands on his shoulders and sat him on the side of the bed.

Jeff watched as Betty began undressing. She started with her blouse, slowly unbuttoning each button. She eased the blouse over her shoulders and let it slide off her back, leaving her silk bra as the only thing between Jeff and her protruding nipples.

In a teasing slow motion, she unzipped her shorts, exposing her matching silk panties. Betty pulled off her skimpy blue jeans as if she was performing surgery, slowly and delicately until she stood before Jeff in her matching silk panties and bra. She leaned over as if she was going to rub Jeff's face with her breasts. Jeff began to open his mouth in anticipation of her pleasures. She bent down at the knees, grabbed both of Jeff's legs, and pulled them up onto the bed.

"If you roll over, I'll give you a full body massage."

"Okay." Jeff tried to hold back his rush of desire. "But only if you promise to let me give you a full body massage when you're done."

"I can't wait." Betty went to her dresser and pulled out two bottles of strawberry body lotion.

Jeff was in ecstasy as Betty kissed and licked his body working her way up from his toes to the bottom of his buttocks. Then she slowly poured the body lotion on both of Jeff's feet and began to massage the same area she had just covered with her tongue. She worked over the entire length of Jeff's back before starting on the front. The pleasure Jeff was experiencing was enough to hold him back from an all-out sexual attack.

When Betty was done, she lay face down on the bed next to Jeff. When she pulled her hair off her back and to the side of her neck, Jeff said, "I hope I can make you feel half as good as I do right now." Then he stood up and reached for the bottle of body lotion.

Jeff followed Betty's lead, first by licking and sucking every inch of her body, and following up with a lotion massage. When he was almost finished, Betty opened her eyes and said, "Now... it's time." She was wet, feverish, and needy.

Betty reached down between Jeff's legs, took his manhood, and directed it toward her wet, pulsating treasure. When Betty and Jeff began their sexual intercourse, an adventure that would last two and a half hours, Betty said, "Good things come to those who are patient."

It was nearly five a.m. when Betty convinced Jeff that he should sleep for a few hours before heading to Michael's. He slept with his head on Betty's shoulder in an unrecognized sign of surrender. For the first time, Jeff had allowed someone else to take control, and he enjoyed it so much he never realized how much time had passed.

CHAPTER 39

The time was eight thirty a.m. Saturday, and Major Anzio and his team were at MFB's HQ reviewing the files that Commander Callaghan ordered them to pick up from George Kane. There were seventeen files in all. Anzio took five of them, and gave four each to Lieutenant Thurston, Sergeant Collins, and Corporal Hunt.

"This is amazing," Thurston said, reviewing one of the files as she sipped on her morning tea. "These guys bought out a lumber dealer in Trenton for a fraction of its value. Jeff Kane hired a private investigator to dig up dirt on the kids. Apparently, two of the half-siblings were sleeping together, and Jeff threatened to expose them if they didn't sell him their shares for a reduced price. After he got the shares from the two kids, he bought out the widow who was still grieving and knew nothing about the business, for half of what her stock was worth. That gave them fifty-one percent ownership and then they forced the sale of the company and made almost six million dollars within two weeks."

"That sounds familiar. In Kane's last acquisition, they also hired a private investigator to dig up dirt on the two brothers who owned the company. It appears as though one of them was having a homosexual affair, while the other was stealing from their inventory and lying to the IRS." Anzio skimmed through the file. "They even got pictures of the brother having sex with his male lover. This guy doesn't mess around, he knows how to make a buck and he goes after it."

Within an hour, the team had assembled a list of people who had enough reason to seek revenge on the Kanes for stealing their businesses. All of the files contained pictures of the owners that had been bought out. Each picture had a file number assigned to it by the team and was placed on a large corkboard that was hanging on the wall. Soon the corkboard was full of pictures and under each picture was a brief description of what happened and a dollar amount of how much Kane profited from the deal. The seventeen files and forty-two pictures told an ugly and scary story of Jeff Kane using every dirty trick in the book to swindle businesses from families. In one case, a business had been in a family for three generations and over a hundred years.

"Any of these people could have gone over the edge and tried to seek vengeance on the Kanes. They all had motive to frame Jeff for murder. They all wanted revenge for loss of their business. In some cases, adultery was exposed, resulting in divorces and broken families due to Jeff Kane's underhanded dealings," Hunt said, as she looked over the board.

Collins agreed. "It's like he left a trail of carnage. Anyone who got in Jeff Kane's way was exposed and destroyed."

Anzio turned away from the board and looked at his team. "I want each of you to find out what you can on each owner, their families or lovers, or anyone else associated with these buyouts. I want to know if anyone has been out of town, filed for bankruptcy, gotten divorced, or anything else that could have triggered these murders. I want this information fast. If one of these people is after the Kane family, then Commander Callaghan and Amanda could be in danger."

The investigative work had begun for the MFB team at HQ.

When Jeff opened his eyes, it was ten. "I should get to Michael's cottage before it gets too late." He rolled out of bed.

"Who's cottage?" Betty rolled over.

"My sister's new boyfriend, his name is Michael," Jeff said indifferently.

"I know several Michaels, what's his last name? Maybe I know him."

Jeff reached for his pants. "Michael Callaghan."

"No kidding? Michael Callaghan." Betty sat up in bed. "Michael and I went to school together at Brownville Elementary School and General Brown High School. Your sister must be special if she landed Michael. He was the most popular guy in school, but he didn't go out with very many girls, and he never slept with any that I know of."

"Why, was he gay or something?" This was Jeff's attempt at dry humor.

"No, there was no one manlier than Michael. He was just so sure of what he wanted and no one around here had it," Betty said, with a sad smile.

"Did you ever date him?" He buttoned up his shirt.

"No. I was too wild for him. We were only friends." Betty got out of bed and slipped on a robe. "I can tell you exactly where his cottage is. A bunch of kids from school used to go there for bonfires during summer vacations."

Jeff's yellow Ferrari Testarossa crept at five miles an hour down the dirt road weaving through Bayshore Estates. Many of the residents were out doing Saturday yardwork. Everyone waved and smiled. At first, he wasn't sure if they had mistaken him for someone else, but as it continued, he decided to start waving back.

When Jeff pulled up in front of Michael's cottage, Michael and Amanda were in his garage working on a boat.

"There's my little brother," Amanda said, walking out of the garage to greet him.

Jeff looked at the boat as he got out of the car. "Hello, Amanda. Are you guys having a boat problem?"

"No, we're just getting it ready for the summer." Michael joined them.

Amanda looked concerned. "Are you all right, Jeff? You look terrible."

"Yes, I'm fine. I stopped at a friend's house in Brownville last night and we stayed up all night playing poker." Everyone knew Jeff liked playing poker, so he used it as an alibi whenever he needed one.

"I didn't know you had friends up this way. Anyone I might know?" Michael could tell Jeff was lying. Reading people was a prerequisite for black ops work and Michael was very good at it.

"No, I asked if they knew you and they said no. They only moved here recently." Jeff tried to cover his tracks. "Say, I'm a little tired. Is there somewhere I can crash for a few hours before the festivities start tonight?"

"Come with me, and I'll show you." Amanda took her brother by the arm. Jeff and Michael nodded to each other as Jeff left with Amanda.

"This is the kitchen, just make yourself at home." Amanda showed Jeff around the cottage. "Here's your room. If we're not here when you get up, it's because we have to go up to Watertown to get Michael's SUV. We'll be late, because Michael's going to take me for a dinner cruise on the St. Lawrence River. If you get hungry, there's plenty of food in the refrigerator, and later tonight we'll have some friends down for a bonfire."

"Sounds good. Have a good time and I'll see you later." Jeff gave Amanda a brotherly hug and headed into his room for some much needed sleep.

When Amanda returned to Michael, he was just coming out of the garage and she asked, "Is everything done?"

"Almost. All we have to do is head into Watertown, pick up my SUV, and then tomorrow we can tow the boat down to the boat launch in Adams Cove and launch it for the summer." Michael was excited to get his boat in the water. It provided another mode of escape, if needed.

"Will we be back in time to go on the dinner cruise?" Amanda wanted to see the sights and learn about the Thousand Islands region.

"Absolutely. We'll have plenty of time to make it to Alex Bay." He put his arm around her and gave her several soft kisses on the lips.

With a puzzled look, Amanda asked, "Alex Bay?"

"Alexandria Bay is called Alex Bay for short. Don't worry, we'll have plenty of time, I promise." Michael resumed his kisses.

"I love you, Michael," Amanda whispered between kisses.

"I love you too, Amanda. Now, let's get going so we can hit the early dinner cruise and get back in time for the bonfire."

When they reached the Coffeen Street Porsche Dealer in Watertown, Michael suggested that Amanda wait in the car while he checked to see if the SUV was ready. Ten minutes later Michael was driving his Porsche Cayenne SUV from around the side of the building. Amanda followed him back to Bayshore Estates where they quickly and quietly cleaned up, and then left for the dinner cruise on the St. Lawrence River.

Amanda was hoping for a fun-filled romantic dinner cruise. She was not anticipating being stalked by two terrorists.

CHAPTER 40

Alexandria Bay is a bustling resort town which feels like a slice of heaven all summer long. Nestled in the heart of the Thousand Islands, this small village is overrun by tens of thousands of visitors from around the world during the summer months. The summers are gorgeous—lots of sun, very little rain, and the mighty St. Lawrence River offers water sports, swimming, and fishing. The Thousand Islands region is truly a summer paradise, unless you're being hunted by terrorists.

Michael and Amanda stopped at Uncle Sam's Boat Tours to purchase their tickets for the early dinner cruise at four p.m. They had just enough time to get their tickets and get down to the docks before cast off.

The *Alexandria Belle* was a fine replica of one of the riverboats that used to run the Mississippi River. The boat had two covered decks and a third deck that, along with having plenty of seating, was open to the fresh air and warm sun. The large rear paddle wheel that propelled the boat, and the front gangplank, along with its riverboat design, gave the passengers of the *Alexandria Belle* a feeling of nostalgia as it cruised up and down the St. Lawrence River.

Michael and Amanda decided to go up to the third deck and enjoy the scenery until dinner was served, and then they would go below to one of the covered decks to eat dinner out of the wind.

As the boat took off from shore, the captain's voice came over the loudspeaker introducing himself and his officers onboard. The captain turned the microphone over to his activities director, who began describing the sights along the St. Lawrence River.

The activities director began giving a history of the St. Lawrence River. "Until the early 17th century, the French used the name *Rivière du Canada* when referring to the upstream portion of the St. Lawrence all the way to Montreal. From Montreal to the Atlantic Ocean they called it the Ottawa River. The St. Lawrence River served as the main route for European exploration of the North American interior. French explorer Samuel de Champlain was the first pioneer to explore the river. Queen Elizabeth II, representing Canada, and President Dwight D. Eisenhower, representing the United States, officially opened an extensive system of canals and locks, known as the St. Lawrence Seaway on June 26, 1959." The activities director took of swig from his water bottle, wiped his mouth on the back of his hand and continued. "The St. Lawrence Seaway now permits ocean going vessels to pass all the way from the Atlantic Ocean to Lake Superior. The river has depths of over two hundred feet, spans a distance of over 1,900 miles, and in some areas its discharge flow is over 593,300 cubic feet per second. Many of the merchant ships that were sunk by European submarines during the Second World War can be found buried in the depths of the mighty St. Lawrence River."

Amanda said, "Wow, what a history, I had no idea that wars were fought up here, and I didn't realize the water was so deep and the river so long."

"Pretty amazing, isn't it? People don't realize how strong the current is." This came out as more of a warning than Michael intended.

Next on the tour director's list of subjects was the Boldt Castle and the legend of George and Louise Boldt. "Boldt Castle, just off the ship's starboard side, is located on Heart Island. Boldt Castle was built by George Boldt for his wife, Louise. When Mr. Boldt left Europe for America, his wife was reluctant to join him and leave the pleasures of Europe behind, so George asked his wife if she would come to America if he built her a castle in the heart of the beautiful Thousand Islands. The island is called Heart Island because it's shaped like a heart." The tour director pointed at the island. "The castle was under construction for seven years when Mr. Boldt received word that his wife had fallen ill, and within the year, she had passed away. Mr. Boldt was so crushed by his wife's passing that he stopped all construction on the castle and left for Europe to visit his family and grieve for his wife, before returning to America. He resumed his life in New York City, and the castle remained unfinished as a tribute to his wife."

"He must have really loved his wife." Michael said. "Could you imagine building a castle for your wife for seven years, and then she dies before it's completed?"

"Look how huge it is. It has a separate boathouse, lighthouse and guest quarters." Amanda was astonished.

"Local legend has it that Mrs. Boldt's spirit came over from Europe in search of her husband, and when she got to the castle, her husband wasn't there," the activities director continued. "So her spirit is said to have remained in this area ever since, looking for her husband. From the day Mr. Boldt left for Europe to mourn for his wife, to the day of his death, Mr. Boldt never returned to the castle because he couldn't bear to live here without his wife. There have been stories over the years that small children were saved from drowning by a mysterious woman in a long white silky gown, just like the gown Mrs. Boldt was wearing when she died."

"Michael, how tragically romantic! Her spirit leaves Europe to be here with him and he leaves here to go mourn for her... and because of his grief he never returns again." Amanda was a softie and it showed.

"I guess there *can* be everlasting love." Michael gazed into Amanda's eyes.

"I love you, Michael." Amanda stared deeply into Michael's eyes.

"I love you too, Amanda." Michael leaned over and gave Amanda a long kiss. He caught a flash of movement over Amanda's shoulder: two men in black suits, black silk shirts and black wing-tipped shoes. They were headed below deck and Michael was sure the Black Blade of Allah agents had seen him.

"Honey, I need to go below deck and use the restroom before we go to dinner. Why don't you stay here and listen to the tour, and I'll come and get you when I'm done?" Michael smiled and rubbed Amanda's arm.

"Okay, see you in a bit."

Michael headed toward the staircase the two terrorists had taken. His mind was racing. Why were Black Blade of Allah agents onboard? Were they looking to blow up the ship? Or take someone or everyone hostage?

He reached into his pocket and pulled out his knife. Its blade was only four inches long, but it would have to do. When he reached the lower deck, he caught a glimpse of them entering the stairway to the engine room.

He opened the stairwell door silently and saw the two men, one carrying a briefcase, exiting onto the lower deck. He grabbed a fire extinguisher attached to a wall and followed them.

On the lower deck, he saw a man lying facedown, bleeding from the back of his head. There were footprints on the oil-stained floor leading away from the man.

Michael could see two men's shadows behind a large generator. The room seemed to be empty of crewmembers except the man lying on the floor. He crept around the back of the generator and took a quick look. One terrorist had his back to Michael, and was on lookout. The second man was arming what appeared to be a bomb in the briefcase.

Michael inched up and slammed the fire extinguisher into the back of the terrorist's head before he could finish arming the bomb.

The man on lookout spun around and faced Michael. He was holding a gun.

The bomb-setter moaned from the floor and when the lookout glanced toward his friend, Michael kicked the gun out of his hands.

Stumbling backward, the terrorist hit a large water pump and dropped to one knee. He snatched up a large wrench and jumped to his feet.

Michael pulled his knife. "You want to dance? If you're sure, then let's get to it."

He went into full attack mode. He charged, and when the man swung the heavy wrench, Michael grabbed the slow moving arm and went to work. First, he sliced the muscle in the terrorist's forearm, disabling his grip. The wrench fell to the floor and the man howled in pain. Then Michael slashed the muscle in his bicep, and the man lost control of his arm. He pulled the man forward, stabbed him in the armpit and leg. He was trying to disable the terrorist, not kill him, until the man pulled a backup gun with his other hand. Michael ducked as the first shot whistled past his ear. Picking up the wrench, Michael swung hard and caught the man on the temple. Death was instantaneous.

He checked the first terrorist for a pulse, but he was dead. Then he checked the crewmember. He was alive but bleeding heavily. Michael bandaged the crewmember as best he could, dragged the terrorists to a loading door at water level, and after tying heavy metal parts and tools to their bodies, he dumped them and the briefcase into the St. Lawrence River. After calling the bridge and asking for help, he left to meet Amanda.

When he returned to Amanda, he said, "We should go below so we can get a window seat for dinner. The boat looks pretty full and I'd rather sit near a window than in the middle of the boat."

"Good idea." Amanda stood and grabbed her Prada purse.

Amanda and Michael went down and got a seat by the window. Shortly before dinner, a pair of crewmembers approached Amanda and Michael and asked if they would like their picture taken. The picture would be placed on a souvenir keychain with a picture of the *Alexandria Belle* on one side and the picture of Amanda and Michael together on the other side.

"Michael, that sounds great! We'll always have a reminder of this dinner cruise and a picture of each other on our keychains," Amanda said excitedly.

"We'll take two," Michael said and they leaned across the table to be closer together.

"Thank you," one of the crewmembers said after the picture was taken. "Your two key chains will be ready when the cruise is over. You can pay for them then."

When Amanda and Michael got their key chains, Amanda pointed to Heart Island in the picture. "How romantic! Heart Island is perfectly centered in the background."

"It looks great," Michael replied, as he handed the crewmember a hundred-dollar bill and raised his palm into the air signaling for him to keep the change.

He looked out over the water for any sign of the two terrorists that he had dispatched. He had a sinking feeling they weren't acting alone.

CHAPTER 41

That evening, Greg Connors walked from his cottage to the bonfire site. Greg was in a good mood; the evening was warm and there was very little wind to interfere with the fire. He started gathering the wood and placing it in the firepit. A short time later, Jeff appeared.

"Hi, you must be Amanda's brother, Jeff. I'm Greg... Greg Connors." Greg extended his hand.

"Hi, Greg. I'm Jeff Kane." Jeff shook Greg's hand. "What are you doing?"

"I'm getting the bonfire ready. Amanda did tell you that we're having a bonfire tonight, didn't she?" Greg continued stacking wood.

"Yes, she mentioned something about bonfires." Jeff watched Greg working. "What do you guys do for fun besides watch the fire?"

"What do you mean?" Greg was defensive, always concerned with their cover.

"You know, drinking and partying, things like that? Just sitting in a chair all night and watching a fire seems like it could get boring after a while." Jeff was smiling.

"Oh, we do plenty of drinking. Some nights we drink so much people have a hard time walking." Greg smiled, trying to read Jeff's face for any sign of a hidden agenda. "We also share stories, catch up on each other's lives, and tell a few jokes here and there."

"I guess Amanda would be a good example of that." Jeff referred to Amanda's sprained ankle. "You know, having a hard time walking."

"That's for sure. She had a pretty good buzz working that night." Greg went back to work.

"So, do you guys like to party?" Jeff asked in a sly, inquisitive way.

"Oh, you mean, do we smoke a little weed or snort a few lines, something like that?" Greg asked.

"Yes, now you're talking about a party," Jeff said with enthusiasm.

"No. No, we do not. In fact, I wouldn't mention this conversation to Michael if I were you. You see, when we were in high school one of our best friends overdosed on his mother's prescription pills, and we made a pact that none of us would ever take drugs, except for booze. In fact there have been several friends that we stopped hanging around with because they started doing drugs. Michael took the overdose hard. I hope you understand what I mean?" Greg went back to gathering wood.

"Yes, I do. Thanks for the heads up. I won't mention it again. In fact, forget I even mentioned it in the first place." Jeff flashed a pearl-white toothy grin.

"Deal—if you help me finish getting everything ready, " Greg laughed.

Reluctantly, Jeff said, "Sure what do you need me to do?" He had no idea what it took to prepare a bonfire.

"Go down to Michael's cottage and bring up as many lawn chairs as he has, for starters." Greg was stacking wood in a pile next to the fire.

"Just one question, how big do these fires get?" Jeff asked, eying the wood Greg had collected.

"They start off about fifteen feet high and then settle down to six or eight feet."

They worked together preparing for the bonfire until Michael and Amanda returned to the cottage.

The empty pizza boxes and coffee cups littering the conference room told the tale of how hard Major Anzio and his team had been working. The printer roared to life. Another piece of the puzzle came across the wire. The IT department had written a program that was collecting intel from every corner of the web. This printout described how Ted Caulkins had committed suicide two days after the meeting with Jeff Kane.

"It appears Ted's wife found out about the homosexual affair from an anonymous letter that contained photos of Ted with another man. According to Sheriff Brown, who interviewed her, Mrs. Caulkins decided to take their kids and leave Ted that day. She confronted Ted with what she called a disgusting and revolting adulterous affair." Anzio read from the fax.

"How did he do it?" Hunt asked with a yawn.

"He hung himself." Anzio continued to read. "And, get this, they found his nude body hanging in his lover's garage—a man named Robert 'Bobby' Sands."

"I can see why Ted felt his life was over; he lost his business, his family and was humiliated in front of his community. It must have been a terrible shock." Sec. Lt. Jamie Thurston realized the gravity of the situation.

"Do you think this Bobby Sands could be the one seeking revenge on the Kane family?" Sergeant Collins questioned.

"He doesn't fit the profile. Most bisexual or homosexual men are passive and nonaggressive. They tend to be victims not murderers," Anzio responded.

"Besides that, the murderer had to have knowledge of this area in order to commit both murders within a short time frame," Hunt added.

"Just to be sure, I want to know more about Robert Sands. I want everything we can get on him since grade school. I want interviews with his neighbors and coworkers about how he's handled the death of his lover in his own home... and I want it done today," Anzio said with authority.

"Good point. He might not have the guts to do something like this himself, but he might have the money to hire someone," Thurston said, adding credence to Anzio's request. "I'll get right on it."

What she would find might save a life… if she found it in time.

CHAPTER 42

By the time Michael and Amanda returned from the dinner cruise, the bonfire was set up and Michael's friends had begun to assemble. Ace brought his car down and parked it ten feet away from the chairs. He removed the customized high-powered speakers from the Cutlass and put them on the hood for some background music.

"Look, honey, Jeff is helping to get things ready. I hoped he would fit in and have a good time while he's here. Everyone seems so nice and Jeff needs to be with some nice people for a change," Amanda said as they pulled up in front of Michael's garage.

"Did you tell Jeff about the porch steps and where to walk?" Michael wanted to avoid another accident.

"I think so, but I'll make sure he knows, just in case."

"I really need to fix those steps tomorrow before we launch the boat. I don't want anyone else getting hurt." Michael parked the SUV and wondered where Jeff had spent the previous night.

Michael and Amanda went into the cottage and changed for the bonfire.

Once everyone assembled at the site, Michael poured gas onto the pile of wood and lit the match. "Here's to friendship and good times." He tossed the match onto the gas soaked wood.

With a loud swoosh, the fire roared to life. The sudden blast of heat and burst of light gave Jeff a feeling of awe.

"Isn't it great?" Amanda asked him.

"Yes, do the flames stay this high all night?" Jeff asked with surprise. "Looks like some of the trees around here could catch on fire if the wind started blowing."

Amanda smiled. "Don't worry, little brother. We won't start any forest fires. These guys have been doing this a long time."

"Very funny. I'm not worried. I was just noticing how close the trees are, that's all," Jeff said.

The rest of the night went as usual. Music floated from Ace's top-of-the-line Bose sound system. It was background music for the dancing fire. Everyone took turns telling jokes and stories, drinking booze and munching on chips, cookies, and popcorn. Amanda was having such a good time, she didn't notice that Michael and his team had cut back on their alcohol consumption. Jeff on the other hand was pounding down beer like there was no tomorrow.

It was about twelve thirty when a slow moving car drove down the dirt road, just forty-five feet from the bonfire. The light from the fire and the darkness that surrounded the car on the road made it difficult for Michael to see it.

"Anyone see who that was?" Michael was clearly suspicious of any unfamiliar cars.

"I couldn't see the car very well. There's not much of a moon tonight." JR had taken notice of the vehicle too.

"How about you, Ace?" Michael asked his wheelman. If anyone knew cars inside out, it was Ace.

"I couldn't see the car either, but it sounded like a nineteen seventy-two Dodge Dart in need of new shocks." Ace and the rest of the group started laughing... everyone except Michael.

"I wonder who it could have been. We normally recognize everyone who drives down this road," Michael said when the laughter died down.

"It was probably someone visiting those people renting the cottage from the Williamses. If it was anyone we knew, they would have either beeped the horn or stopped to say hello," Karen Miller dismissed it.

Michael waited to see if the car would turn around at the end of the road and come back, indicating a possible recon mission. Fifteen minutes passed, and the car didn't come back. Maybe it *was* a late arrival for one of his neighbors. Michael's concerns diminished, knowing that he had a team from HQ at the top of the road and there were no reports of suspicious activity. Surely the car must have parked down the shore and the occupants were spending the night.

He coasted the car the last hundred feet, so as not to wake anyone up. He parked his Dodge Dart across the street from the cottages, grabbed his rifle and slipped into the cow pasture. The going was much tougher coming from this side of the pasture; it was loaded with briar bushes and burdock patches. He had made it most of the way to the bonfire site when he came across a herd of cows.

His stealth approach became nearly impossible. If they woke up or started to moo, the men at the fire would surely become suspicious. He was too far away and there were too many trees for a clear shot. He backed off and started to formulate another plan. He headed back to his car and decided to wait until the group split up. Maybe an opportunity would present itself then.

The bonfire went on with its bright glittering light and warm glow. The large consumption of alcohol was evident by the stack of beer cans that were piling up on the lawn. Lots of talk and laughter flowed from everyone except for Jeff. Jeff, whether being unfamiliar with the people or just having his mind on other pressing matters, seemed to be abnormally quiet.

By three a.m. the party was winding down. Michael put out the fire while the others picked up their chairs and headed for their own beds.

When Amanda and Michael climbed into bed, Amanda leaned over and whispered, "I wish we could make love tonight, but Jeff is just down the hall. I would be so embarrassed if he heard us."

Damn, Michael was hoping this would be the night. "I know, babe. We can wait a little longer. Don't worry." He could wait, but a quickie was out of the question. He was intent on a full-blown lovemaking session, a heart pounding, sweat dripping sexual romp… oh yeah, he could wait.

"We'll be here for the next eight days and I promise, the wait will be well worth it." Amanda kissed Michael on the cheek, snuggled up next to him, and laid her head on his chest.

When the early morning sun shone through the window, Amanda opened her eyes. Her first thought was to get up and close the curtains and climb back into bed. The last time they had a bonfire, Michael picked up the empty cans and cleaned up around the fire while she slept. Amanda lay in bed watching Michael sleep, thinking about their future together. She wondered when he would ask her to marry him, and how many children they would have.

After a few moments, she decided to go clean up the empty beer cans and any other mess around the fire so the yard would look nice for any early rising neighbors that might wander by.

It was the worst thing she could have done.

CHAPTER 43

The whir of the printer woke up three MFB operatives and caused the fourth, Major Anzio, to put down the coffee he was about to pour. He went to the printer in anticipation of what he was about to read.

"All right, get this..." Anzio read the first page. "Our boy, Robert 'Bobby' Sands, has not been back to work at the paint store since Ted Caulkins committed suicide. His neighbor last saw him packing his car with clothes. He claimed he was going to visit some family. The odd thing about that is he once told the neighbor that he had no family."

"That's understandable. The guy's lover just committed suicide in *his* house. I'm sure I would want to get away too." Lt. Thurston poured two cups of coffee, one for herself and one for Anzio.

"Yes, but according to this police report, the paint store owner was not notified by Sands that he would be missing work or going on a vacation." Anzio took the second page from the printer. "It says here that a background check on Robert John Sands Jr. came up with the fact that he was in the Marines for three years and then was deployed as a special ops Marine sniper for two years before being court-martialed on rape and sodomy charges. Apparently he was a sniper in the Marines when he was caught having sex with a major who had been jailed for public drunkenness. Sands claims the major consented to the sex, but the major claims to have been sleeping and knew nothing about what had happened. The MP who walked in on Sands couldn't tell if the major was awake or asleep."

Corporal Hunt looked grave. "That changes the picture on Sands. An ex-Marine sniper could have certainly committed two murders."

"Sands served two years in a military prison before being dishonorably discharged, and then he headed north to Minnesota where he met Ted Caulkins." Anzio took coffee from Thurston and took a sip. "Mr. Sands was born in Redwood, New York, a small hamlet just northwest of Alexandria Bay. After graduation from high school, he lived in Rochester for sixteen months before joining the Marines."

Lt. Jamie Thurston said thoughtfully, "That's not much time served, considering the crime. Maybe someone pulled some strings, or maybe he wasn't guilty after all."

"It sounds like Sands knows the Rochester area," Sergeant Collins mused.

Anzio put down his coffee. "Wow, get this one. Both his father and grandfather were in the Marines. His grandfather was a major and his father was a lieutenant colonel when he retired, with twenty-seven years of service that included being a military advisor and intelligence officer. That explains why Bobby Sands would join the Marines—just think of the pressure his family put on him to join."

"Sir, didn't you say that Jeff Kane was going up to the Thousand Islands region to visit his sister and Commander Callaghan at his cottage?" Thurston asked.

"You're right. If this is our guy, he could have followed them up there. He could be setting up something right now. Get Commander Callaghan on the phone," Anzio directed. "This also says that Mr. Sands's parents are still alive and live in Redwood, New York."

Commander Callaghan's cell phone went straight to voicemail. "I have his cottage phone number, sir, I'll try it now."

Michael heard the cans clanging together. He opened his eyes and Amanda was gone. She must be the one picking up the cans. "I love you, babe," he said with a grin. "I guess I should get up and get our vacation started."

Michael was watching Amanda out his bedroom window; the cottage phone startled him.

Before Michael turned away from the window, he noticed a dark green Dodge Dart slowly driving past his cottage. "So you were a Dodge Dart after all. God, Ace really knows his cars."

While Michael walked into the kitchen to answer the phone, the dark green car came to a stop in front of the bonfire site. Amanda didn't hear the man walking up behind her.

He slapped a soaked handkerchief over Amanda's nose and mouth. The stinging chloroform sent her into a spiraling darkness. The garbage bag, half-full of empty cans, slid from her hands as she went limp.

He dragged Amanda back to his car, leaving a drag mark across the grass and a tennis shoe.

Within seconds, Amanda was lying unconscious in the backseat of the dark green Dodge Dart as it headed out of Bay Shore Estates, leaving a dusty trail in its wake.

Michael answered the phone. "Good morning."

"This is Major Anzio. Commander Callaghan, are Amanda and Jeff Kane staying with you this weekend?"

"Yes, they are. Why do you ask?" Michael yawned and stretched.

Anzio explained what they had learned about Bobby Sands and his connection to the Alexandria Bay area. "The man is a trained killer, an ex-Marine sniper."

"I want you to track down Sands. Find out where he is and where he's been in the last two weeks. Also, contact his parents and find out if he has been in touch with them recently." Michael hung up the phone and tried to put the pieces of the puzzle together.

He stood there for a moment considering what he learned from the phone call as he looked out over the water in Guffins Bay. The lake was so calm, it looked as flat as glass. A stark contrast to what would happen next in his life.

"Listen up, people. I want to know everything about Mr. Bobby Sands, where he is, what he's doing, everything, even what he's eating. Hunt, you check his credit cards, see if he's charged any meals, gas, clothing, or anything else in the last two weeks. Collins, check his bank accounts, money market funds, stocks, CD or any real estate he might own. I want to know if he's made any unusual deposits or withdrawals since Kane's takeover of Caulkins Lumber. Thurston, get me a map of the Thousand Islands region and a road atlas of New York State." Anzio picked up the phone and dialed information.

"Operator, please connect me with a Robert John Sands in Redwood, New York."

"One moment please."

After several rings, a man with a deep voice answered. "Hello."

"This is Major Anzio, is this Colonel Robert John Sands Sr.?"

"Yes, this is Colonel Sands, and what can I do for you, Major Anzio?" Colonel Sands wrongly assumed that Major Phillip Anzio was still in active duty.

"Colonel Sands, I need to know if you've talked to your son Robert lately."

"There must be some mistake, sir, my son is dead. He died while serving his country in the United States Marine Corps," Mr. Sands spoke with finality and pride.

"Colonel Sands, I know your son is alive and so do you. I also know what he did to get a dishonorable discharge twenty-three years ago, so let's cut the crap, and just answer my question." Anzio was irate.

"Look, Major Anzio, that man disgraced our family. My wife and I buried my son a long time ago," Colonel Sands said angrily into the phone, attempting to pull rank, even if he was retired.

"Does your wife know your son is still alive?" Anzio trumped with the wife card, trying to get the man to start talking.

"The man that used to be my son is dead, sir." All Colonel Sands wanted was to get off the phone before his wife overheard the conversation.

"Colonel Sands, does your wife know that the child she gave birth to is still alive?" Anzio was no pushover, and he was not going down easily.

"I don't have to answer any more of your questions, sir, and this conversation is over," Colonel Sands declared.

"That's fine, Colonel. I guess I'll have to get on a plane and ask her myself if she knows that her son is still alive." Threatening to drag the wife into the situation was playing it the hard way, but Anzio was out of options.

There was a long silence before Colonel Sands answered. "Yes, the man you call my son called here Friday evening. It was the first time he's called here since he disgraced our family twenty-three years ago. I told him that we buried him and the memory of him a long time ago and to never call back."

"What did he want when he called?" Anzio was skeptical.

"He said he was leaving for good and wanted to say goodbye to my wife. I said absolutely not."

"Did he say where he was calling from?" This was a critical piece of the puzzle and Anzio would get it, one way or another.

"No. Did he do something wrong?" Colonel Sands asked. He almost sounded concerned.

"We don't know, Colonel, but if he calls again, try to find out where he is and call me at this number." Anzio gave his cell phone number to Colonel Sands and said, "If he tries to come to your house, remember he's been through a lot and he may be dangerous. Do not provoke him or threaten him, just call me right away."

"Major Anzio, one more thing. My wife doesn't know that Bobby's alive, or what he did to get his dishonorable discharge. I told her that he was killed in Operation Desert Storm and he died a war hero. If there is any way I can keep her memory of him as a hero intact, instead of knowing what he became, then I would do whatever it takes to make that happen. Do you understand me, sir?"

215

"I want you to understand that your son may be in a lot of trouble, and he may try to reach out to his mother. If you plan to tell him that he does not matter to you, that's your business, but if he contacts you or your wife, I expect to be notified. Thank you for your help, and please call me if you hear anything." Anzio was pissed off at Colonel Sands's attitude.

Michael made a quick detour into the bathroom and headed up toward the back lot to help Amanda. He couldn't see her anywhere. His heart started to race and his mind flashed back to the dark green Dodge Dart.

He took off on a full sprint toward the bonfire site. As he crested a small hill just before the paved road, he began calling her name. There was no reply.

Crossing the road, he looked in both directions. There was no sign of Amanda or the dark green Dodge Dart. He looked around the bonfire site with the scrutinizing eye of a seasoned black ops commander. Amanda's garbage bag lay half-open in front of the pile of cans. The lawn chairs were just as they had left them the night before.

Then Michael noticed the rut left by Amanda's cast. One of her tennis shoes lay upside down next to the drag mark. Michael's face flushed red and he broke into a sweat. "Oh my God, Amanda! What happened to you?" Michael's thoughts went to Jeff. He never showed up on Friday night and when he arrived on Saturday morning, he looked like he had been up all night.

Michael ran back to the cottage, up the porch stairs, through the side door and bolted down the hallway. He slammed open Jeff's bedroom door.

"What's going on?" Jeff asked blearily as he sat half up in bed.

"Where is she?" Michael demanded.

"Where is who?"

Michael was so upset, he dragged Jeff onto the floor. "I am not playing games. If anything happens to Amanda, I'll hold you responsible. Now, for the last time, where is she?" he shouted.

"I have no clue, get off me!" Jeff snapped back. "Fuck off and leave me alone."

"You never showed up Friday night, is this what you were planning?" Michael slammed Jeff back down. "Was that guy in the Dodge Dart your mysterious friend that none of us knew?"

Jeff didn't reply. He tried unsuccessfully to wiggle free from Michael's grip.

Michael placed his left knee over Jeff's throat. "I want to know where she is, and if you don't start talking now, you'll never be able to talk again."

Jeff began to gasp for air at the pressure from Michael's knee. "I don't know anyone with a Dodge Dart and I did stay with a friend on Friday night," he grunted.

"Who did you stay with on Friday?" Michael let off a little of the pressure.

"I stopped on the way here to get some beer and ended up meeting this good-looking bartender. We drank some beer and did some shots, and when she closed up early, she asked me up to her place for a little fun. That's all that happened. I didn't meet anyone else," Jeff pleaded.

"Where did you stop and what was the girl's name?" Michael applied more pressure.

"I stopped at the Brownville Hotel," Jeff groaned under Michael's weight and realized there was nothing he could do to free himself.

"What was the girl's name?"

"I don't remember," Jeff said, trying to wipe the cobwebs from his mind. "I can't think of it. I just woke up—cut me some slack, you're breaking my neck."

Michael applied more pressure. "You're lying."

"Wait, wait, her name was..." Jeff whimpered.

"I want the name, and if you're lying, I'll know it."

"Betty, her name was Betty, Betty Macaroni… no, it was Betty Spaghetti. She said she knew you. That's why I didn't want you and Amanda to know where I was. I didn't want my sister to think I was cheating on Cathy again. Betty said she knew you and I thought you would figure out what happened." Jeff's tone was sincere, he had too much information to be lying, and Michael knew it.

Michael got off Jeff and helped him to his feet, and a realization came over him. "Someone in a dark green Dodge Dart just took Amanda. I didn't see it happen, I was on the phone…" Michael stopped in mid-sentence, and then he ran for his cell phone on his dresser.

After turning his phone on, Michael hit speed dial for his man at the lookout post positioned at the top of Bayshore Estates dirt road. "This is Anderson, can I help you, Commander Callaghan?"

"Did you see a green Dodge Dart leave Bayshore yet?" Commander Callaghan was all business with his man.

"Yes, sir, just a few minutes ago, it went east on North Shore Road… in a real hurry, too," Sergeant Anderson said nonchalantly.

Michael was angry and it showed. "Why in hell didn't you stop it?" he demanded. "Did you see a woman in the car?"

Sergeant Anderson knew something was wrong and began to spit out protocol. "The vehicle didn't fit the profile, sir. A white male in his early forties, he was alone, and it had apparently spent the night at one of the cottages. Nothing suspicious or alarming until it hit blacktop, then it accelerated quickly."

"Did you get a plate number?"

"No, sir, too much dust coming off the dirt road."

"Maintain your post, and check *all* cars coming and going. Amanda is missing," Michael ordered.

Michael called HQ.

"Anzio here."

"This is Commander Callaghan. Amanda was just taken by a man in a dark green Dodge Dart. Mobilize your team and get up here ASAP."

"We'll take a chopper and be there in an hour." Anzio hung up the phone.

"Guess what I just got?" Collins announced as he hung up his phone. "Robert Sands and Ted Caulkins had a joint savings account that was closed out two days after the suicide. Between that account and Sands's checking account, which is now closed, Sands has over twenty thousand dollars in cash on him."

"It sounds like Sands is our man, and he's at it again. He just took Amanda Kane. Thurston, call our private airfield and have a chopper ready in fifteen minutes. Hunt, I want you to call the state police offices in the Thousand Islands area and have them work with the local police and the sheriff's office to set up roadblocks on every road in a sixty-mile radius from Commander Callaghan's cottage. Contact the Coast Guard and have them increase security on the St. Lawrence River. Give them the description of Sands, his car and Amanda Kane. Get the local TV stations to put Sands's face on TV and keep it there. List him as armed and dangerous. Put out a ten thousand dollar reward for any information leading to his whereabouts." Anzio was gathering his paperwork in preparation to leave.

"Collins, contact our liaison at the White House and have them get a court order for a phone tap and surveillance on Robert Sands's house in Redwood, and have them pave the way for local law enforcement backup," Anzio said hurriedly. "Get your gear, team. We're moving north to the Thousand Islands. A woman up there needs our help."

CHAPTER 44

Michael hung up the phone, turned to Jeff, and said, "Go up to the bonfire and don't let anyone touch a thing. Keep all dogs, kids, birds, or anything at all from going near the whole area. I'll be out in a few minutes."

Without a word, Jeff walked out the door and headed toward the site. His head was pounding.

Michael picked up the phone and called Connors. "LT, Amanda has been taken by a white male in his early forties, driving a dark green Dodge Dart that is traveling at a high rate of speed and heading off of Pillar Point. Get on our security cameras and find that car."

"I'm on it." Greg leaped out of bed and headed into his computer room. He slid open a panel on the wall behind his computer, revealing a large monitor displaying satellite feeds coming from the MFB HQ in Rochester and his own security cameras. Greg hit the speed dial on his phone.

"Yankee Stadium, third base." This was the standard salutation from HQ.

"Johnson, this is Lieutenant Connors, we need an emergency diversion of our satellites over this area. This is a code red. We're looking for a dark green Dodge Dart leaving the Pillar Point area within the last hour."

It would take time to relocate the satellite orbit and an emergency protocol would need to be implemented.

"What's the name of the operation, sir?" Johnson was already preparing the protocol implementation for a code red, allowing Lieutenant Connors remote access to the satellite.

Connors thought for a moment. "Call it: Save the Angel." Connors officially declared operation Save the Angel, and every resource at the MFB Black Ops HQ was at his team's disposal. At that very moment, hundreds of people at HQ were scrambling to prepare for departure in case they were called upon. Dozens of technicians were looking for every dark green Dodge Dart within fifty miles of Pillar Point.

"Roger that, sir, Operation Save the Angel is underway." Johnson began redirecting two MFB geosynchronous satellites.

Michael called the rest of his team, told them what had happened, and asked if anyone had seen the dark green Dodge Dart leave Bayshore in the last fifteen minutes. Nobody had seen a thing.

Within three minutes, everyone, with the exception of Greg, was assembled on the road in front of the bonfire site. There was no way the women were going to sit this one out.

Michael explained to everyone what Major Anzio had said to him. "What we need to do while we're waiting for Anzio's team is to check with everyone on this road to see if anyone got a good look at the man in that Dodge Dart."

"Should we wake people up if they're still sleeping?" Karen Miller asked.

"Yes, maybe someone saw him at some other time. We need to find out as much as we possibly can about this guy in the next fifty-five minutes, and I want Lou to start with those people renting the cottage where that car was parked last night." Michael looked worried.

Michael ran to LT's place. Finding Greg in his computer room busily tapping keys, Michael looked over his shoulder. "What did you find?"

Without looking up, LT said, "I've called in 'Operation Save the Angel' to HQ, they're redirecting our two satellites over this area, and they're tapping into the Department of Defense's satellites as we speak."

"Operation Save the Angel. She would like that. Thanks, LT." Michael stared at the screens as LT Connors flew through hours of data pictures coming in from the security cameras, while they waited for live satellite feeds.

"I have a Dodge Dart turning off of Route Twelve last night onto Moffit Road. He was heading east… it's the same car we saw drive by. Thirty minutes ago I have the same car turning off Moffit Road and heading West on Route Twelve." Greg pulled up the camera feed. "There he is and he's hauling ass."

"Can you freeze frame and get a plate number?" Michael knew he was asking a lot of his number two man.

Greg stroked the keys like a concert pianist. The car had taken the corner at a high rate of speed. Even with state-of-the-art, high-definition, military-grade equipment, the image of the license plate was still blurry. "Hold on, Commander, let me try to enhance the picture."

When the plate became readable, Connors cursed. "Damn it, he went too wide on his turn, it's only a partial plate."

"It was probably a stolen plate anyway," Callaghan replied. "At least we know where he's going." Michael gave LT the details of his conversation with Anzio as well as what the other team members and the women were doing.

"I don't like the women getting involved," Greg said.

"I don't either, but right now we need boots on the ground canvassing the area. Start a background check on this Bobby Sands character, I want to know everything about him ASAP."

"Shall I call in more men, now that we have a mission protocol?" Connors was already typing in the request when he asked.

"Yes, I want to have a picture of Amanda… I mean the asset, distributed to our field agents at HQ. We're less than thirty miles from the Canadian border, and I want two MFB agents at every border crossing between Buffalo and Vermont within ninety minutes. Also, have a team on standby in case we need them here."

Commander Michael Callaghan left Connors and helped canvas the area cottages to see if anyone had seen Amanda being taken, or if she was seen in a dark green Dodge Dart.

Michael knew help was on the way, but with the speed and brutality of the last two murders, he could only pray they would find Amanda in time.

CHAPTER 45

The team of four MFB operatives had gathered their gear and left HQ within minutes. When they arrived at their private airstrip, the chopper was waiting for them. The fifty-five minute helicopter ride to Bay Shore Estates on Pillar Point took the crew across Lake Ontario and they were now hovering above Michael and his friends.

"There's no place to set us down, sir." Anzio heard the helicopter pilot in his headset.

"This is fine. If you open the side doors, we'll drop some rope and we'll be on the ground in a minute." Anzio nodded at his team to get moving.

The pilot hit the release button, opened both side doors, and two ropes dropped from both sides. A few seconds after that, four MFB operatives were rappelling down the ropes with their duffel bags of gear across their backs.

Once on the ground, Anzio signaled the pilot to take off, and the search began.

Michael met Anzio a short distance from the bonfire. "We found this handkerchief, the tennis shoe, and those drag marks on the grass. It sure looks like abduction to me."

Anzio lifted the handkerchief to his face and sniffed. He jerked his head back from the pungent scent.

"Chloroform. He picked that up as part of his military training." Anzio placed the handkerchief into a clear plastic bag.

"Do you have any more information on this man, Sands?" Michael was growing impatient. In another few minutes, his satellites would be overhead and his teams would be starting a real-time search.

Anzio turned around to respond to Michael's question and saw the group of people standing behind him. "Who are all of these civilians?"

"These people are friends of mine and Amanda. Now tell me what you've got," Michael replied impatiently.

Anzio pulled out a folder with a picture on it and said, "This is a picture of Robert John Sands Jr., aka Bobby Sands. I turned it into a wanted poster. We should have them plastered on every store window, telephone pole and post office between here and Ogdensburg."

Michael looked at the picture of Bobby Sands and his Marine record listed below it. "Why would this guy want to kidnap Amanda?"

"Sir, we have reason to believe this man wants vengeance on the Kane family because they played dirty taking over a lumberyard in Minnesota that Sands's lover owned. His lover, who had been in the closet, lost his business, his family, and his reputation in the community before committing suicide." Callaghan speed-read the file.

Jeff Kane sheepishly lowered his head and moved back in the crowd. Even now, with his sister missing, he couldn't find the courage to take responsibility for what he had done.

Michael closed the folder and said, "Good job, Major. Take your team and go interview Colonel Sands and his wife in Redwood. We have a stakeout van equipped with wiretapping devices and surveillance equipment for you to use. Ace will show you where it is."

Major Anzio and his team followed Ace at a jog. Michael turned to the women and said, "I need you people to meet me in Alex Bay, at the liquor store off Main Street, in one hour." He turned back to his team and said, "JR, you and Ace take my SUV while LT and I

225

launch the boat. We'll take the boat over in case we need water transportation. Okay, men, mount up for action." They all understood he meant to bring weapons with silencers, night vision goggles, Kevlar vests and other black ops gear.

"LT, is there any word from HQ on the satellite search?" Michael checked his watch.

LT Connors checked his cell phone for an update. "They're searching a five hundred square mile area now. They have nothing to report yet, Commander."

"Keep me posted. Bring the mission laptop with sat-links and walkie-talkies," Michael directed.

"What can I do to help find my sister?" Jeff asked, completely missing the fact that Michael was called commander.

Michael felt like knocking Jeff out. "You've already done enough—you and your dirty little corporate tricks," Michael sneered. "This man Sands is getting even because of you."

"Please, Michael, she's *my* sister," Jeff implored him.

"He's right, Commander, let him help. We need everyone we can get to help find Amanda." JR was already in black ops mode. "Even if he is nothing more than a pair of eyes on the ground, we need human intel."

"Okay, fine, you can ride with the women and help put up the wanted posters," Michael snapped.

Commander Callaghan addressed everyone, "We're going to need standard gear, food and water in case anyone gets hungry, and flashlights for when it gets dark, staples and staple guns. Anyone have questions?"

They shook their heads.

"Good. We'll meet you in Alex Bay as soon as we can, and thank you so much for your help." Michael turned around and headed for his cottage.

The rest of the Bayshore gang headed for their cottages to gather supplies and get ready to leave.

Michael stood in his bedroom staring at the picture of Bobby Sands. He was committing his face to memory—his eyes, his chin, and all of the biographical information listed in the report.

Jeff had followed Michael into his cottage. "You probably hold me responsible for what happened to Amanda, and I don't blame you for that. But I would at least like to know what I did that would make someone want to kidnap my sister!"

"We have reason to believe that Bobby Sands wants vengeance on your family because his lover committed suicide after you played dirty pool in order to take over some lumberyard in Minnesota," Michael replied.

"You think it could be because of Bobby Sands's lover? There wasn't any woman involved with that deal, there was Ted and his brother Randal Caulkins, there wasn't any...." Jeff's face went blank as he stopped talking mid-sentence. "Did you say his lover was a man or a woman?"

"Ted Caulkins committed suicide after he lost everything he had." Michael looked at Jeff with narrowed eyes.

"Oh my God, that means that Ted Caulkins committed suicide." Jeff was shocked.

"What happened out there?" Michael asked, as he turned his attention back to the report.

"Two brothers owned a lumberyard. One of them was stealing inventory to build a new house without reporting the inventory shrinkage to the IRS. With inflated sales costs, there was less profit and fewer taxes to pay, which is illegal, not to mention the theft. The other brother, Ted, was married with kids, and he was cheating on his wife with a man. I had a picture of the other man and Ted having sex, but you could only see the back of the second man. That man must be Bobby Sands."

"So you blackmailed both of them so you could buy their business really cheap?" Michael sneered. "You leave no stone unturned... is that it?"

"Did I use blackmail? No, I just brought out the truth and they decided they wanted to sell," Jeff protested.

"Yes, I'm sure it was a really easy decision. One faces possible charges of tax evasion, and the other is threatened with exposure of his homosexual affair. Which must have happened anyway, if he was so depressed that he committed suicide." Michael turned away from Jeff in disgust.

"I want you to know that I was just doing my job. It was nothing personal." Jeff attempted to absolve himself of any blame.

"Doing your job?" Michael shot back. "How does interfering in someone else's life become your job? What business is it of yours what those people did in their personal lives? Who appointed *you* the guardian of morality and decency? No, you weren't doing your job. You were looking for some low-down dirty way of making a buck at someone else's expense." Michael's voice was getting louder. It was clear that he was upset with Jeff and his way of doing business. "Because you think you've got the right to take advantage of people and ruin their lives, all in the name of the almighty dollar, three people are dead and Amanda has been abducted. How does that dollar feel now?"

There was a long silence and Michael went back to looking at the biography of Bobby Sands.

Jeff said, "Michael, you're right. I started out by helping lumberyards that owed a lot of money and were on the verge of bankruptcy. Somehow I got caught up in the world of acquisitions and my greed got the best of me."

"Let's hope your greed doesn't kill Amanda." Michael packed his gear and escorted Jeff to Karen Miller's car.

The clock was ticking and time was against the MFB team. Amanda's life was hanging by a thread.

CHAPTER 46

The doorbell rang with a sound like Big Ben. Second Lieutenant Jamie Thurston waited in front of the door with the rest of the agents behind her. They were all wearing military uniforms. After several minutes, Mrs. Sands came to the door. "Can I help you, miss?" she asked pleasantly. Mrs. Sands was a petite sixty-three-year-old woman who had spent her life volunteering to help other people while her husband was away in the military.

"Mrs. Sands, I'm Lieutenant Jamie Thurston. We would like to talk to you and Colonel Sands for a while, if that would be all right?" Thurston was polite, hoping her military title would gain her entry into the house.

"Is there something wrong?" Mrs. Sands held a trembling hand to her mouth.

"This is a personal matter. May we come in and talk?" Thurston pressed.

"Yes, I'm sorry, please take a seat in the living room." Mrs. Sands motioned toward the living room. "I'll get the colonel. He's out back chopping some wood for the fireplace."

A few short moments later, Colonel Sands entered the room and said, "I'm Colonel Sands, who are you?"

The team jumped up and stood at attention. "I'm Major Anzio, and these are Second Lieutenant Thurston, Sergeant Collins, and

Corporal Hunt. We need to talk to you in regards to our discussion this morning," Anzio said.

"I see." Colonel Sands pursed his lips, and then turned to his wife. "Honey, could you make us some coffee or tea and perhaps a little snack? I'm sure these fine people could use a little something to eat and drink."

"I'll be back in a few minutes," Mrs. Sands politely excused herself.

After Mrs. Sands left the room, Colonel Sands sat down next to Anzio and said, "Thank you for not burdening my wife with this delicate issue."

"Well, Colonel, I'm afraid she's going to have to know, now. Earlier this morning, Bobby kidnapped a woman not more than thirty miles from here. We believe he intends is to kill her before he makes a run for Canada. Before he does, it's likely he will try to contact your wife to say goodbye. We need to be here with a phone tap and surveillance on your house. We have a court order allowing us to do so, but we need both your help and your wife's if we're going to keep that girl alive."

"You mean my Bobby is still alive?" gasped Mrs. Sands, standing in the doorway with a plate of cookies. The look of shock on her face was unsettling to everyone.

"Honey." The colonel quickly got up and walked over to his wife. "There is something we need to talk about." The colonel guided his wife by to the couch where she sat down with the plate of cookies on her lap. The colonel gently took the cookies from her lap and put them on the table.

"You see, Mrs. Sands," Anzio said, "We don't believe that your son was killed in a training exercise overseas. It appears as though his dog tags were exchanged with someone else's. He is in some trouble, and he needs your help."

"Trouble… what kind of trouble?" Mrs. Sands was in shock.

"We believe that he abducted a woman earlier today, and before he leaves the country for Canada, he may try to contact you," Anzio said.

Mrs. Sands raised both hands to her mouth. "Why would my Bobby abduct a woman?"

"Please, Mrs. Sands, this is a military matter and I'm not at liberty to discuss the details of the case with you. But we believe that your son has been through a lot recently, and he may attempt to hurt the woman or himself. We would like to end this ordeal before anyone gets hurt. Can we count on you to help us save this woman and protect your son from harm?" Anzio was careful with his choice of words.

"What can I do?" Mrs. Sands's voice quivered, her face was pale and her hands were shaky.

"We believe that your son will try to contact you either by phone, or in person over the next few days. We will be setting up a phone tap inside the house and surveillance both inside and outside the house. If Bobby tries to call you, we need you to keep him on the phone long enough for us to get a fix on his location so we can bring him, and the woman, in before anyone gets hurt."

"I'll do what I can to help." Mrs. Sands got up and went into the kitchen to retrieve the kettle of water whistling on the stove. Colonel Sands followed his wife into the kitchen, and shortly, they could hear Mrs. Sands begin to cry and her husband's attempts to console her.

CHAPTER 47

Commander Michael Callaghan and Lieutenant Greg Connors pulled into the public docking area in Alex Bay and walked to the liquor store where his friends from Bayshore were waiting. Teresa Bernard, Karen Miller, Sue Miller, and Mary Cormine were waiting to help find Amanda. Standing behind the women was the rest of his MFB Black Ops team, Billy 'Ace' Bernard, Jimmy 'JR' Ryan, and Lou 'Cool Hand Lou' Petrone. Jeff Kane disconnected the call on his cell phone and got out of Karen's car when Michael arrived.

"Hi, guys, thanks for helping," he said.

Michael was holding some of the wanted posters. "This is the man who took Amanda, and he's the same person who has been driving a dark green Dodge Dart up and down Bayshore. We need to put these wanted posters on every telephone pole, store window and on every mailbox from Clayton to Ogdensburg." Callaghan handed out the posters.

His tone turned deadly serious. "I've already sent copies to all border patrol, customs agents, and coast guard personnel in the area. We also need to ask store clerks if any of them have seen him in the last two weeks. His name is Bobby Sands. He's wanted in connection with two murders in Rochester. He's considered armed and dangerous. We need to travel in pairs for our own protection. If anyone sees him, or gets any information regarding him, call me on my cell phone." Michael nodded. Karen and Sue left in one direction, and Teresa and Mary took off in another direction, leaving the MFB Black Ops team and Jeff with Michael. Michael was hoping that Jeff would leave with the women.

Michael pulled out his cell phone and scanned the photo of Bobby Sands. Then he dialed a number. It was answered on the first ring. "This is Michael Callaghan. I would like to speak to the president on an urgent matter."

"Please hold, Commander, I'll put you right through." There was a standing order from POTUS when any of his kitchen cabinet called, to interrupt him and put the call through.

"Commander Callaghan, what can I do for you today?" POTUS was sitting in the Oval Office with his Chief of Staff and the Secretary of State—his meeting was put on hold.

"I need a favor, sir. Amanda has been taken hostage in upstate New York, and I need every border crossing from Alexandria Bay to Ogdensburg to receive a BOLO for a man named Bobby Sands and Amanda. I'll send you a photo of each when we're done." Michael was all business. "Also, I've dispatched some of my men to aid the border patrol in searching every car for Amanda."

"Consider it done. If there's anything else you need, let me know. Good luck, Commander." POTUS made a note on his personal pad.

"There's one more thing. I'll need special ops executive orders authorizing wiretaps, and access to sheriff department and Coast Guard resources. I've indicated that I already have this in place." Michael knew POTUS would cover for him.

"I heard about that from your liaison. I'll have it done within the hour and dated yesterday." POTUS knew how to take care of his men.

"Thank you, sir. I'll send the information now." Michael disconnected the line and sent the picture of Bobby Sands and a picture of Amanda to POTUS.

"What was that all about? Holy shit and fuck me… was that the President of the United States?" Jeff couldn't believe his ears.

"I was just calling in a favor, that's all." Michael punched a few buttons on his cell phone.

The line was answered on the first ring. "Yankee Stadium… third base."

Michael said, "Johnson, this is Commander Callaghan. I want an update on the satellite imaging for Alexandria Bay. We're looking for that dark green Dodge Dart, the man, and the woman that Lieutenant Connors called in. What have you got for me?" Michael was impatient with the lack of satellite success.

"I have the photos, sir." Johnson recognized Amanda. "I've put every available man on this and so far we haven't found the asset or the target. We'll keep looking and if they pop up their head, I'll get back to you with a location ASAP."

Michael rolled his eyes in frustration. "Use infrared and radar to penetrate every house in the area if you have to, but find Amanda and that damn car." Callaghan took a deep breath and blew it out. "Thank you, Johnson. I'll be on my cell." Michael hung up and turned to his team.

"The car hasn't been spotted yet. We need to canvas the area, they must be close by."

"What do you want us to do?" Ace made sure no one was watching then pulled out a .45 caliber Glock model 30 semi-automatic pistol with a silencer and handed it to Michael.

Tucking the pistol into his waistband at the small of his back, Michael said, "I found out that this guy's parents live in Redwood, just fifteen minutes up the road. My guess is that he's somewhere between here and Clayton, and if I'm right, it might be just as easy to spot him, his car, or Amanda from the water as from the local roads," he said. "I thought that Ace could start looking in Clayton while JR starts in Ogdensburg."

Michael went to his SUV and pulled out binoculars with infrared and radar penetration capabilities. He handed a set to each of his men. "Use these if need be. Time is running out and we need to find Amanda before the storm hits." Michael looked up at the darkening clouds.

Turning to Lou Petrone, Michael said, "I need you to start canvassing this area."

"How about us, what are we going to do with the boat?" Greg was ready for action.

"We'll take it down to the Bonnie Castle Resort and see if we can rent some dock space for a few days. Then we can start searching from as close to shore as possible in case we can see the car parked down in front of any of the cottages—or anything else unusual," Michael replied.

"What do you want me to do?" Jeff asked. "Should I go with you and help you with the boat?"

"Do you have any experience with boats?" Michael didn't want Jeff to get in his way, but he didn't want to insult the man either.

Jeff thought about bluffing, and decided against it. "Not really."

"Then you can go with Lou." Michael had taken charge and his men followed orders.

"Do I get a gun too?" Jeff looked hopeful.

Michael turned and looked him in the eye. "No chance." *What a dumbass.*

"Ah, really? That would be really cool if I could get a gun with a silencer," Jeff begged.

Michael rolled his eyes and walked away. The rest of the team set out on their missions.

Dark cumulous clouds painted the sky. Michael prayed he would find Amanda before the weather made traveling by water impossible. He knew if the clouds got worse, it would interfere with his satellites' ability to find Sands. Time was running out and a feeling of dread came over him. It was an unfamiliar feeling for Michael Callaghan.

There was a storm coming, and before it was over, someone would be dead.

235

CHAPTER 48

Amanda was beginning to wake up. The combination of the chloroform and the booze she drank the night before was making her extremely nauseated. Slowly opening her eyes, she saw a man with short dark hair in his early forties sitting across from her. Her head began to clear and she realized that her hands were tied behind her back with a coarse rope and her feet were tied together. She was having difficulty breathing because of the gag in her mouth. She looked around as much as she was able. All there was in the dimly lit room was the chair that she was sitting in, and the chair her captor was sitting in.

Amanda began to choke, and the urge to vomit came over her.

"What's the matter, princess, are you feeling ill?" Bobby Sands got up from his chair. "Do you realize that if you throw up while you're gagged, you'll no doubt inhale the vomit into your lungs and suffocate?"

Amanda's chest began to heave. She was doing all she could to keep from vomiting. She began to plead with him though her moans and body language to remove her gag.

"If you promise to be a good princess, I'll help you. Do you promise?"

Amanda nodded. She closed her eyes and tried to hold back the vomit while her chest and stomach continued to fight against her.

Her mind was coming out of the chloroform-induced fog. She needed to take deep breaths to calm her stomach and plan an escape.

Bobby Sands untied her gag. Once it was pulled from her mouth, Amanda began to throw up violently all over herself and the floor in front of her.

"Now, do you see the mess you've made?" Bobby Sands whispered into Amanda's ear. "Naughty girl, you're such a naughty girl."

Amanda tried to lean forward as she vomited, but a rope tied around her neck prevented her from doing so. The rope was tied to the rafters in the ceiling. When she finished heaving, and her feeling of nausea subsided, she sat upright in her chair, sucking deep breaths into her burning lungs.

"Now remember, you promised to be a good little princess. If you aren't, then I'll put the gag back on again," Bobby said in a patronizing voice.

"Who are you and what am I doing here?"

"I am a man who has finally had enough of society and all of its biased sexual referendums, unforgiving idealisms, judgmental finalities and greed." Bobby Sands started pacing. "You people think that you can sit back with all your money and power and destroy everybody else's lives as long as you create more money and power for yourself. Well, little princess, this time you picked the wrong man to screw over. You and your greedy little family are going to pay the price for what you did to my Teddy. For the first time in my life I found happiness—I found love, unconditional love. I found someone who accepted me for who and what I am, and now he's dead because of you." Bobby's tone was harsh and unforgiving. The gentle man who took off her gag was gone. Before her stood a man in a rage, and she knew it.

"I'm sorry. I didn't mean to upset you. I just wanted to know your name." Amanda tried to calm Bobby down.

"My name is Bobby Sands, and you and your family took the life of my best friend and lover, Ted Caulkins. Now *you* are going to pay the price."

"Ted Caulkins… are you talking about Ted Caulkins from Caulkins Lumber in Minnesota?" Amanda put the pieces of the puzzle together.

"Yes, and you killed him." Bobby dragged his chair over and sat down across from her.

"How did I kill him? I've never met him!" Amanda wanted to keep him talking, maybe she could reason with him.

"Don't be coy with me," Bobby snapped back. "After your family stole his business and exposed him as a bisexual, he was disgraced to the whole community. He lost his business. His wife and his kids abandoned him. All of his friends and neighbors disassociated themselves from him. He felt that the only thing good in his life that was left was me." Bobby's voice turned sad as he recalled everything that happened as if it were yesterday. "His suicide note said that he loved me too much to put me through that pain." Tears began to well in Bobby's eyes. "He said that no one knew who I was, and that I was young enough to still have a good life. He took off all of his clothes because he felt that the Kane family had stripped him of everything that was good in his life, and he wished me happiness. I found him hanging naked in the garage, the garage attached to *my* house, the house that he helped me buy." Tears were streaming down his face.

"I am sorry, I didn't know about Ted." Amanda tried to console Bobby.

"Sorry, my ass." Bobby's anger flared again. "People like you don't know what sorry is. Well, it's time that you learned. It's time that society learned."

"Maybe we can make it up to you. We can give Caulkins Lumber back, and we can help you financially. Please, we didn't mean to hurt Ted, or you. What can we do to help?" Amanda pleaded.

"You really shouldn't be sitting in those clothes with all that vomit on you, besides it really smells. Let me help you take them off." Bobby's face had turned red and his lips were curling up.

Bobby pulled out a long hunting knife and went behind Amanda. "Now, don't make any sudden moves or utter a sound. You might get cut." Bobby began to cut her T-shirt. He pulled her shirt off and said, "Now doesn't that feel better? It certainly smells better."

Amanda sat motionless in her bra and shorts. She didn't know what to say.

"Oh, you're right, you still have vomit all over your shorts. They must go too. How silly of me to forget." Bobby cut the side of her shorts. Within a few seconds, Amanda was wearing only her bra and panties.

"What can my family do to help? I realize now that we did something very wrong. Let us help to make up for it," she said.

Bobby started yelling. "You want to help? Do your really think that you can wave your magic wand and make everything all right?" Bobby's mood had swung again. "Can you bring back Teddy? Can you bring back that man in Mount Morris or Jeff's sleazy little lover? Can you turn back time and change the fact that I was kicked out of the Marines? Can you change the fact that my father has disowned me and told my mother that I'm dead? Can you take me back to the time when I was fourteen years old and I confessed to a priest in Ogdensburg that I was gay and he denounced me and called me a sinner and a degenerate?" His rage was in full swing. Sweat dripped from his face. His shirt was drenched with perspiration.

He had a strange tattoo on his neck. A waning crescent moon with two black daggers crossed under it. The tattoo looked new—maybe he was in some kind of cult. She realized who had killed Gino Torchia and Ann Chantel. "Were you the one who tried to run us off the Chaumont Bridge with the cement mixing truck?"

Bobby Sands tilted his head in thought. "I don't know what you're talking about. I would never do something so impersonal. I want to see you die, to look into your eyes as life slips away, but my new friends have something different in mind. They want me to bring you to one of their locations in Kingston, then they will slowly take over your companies. Then I'll get to have my revenge."

"Why did you kill that man in Mount Morris and Ann... the woman in Rochester? What did they ever do to you?" Sands was an emotional wreck. Maybe if she changed the subject, she could reason with him and talk her way out of this.

"I wanted to ruin everything your brother touched. Make him pay for what he forced Teddy to do. I want Jeff Kane to live with the pain and suffering that I have lived with." Bobby Sands wiped sweat from his brow. "I could have killed your brother. Would you prefer that?"

"How could you have killed Jeff? He wasn't in Mount Morris." Amanda was playing a dangerous game. Bobby Sands was talking, opening up, but he was also becoming more erratic in his speech and actions.

Bobby Sands licked the hunting knife absently. "I was standing fifteen feet from him in his own house. I was holding his loaded gun. I could have shot him dead, and I almost did. But that would have been too easy." He began to walk in circles around Amanda, staring at her body.

"I wanted to kill his wife in Mount Morris, but she wasn't in the van when I opened the door. The damn rain blurred my vision. I saw them together at the bar, hugging, kissing, flirting with each other. I knew they were going out to fuck." He slid the knife across Amanda's buttocks as he circled his prey. "I saw them leave together. I never saw that bitch wife of his stop in the bathroom on her way out. Most unfortunate for me. I had to settle with killing her would-be lover, and leaving your brother's gun. I was hoping for so much more fun."

"Why Ann Chantel? She wasn't involved in this. She was just an employee trying to do her job." Amanda was trying to find some shred of guilt that would give Sands room for pause.

"Are you fucking crazy?" Bobby Sands yelled so forcefully that spit hit Amanda's face. "She was there with Jeff when he humiliated my Teddy. She helped him plan the whole thing."

"No, she only went on the trip because Jeff's regular assistant was away on business. She had nothing to do with gathering information and humiliating Ted. She was just doing what Jeff told her to, she didn't even know the details. Only Jeff knows the details of a buyout, until it's already done." Amanda saw a flicker of understanding in Sands's eyes.

Bobby Sands stepped back from Amanda and stared at her in silence for a few moments. "I bet you didn't know Jeff was fucking her, did you?"

Now Amanda looked stunned. "What are you talking about? Jeff is married and Ann is dating someone else. They were not having sex."

Sands shook his head. "That little slut was fucking Jeff the night I killed her. I saw them, I waited for them to finish and leave before I went into her apartment. I could smell the sex, see it on the bed, I could almost feel it." Bobby Sands licked his lips at the memory of being in Ann's apartment.

Sands had calmed down a bit, and Amanda took a chance. "Don't you think there's been enough killing and death? I can't change the past, but maybe I can help with the future," Amanda implored Bobby.

"No thank you. I already have my future planned, and yours for that matter." Bobby smiled. "Do you know what an unforgivable act is?"

"An unforgivable act? I don't understand. What do you mean?" Amanda was speacking calmly, trying to soothe Sands.

"Unforgivable acts, deeds that are so wrong that they simply cannot be forgiven... an act of vengeance must be taken in order to set things right again." Bobby was tapping the knife against his leg.

"I don't know. I've never heard of it before." Amanda had to find a way to make a connection with Bobby.

"Suicide is an unforgiveable sin," Bobby gritted through his teeth. "My Teddy will never go to heaven. But when my work is finished here and your brother has to live with his everlasting pain, then justice will be served. Then I'll join my Teddy in purgatory, but until then I must leave a legacy so society learns to treat people like people, not just numbers, or dollars, or to alienate them because of their beliefs or preferences." Bobby Sands absently lifted the knife up to his tongue and licked it again. "I'll balance the scales for the unforgivable act that your family did."

Amanda realized two things, first that Bobby intended to kill her, and second, he planned to commit suicide so he could be with Ted. "There must be a better way, let me help you find it."

"Enough chitchat. On your feet!" Bobby snapped. "Come on, princess. I have something to do and you have your own little worries ahead of you." Bobby grabbed Amanda by the arm and dragged her to her feet.

Some of the vomit on Amanda's leg rubbed off on Sands's leg. "Damn it, you stink like hell. You are a naughty little piggy. A naughty dirty little piggy, that's what you are." He pushed Amanda roughly back into her chair.

He tied her hands to the back of her chair and left the room. A short time later, he returned with a metal pail full of water and suds. He slid the bucket next to her feet and tossed the rag onto her lap. "Do you promise to be a good little piggy if I let you wash up?" Sands pulled his knife and his lips curled into a devilish grin.

Amanda looked at her arms and legs. The stench was disgusting. "I promise."

Sands untied her.

Her wrists and ankles were red and raw from rope burns. This was her only chance. Her heart began to stammer in her chest. She flexed her muscles in preparation.

Sands walked toward the door. "You have thirty seconds to clean up… little piggy."

Amanda sprang from her chair and sprinted toward him. She leaped into the air, planted a foot against the wall, and flew at Sands with a superman punch.

The punch landed squarely on Sands's jaw. He staggered back several yards and regained his balance. "You little bitch." He rubbed his face and got between Amanda and the door. Holding the knife in an attack position, he locked the door and slid the key into his pants pocket.

"Okay, princess, let's dance." Sands moved toward Amanda with the knife swinging from side to side.

Amanda had taken kickboxing; now it was time for those skills to pay off. She backed up, waiting for an opening. When Sands was in motion, she executed a perfect kick, knocking the knife from his hand.

The knife flew up and stuck in the ceiling. Sands charged at her with forward kicks and reverse spinning punches. His rage was out of control; he threw all of his one hundred and ninety pounds into his attack.

Amanda was able to block some of the punches, and even land a few. A heavy-handed right cross struck hard on the side of Amanda's face and she went down with a crash. Her chair skidded across the floor.

Sands pounced on her. She hit him with an up-kick that sent him tumbling. Dazed, she staggered to her feet.

Sands went on the attack. Several hard hammer fists knocked her down. He got her in a rear-naked chokehold, and choked her unconscious.

Amanda woke up and could taste the blood in her mouth. Her vision was blurry and her entire body ached. He'd bound her hands behind her back.

Sands pulled hard on a rope tied around Amanda's neck. "I want you to stand on the chair," he ordered.

"Stand on the chair?" Amanda said in a frightened voice. "What for, what are you going to do to me?"

"Just stand on the chair. If you don't do it, I'll hoist you onto the chair by the rope around your neck." Bobby's patience was running out.

The rope around her neck was draped over one of the ceiling rafters and tied to a cleat on a support beam a few feet away.

When Bobby started to pull on the rope, Amanda said, "Okay, okay, I'll get up on the chair."

When Amanda stepped up onto the chair, it wobbled under her weight.

Bobby retied the rope around the metal cleat, tight enough so Amanda could barely move. "I want you to look at the floor beneath you. Do you see a large rectangle around your chair?"

"Yes, what is it?"

"This room is part of a very old house, and years ago, when my uncle built houses close to the water, as this one is, he would build a boat access. During the winter months, he would hoist the boat into this room. Your chair is actually on a trapdoor." Bobby's tone had turned cold and detached. "That lever over there on the wall is the release mechanism. All I have to do is pull that lever and the trapdoor drops open and the boat is right below you—or in your case, your chair will drop down and you'll hang."

Horrified, Amanda's eyes filled with tears and she couldn't think of anything to say. Her legs began to tremble and she began to panic.

Bobby said, "I have to leave for a while and I want you to be a good little princess and stand real still until I get back." He pulled the gag back over Amanda's mouth and tied it around the back of her head. "But just in case you lose your footing and knock your chair over, I want you to feel the way my Teddy did when he died." Bobby pulled out the hunting knife and cut off Amanda's bra and panties. "Now you know how my Teddy felt before he died. I want you to think about that until I get back."

Amanda stood naked on the unsteady chair, tied up and gagged, with a rope around her neck. The tears streamed down her face. She began to pray to God for help. She prayed that Michael would find her and save her from certain death.

CHAPTER 49

A nine-year-old boy named Chucky and his dog Lucky were walking down the street on their way to the store. His mom needed some bread for dinner. Lucky got his name when Chucky's parents told him that his new puppy was lucky to have Chucky as his master. When they asked him what he wanted to name the dog, the answer was Lucky.

Chucky would throw his ball into neighborhood yards; Lucky would fetch the ball and return it to Chucky for another round of fun. Chucky and Lucky were passing by old man Mitchell's house, a house that had been vacant for six months because the old man left his house to a nephew in his will. Chucky threw the ball as far as he could and Lucky took off after it. The ball bounced on a rock and rolled along the side of the house down near the water.

A few moments later, Lucky started to bark and Chucky decided to investigate. As he drew closer to the house, he saw Lucky looking into a cellar window. "What's the matter, Lucky, did your ball roll into the basement?" Chucky walked up next to Lucky and found that the window of the basement was mostly covered with cardboard. A small corner section of the window was exposed.

Chucky looked into the window. "Lucky, there's a naked lady in there standing on a chair," Chucky whispered. "She sure is pretty." Chucky had never seen a naked woman before; it was mesmerizing.

Amanda heard a noise outside of the only window in her room. She turned her head and saw the boy and his dog. When she tried to motion to them for help, they disappeared.

Chucky pulled Lucky back from the window. "Lucky, I think she might have seen us. We better get your ball and get out of here before we get in trouble."

Michael's cell phone rang. "What do you have for me?"

"This is Johnson at HQ, sir. We just received a call from the manager of Bonnie Castle's boat sales. He saw Sands's picture on the five o'clock newscast and recognized him as the man who bought a seventeen-foot used tri-hull boat yesterday morning. He paid cash."

"I want you to contact the Coast Guard, the local sheriff's office, and get every available boat in this area to patrol the river between here and the Canadian border," Commander Callaghan ordered.

When the Sands's phone rang for the first time, the tape recording machines and the monitors automatically turned on.

"Are you ready, Mrs. Sands?" Major Anzio motioned for Mrs. Sands to sit at the dining room table and answer the phone.

"What do I do if it's not Bobby? What if it's just one of the neighbors?" Mrs. Sands was panicky.

"Just act normal and keep the conversation short." Anzio smiled. "Answer any questions they have, and tell them you can't talk right now. Promise to call them back, and be polite."

The phone rang for the fourth time. Mrs. Sands picked it up. "Hello."

There was a long silence.

Mrs. Sands said, "Hello, is there anyone there?"

"Mom, it's me... Bobby." Bobby Sands sounded quiet and withdrawn.

"Bobby? My Bobby, is this really you?" Mrs. Sands had been told that her son was alive, but hearing his voice again after

246

believing he was dead for so long, came as a shock. "Oh dear Lord, is it really you, Bobby?" Her face reddened.

"Yes, Mom, it's really me." The sound of her voice somehow made Bobby feel better.

Mrs. Sands began to sob. "Oh Bobby, I've missed you so much. I prayed to God to let there be some mistake, and to let you be all right."

"I am all right, Mom. I love you, Mom. No matter what happens to me, I want you to know that I'll always love you." Bobby Sands looked over his shoulder through the dirty windows of the phone booth. No one was watching.

Anzio motioned to Mrs. Sands to keep talking to Bobby.

"Bobby, when are you coming home?" Mrs. Sands sobbed. "I can't wait to see you again. I've missed you so much."

"Mom, something has happened, and I'm not going to be able to come home."

"Well, if you can't come home now, then when will you come home?" Mrs. Sands pleaded with her son.

"I... I don't know, Mom. I've gotten into a bit of trouble and I may not be able to come home." Bobby Sands's voice cracked and a tear slid down his face.

"Please, Mrs. Sands just a little longer, just a few more seconds," Anzio whispered.

"Listen to me, Bobby, I know you've been through a lot, but please don't hurt that poor girl, she—" Mrs. Sands couldn't control herself. She wanted her son to be safe. She couldn't bear the thought of him hurting someone.

Bobby interrupted his mother, "The police have been talking to you, haven't they, Mom? Don't lie to me, Mom. The police told you about the girl."

Mrs. Sands held a hand to her mouth. "No, honey, a man from the Army told me they could help you. It's not too late, please come home. I want to see you and keep you safe."

"Mom, I have to go, they're probably tapping your phone right now. I love you, Mom, always remember that." Bobby hung up the phone and wiped the tears from his eyes.

"Did you get it?" Anzio shouted to his man operating the call trace.

"Yes. He's at a phone booth in Alexandria Bay," Hunt replied. "Here's the address."

"Colonel and Mrs. Sands, we'd like you to come with us in case we need to talk him down. Would you be able to do that?" Anzio asked.

"Yes," Mrs. Sands replied. "I'll do anything, just please don't hurt my Bobby."

Bobby Sands was furious that someone was harassing his mother and interfering with his plans. He needed to move up his timetable. The end would be here soon.

CHAPTER 50

Anzio's MFB operatives left for Alexandria Bay. Once inside the car, Anzio picked up his cell phone and called Commander Callaghan.

"What have you got?"

"Bobby Sands just called his parents from phone booth in Alex Bay. I'm sending you the address now."

"Thanks." Commander Callaghan knew they were getting close.

The first to arrive at the phone booth was Lou Petrone. The phone was hanging in the air and there was no sign of Bobby Sands.

When Anzio arrived at the phone booth, he checked his watch and realized that from the time of the hang up, until now, sixteen minutes had lapsed. "He must be on foot. That means he must be close to here."

"I don't follow you, sir?" Thurston asked. "Why can't he be in a car?"

"Sands hung up sixteen minutes ago. Sixteen minutes would have given him enough time to hit one of the road checks in town if he was driving. But if he's is walking, he might not have been noticed, and that means he must be somewhere around here." Anzio looked for anyone to disagree. "Let's spread out on foot in teams of two and work toward the water. If you see him or his car, call me on my cell phone. Mr. and Mrs. Sands, you can stay here with one of my men, and if we find Bobby, we'll call for you."

Michael and Greg parked the boat at a public dock and walked into the heart of the village so Greg could grab a drink and urinate, while Michael checked on the other members of the team. Michael sat on a park bench just outside of the grocery store. He was on his walkie-talkie, filling in the other members of the MFB team on what he had learned so far. No one had any solid leads and Michael directed his team to move their positions closer to the phone booth and start a street-by-street recon of the area.

HQ was still searching live satellite images with no luck. His men from HQ had arrived at the border crossing via helicopter and were checking every car, regardless of make or model.

Michael sat looking at the wanted posters and feeling anxious when a little boy came out of the grocery store and untied his dog from the bike rack next to him.

"What's wrong, mister? You look really sad," Chucky said, as his dog Lucky began to lick Michael's hand.

Michael pet the dog. "I am. I've lost someone that I love very much, and my friends and I can't find her anywhere." Michael put his walkie-talkie back in its carrying case.

"Is that man in the pictures the person that you lost?" Chucky was looking at the wanted posters of Bobby Sands.

"Why, have you seen him?" Michael asked in an excited voice.

"Nope, just in those pictures you're holding." Chucky had an innocence that made Michael smile.

"Here comes one of my friends," Michael said as Greg came out of the store. "You and your dog be good, and if you see the man in this picture, run away and call the police, okay?"

"Sure thing, mister. Good luck finding your friend."

"Thanks for your help." Michael got and started toward Greg.

Chucky noticed that Michael's keys had gotten wedged between the slats of the bench and remained stuck there. "Hey mister, you left your keys here." Chucky started to pry the keys loose.

Michael walked back to get his keys. "Hey, thanks, little buddy. I wouldn't have gotten too far without them, would I?"

Chucky stared at the picture of Michael and Amanda attached to the keyring. "She's pretty even with her clothes on," Chucky said to Lucky as he showed the dog the picture of Amanda.

"What did you say?" Michael narrowed his eyes.

"Oh, nothing, mister—I was just telling Lucky that she looks pretty!" Chucky said nervously.

Michael sat down on the bench next to Chucky and said, "Hey, little buddy, I'm not mad at you. This is the friend I'm looking for. I've been so sad and lonely and I'd be really happy if you could tell me where you saw her."

"Honest, mister, I wasn't peeping in people's windows. Lucky couldn't find our ball and I went to help him find it—that's when we saw her," Chucky explained.

"I wasn't thinking like that at all. I know how dogs sometimes need a little help finding their balls. Can you tell me where you saw her?" Michael smiled.

"Commander, what's up? Are you coming?" Greg was twenty feet away.

"Hang on." Michael never took his eyes off the boy.

"Do you know where she is?" Michael asked again.

"Sure I do. She is down at old man Mitchell's place in the basement," Chucky said cheerfully.

"Oh that's great! Can you take me to old man Mitchell's place so I can get her?" Michael asked carefully, trying not to spook the boy.

"I don't think so. She didn't have any clothes on and I don't want to get in any trouble." Chucky petted Lucky.

"I promise you won't get in any trouble. I'll give you and Lucky a reward if you help." Michael reached into his pocket and pulled out a twenty-dollar bill. "How about a twenty-dollar reward if that really is my friend at old man Mitchell's?"

"It's her all right, Lucky and I got a good look at her… Just her face though, all we looked at is her face," he said guiltily.

"How far is old man Mitchell's cottage from here?"

"Just down past the Bonnie Castle, it's right on the water." Chucky was being as helpful as possible. He wanted the reward money.

"Get the boat and head north just past Bonnie Castle and look for me onshore." Michael tossed the keys to Connors.

"What's up?"

"We may have a lead. Just get the boat and look for me onshore." Greg nodded and left for the boat.

"Are you ready, little buddy?" Michael asked Chucky.

"Yup, I'm ready." Chucky got up from the bench and tugged on Lucky's leash.

"Good, let's race. I'd love to see how fast you can run." Within seconds Chucky, Lucky and Michael were running toward old man Mitchell's cottage and Greg was racing toward the boat docks to get Michael's boat.

Michael knew from experience that black op missions never went according to plan. There were always elements out of the team's control. With all of the technology and human resources being utilized by the MFB team, Michael knew this little boy could be his best chance at finding Amanda alive. Human intel from local sources often meant the difference between success and failure.

CHAPTER 51

Bobby Sands had casually and inconspicuously walked back to old man Mitchell's cottage, listening for sirens and keeping a sharp eye out for police cruising the streets. As Bobby began walking up the driveway to his late uncle's cottage, he decided to go down around the front of the cottage and prepare his boat for a quick getaway in case he needed it. Once Bobby got around to the front and stood next to the boat tracks, he stopped and gazed out across the mighty St. Lawrence River. "Only four or five miles from here to Canada, then I'm home free. If I'm forced to, I can dump the body in the middle." Bobby saw freedom and his new associates on the Canadian side. "And actually only two, two and half miles to international waters."

Bobby checked the darkening sky. The forecast called for showers. "Everything looks good for a midnight run. I had better get Amanda ready for her meeting with destiny."

He untied the ropes from the dolly the boat was sitting on—when he got into the boat, all he had to do was release the brake and the dolly would slide down the boat tracks into the water. The momentum from rolling down the tracks would push the boat out far enough into the river, all he had to do was drop the motor, start it up, and be on his way. It was a quick and quiet way to escape. When the boat was ready, he walked up a narrow set of stairs to a small trapdoor that led into Amanda's room.

Amanda was surprised when Bobby came up through the trapdoor in the floor and nearly lost her balance.

"What's the matter, princess, did I forget to tell you about the second trapdoor entrance from the boat lift?" Bobby laughed cynically.

Amanda's legs were trembling from the fatigue of standing perfectly still for nearly an hour. The gag in her mouth was hurting her. Perspiration ran down her face and dripped down her naked body. Her split lip and black eye were the least of her problems.

Sands stared at Amanda's naked body. She was sweating, and her body glistened in the sunlight filtering in from the front windows. It was a pity that he had kill something so beautiful. But Jeff Kane needed to feel the loss of someone he cared about, and Bobby would have his revenge.

"Listen, princess, I can tell that your legs are getting a little wobbly and they must hurt like a bitch. How does it feel to be stripped of everything in life? Can you possibly imagine what Teddy must have felt like?" Bobby stared into Amanda's eyes.

"It's another couple of hours before we leave. Personally, I don't think you can make it another hour." Bobby walked over and looked out the window toward the road.

Amanda's legs burned as she stood on the chair. Blood had formed at the corners of her mouth from the gag being too tight. She blinked away tears.

Michael and Chucky were walking up the driveway toward old man Mitchell's house when Michael said, "Now where exactly did you see my friend?"

"Right over there." Chucky pointed to the side of the house. "Lucky was chasing the ball and it hit something and bounced down the side of the house."

Michael's phone rang. "Commander, we have Amanda and Bobby Sands on sat images. I'm sending you the location now," Johnson at HQ spoke rapidly. "We used radar to sweep the location and we have a positive ID on the car in the garage and there are two people inside the building."

Michael ran to the garage and looked through the window. He saw the dark green Dodge Dart. "I'm on them now. Lock on my location and send the rest of the team here, now." Michael pulled his silenced Glock from the small of his back.

Michael turned toward Chucky and said, "You've done great, pal. Now run home with Lucky as fast as you can."

"What about my twenty dollars?" Chucky looked hurt. "You promised me a reward."

"Oh, here you go, you deserve it. Now run home." Michael handed Chucky the money and waited till the boy and his dog were gone.

Michael crept along the side of the house where Chucky had seen Amanda. He peered into the window, and caught his first glimpse of Amanda and Bobby. His phone vibrated on his belt and he jumped away from the window.

LT had received the message from HQ and the address of old man Mitchell's cottage. "Talk to me, Michael. What have you got and what do you need me to do?" Talk about timing.

"I found Amanda. Sands has her at a cottage, about a half mile northeast of Bonnie Castle," Michael whispered in an excited tone.

"I'm in the boat. I can be there in five minutes." Connors gunned the motor and the boat sped forward.

"There's no time to wait, I'm going in now." He was not about to wait for anyone.

Michael sprinted to the front door and picked the lock. He crept toward the basement door. An old wooden floorboard squeaked and he froze and waited. Hearing nothing, he entered the stairwell and started down into a cluttered basement. On his left, at the end of a hall, was a closed door. Michael headed for the door with his gun drawn.

Bobby had seen Michael approaching the house and had heard the floorboard groan under his weight. He knew Michael was younger and stronger, so he set a trap.

Michael approached the door and listened. He could hear Amanda whimpering in pain. His mind raced. He knew he was walking into an ambush, but for the moment, Amanda was still alive and he couldn't afford to wait.

He gently took hold of the doorknob and turned it. It was unlocked. With his pistol ready and adrenaline pumping, he burst through the door prepared to take a quick shot.

Everything happened so fast, yet time seemed to slow to a crawl.

There was a rope attached to the door he just opened. The rope connected to a lever. The lever released a trapdoor under Amanda, who had another rope tied around her neck and attached to a ceiling joist. Amanda was about to hang.

Michael had absorbed almost everything in a split second, and he reacted. He fired twice. He hit the rope before it tightened around Amanda's neck. But her arms and legs were still tied as she dropped through the trapdoor.

Pain exploded in the back of Michael's head. It felt like his teeth were vibrating.

Bobby Sands had waited behind the door with a piece of wood and he hit Michael with everything he had in the back of the head.

Michael staggered forward, dazed and off-balance.

Sands attacked, swinging the two-by-four wildly, knocking the gun from Michael's hand. Sands swung the wood again, aiming for his head.

Michael ducked and landed a clean punch to Sands's solar plexus, and Sands dropped the wood and stumbled backward.

Michael was bleeding heavily from the head wound and he was dizzy. He circled closer to the trapdoor, trying to check on Amanda. He caught a glimpse—she was lying facedown in a boat. "I have backup on the way. Let Amanda go and you can leave."

Sands pulled his knife. "No chance. She's coming with me." He lunged at Michael and sliced his arm, causing him to trip on the loose ropes.

Even hurt, Michael was dangerous and Sands knew it. He scrambled to the trapdoor and jumped through it, landing next to Amanda's limp body.

Sands hit his quick release lever and the boat raced down the tracks. He started the motor before the boat hit the water.

Michael got up, ran across the room and picked up his gun. He threw himself through the trapdoor—too late. Sands was already heading for deep water.

"LT, which way is Bonnie Castle?" Major Anzio asked over his walkie-talkie.

"It's two klicks northeast of your position." Connors saw Anzio from the water as his boat raced toward Michael.

Anzio double clicked his walkie-talkie and said, "Attention all units, Commander Callaghan has made visual contact with Amanda Kane and Bobby Sands one klick north of the Bonnie Castle Resort. I want all personnel, all available Coast Guard and Sheriff Department's boats to head to that area now."

Michael ran toward the dock with his Glock raised; there was no shot. Sands was using Amanda as a human shield.

Michael saw Greg in his boat, heading his way. Michael yelled and waved to Greg, who in turn floored the boat and raced toward Michael as fast as he could.

Anzio and his team ran northeast on the street closest to the water. As they approached old man Mitchell's cottage, they could see Michael down on the dock waving to someone. "That's it, let's go," Anzio yelled. The team pulled their guns from their holsters and began to sprint toward the house.

As the operatives reached the house, they heard Michael yelling to Greg down on the riverfront. "This way, men, on the double, head toward the dock," Anzio shouted.

LT Connors barely reached the dock before Michael jumped in the boat. "Follow that boat." Michael pointed at the tri-hull carrying Amanda and Bobby.

Anzio reached the dock in time to see Michael and Greg pull away. He watched Commander Callaghan chase a red and white tri-hull boat with two people in it. He radioed the Coast Guard and sheriff department's boats, gave them descriptions of both boats, and ordered one of the Coast Guard boats patrolling the shoreline to pick him up. The rest of the boats were to prevent Sands from crossing into international waters. Within minutes Anzio and his team were aboard a Coast Guard cutter and they joined the chase.

Michael's boat was a twenty-six footer with twin Mercury cruisers. He had extra horsepower put for high-speed water chases. He floored the accelerator and began to narrow the gap to the slower boat. The chase took them into the middle of the river. It was clear that Sands was making a break for the Canadian side. The winds had kicked up, and the river was choppy with the waves of two to three feet. The boats bounced over the whitecaps and waves splashed high, making visibility difficult at times.

"Commander, the waves are getting too rough out in the middle—this boat will never hold together with this type of pounding." Connors knew his opinion wouldn't matter to Michael, but he felt obligated to voice it.

"Put on a life preserver, they're below deck," Michael yelled back, continuing his high-speed pursuit.

The Coast Guard and Sheriff Department boats, being much bigger and much slower, headed toward Bobby and Amanda from the borderline of international waters. There were three Coast Guard and two Sheriff Department boats in the chase. They began to form a containment perimeter around the tri-hull and closed in on Bobby Sands with their lights on and sirens blaring.

"This is the US Coast Guard, stop your boat or you will be fired upon. Repeat, stop your boat or you will be fired upon," loudspeakers blared across the turbulent water.

Bobby Sands heard the warnings, looked at how rough the water was getting, and knew he would never make it to the Canadian side. It was time for plan B.

As Bobby slowed the boat, he reached over and grabbed the rope that bound Amanda's hands behind her back and tied it to the anchor rope. "Don't get any ideas, princess, you're staying with me."

Anzio and his crew circled around the front of Bobby's boat and stopped two hundred yards away. "Bobby, this is Major Anzio. We don't want anyone to get hurt here. We're going to approach your boat. You and Amanda Kane will climb aboard this boat. Do you understand me?"

Bobby grabbed the anchor and placed it on the seat next to him. "Okay, princess, it's time to teach the world a lesson on dignity. Now stand up on the seat."

Amanda was shaking her head no and resisting Bobby, until he pulled a flare gun and held it to her head. "Either get up, or die right here."

When Amanda stood up on the seat, Bobby was standing in front of her, facing the police boats. He had pinned Amanda against the side of the boat and pressed up against her so she couldn't move. Bobby took the gun away from Amanda and put it to his head. "You people have taken everything in life that was ever good for me, and destroyed it," he yelled.

Michael could see that Amanda was tied to the anchor rope, and he slowly approached Sands's boat from behind. There was still no clear shot at Sands. The turbulent water made shooting too risky and Michael began to formulate another plan.

"What are you doing?" Greg whispered as their boat crept closer.

"Get ready to take the boat when I say," he replied.

Anzio tried to reason with Bobby. "Bobby, I know you've been through a lot in your life and I know that you feel the world has been unfair, but think about your mother. She knows you're alive and she loves you very much. Your mother is on shore waiting for you. I can guarantee your safety if you give up now."

The snipers on the Coast Guard boats found it impossible to keep their sights on Bobby in the rough water.

"My life is over. Whether I go to prison, or end it now, I'll never be with my mother again. At least this way, I can be with Teddy forever." Bobby Sands opened his mouth and began to cry as his finger squeezed the trigger on the gun.

The flare burst into flames as it entered Bobby's mouth and the impact drove him and Amanda overboard into the rough waters of the St. Lawrence River. As Amanda flew over the side of the boat, the anchor went flying over with her. With the gag over her mouth, she got little oxygen before being dragged down under the water by the anchor.

Michael watched as the anchor rope continued to unwind into the water. "One, two, three—" Michael quickly gunned his boat to close the twenty-foot gap between the boats. "... Fourteen, fifteen. Fifteen seconds, that means Amanda is down over one hundred feet. LT, tie them together," Michael yelled as he pulled Greg into the driver's seat.

"Michael, what are you doing?" Greg moved the boats closer together.

"I'm going down after Amanda," Michael snapped back.

"Michael, you can't go down there. The current is so strong that if you lose your grip, the undertow will suck you down. We were SEALS for years—you know I'm right," Greg shouted.

"The pull from the undertow, the weight of the anchor, and Amanda's weight will be too much to pull her up by hand. I have to go down and cut the anchor line so you can pull her up." Michael put on fins and grabbed a fishing knife.

"I'll be pushing her up after I cut the anchor. When you feel the line get lighter, start pulling her up." He climbed up onto the seat with his anchor in one hand and the fishing knife in the other.

The rest of his team raced toward them in a boat they commandeered from a local dock. Their weapons were drawn.

Anzio and his team could see Michael moving closer to the Sands's tri-hull boat, unsure of what Michael was planning to do.

"Michael, this is crazy. The water temperature at that depth is so cold that you'll never be able to hang on, what are you doing?" Connors was almost frantic at Michael's decision.

"I don't have time to argue with you! Get in that boat and grab Amanda's anchor line, and that's an order. I'm not going to let her die now," Michael yelled.

Michael grew impatient while Connors was tying the boats together. "LT, she's has been down too long as it is now. I can't wait any longer." Michael jumped off the boat next to Amanda's anchor line.

Michael descended quickly and he could see the strong current pulling Amanda's anchor line hard to one side. He tried to control his dive and stay alongside Amanda's rope, as the current pulled at him. He slid one hand along Amanda's rope while holding tight to the anchor with his other hand. Dropping swiftly he could feel the rope tearing up his hand. The water grew darker and colder and memories of other missions crept into his mind as his body fought for control against the pain of his rope burns and the icy cold water. His lungs burned and his chest ached from the pressure of his quick descent.

When Michael was within ten feet of Amanda, he could see her body waving with the current like a blade of grass bent by the wind. His heart sank.

When he reached her, he dropped his anchor and began cutting the rope that held her. The currents buffeted him, making the cutting difficult.

When he cut Amanda's anchor free, he could feel the power of the current thrash him about like the end of a whip.

He used every ounce of strength and began kicking. Slowly, he and Amanda began their ascent. Within seconds, he could feel Connors pulling the line. Michael looked into Amanda's wide-open eyes. He leaned over and tried blowing some air into her mouth, hoping for a response. It was no good, the air leaked out. Nearly out of air, Michael reached deep within and poured every ounce of energy into his ascent. His lungs were burning, and his legs were beginning to cramp.

Thirty seconds later, Michael and Amanda were hoisted out of the water and into a Coast Guard cutter which had pulled up next to Michael's boat. Two men had helped Connors pull the anchor rope to the surface. The crew immediately started working on Amanda. Michael had blood seeping from his ears.

"Commander, that was a foolish thing you just did, even for a Navy SEAL. You could have been killed," Major Anzio said. The crew continued working on Amanda.

Nothing seemed to be working. They shocked her four times with a defibrillator and the mouth-to-mouth resuscitation was not working. Michael prayed to God to bring her back.

"I'm sorry, sir, she was down too long. I'm afraid she's gone," one of the medics said in a quiet voice.

"Bullshit, she's tough, keep on trying." Michael wasn't willing to give up.

The medics continued to work on Amanda. They poured every ounce of energy into trying to bring her back. Precious seconds ticked by and there was no response from Amanda's lifeless body.

The lead medic looked up at Michael. "I'm so sorry, sir. She's nonresponsive."

Michael stood looking at Amanda's body, half-covered with a blanket. Her wide-open eyes were staring up into the heavens. His eyes began to fill with tears and his legs began to shake.

"You did everything you could, Commander." Anzio put his arm around Michael trying to console him.

Michael looked away as tears streamed down his face, and he saw that they had drifted down in front of Heart Island and Boldt Castle. He remembered Amanda saying they would always be together, always and forever. "No, no, no," Michael cried out. He rushed over to Amanda, and began CPR. Her chest was heaving up and down with every thrust from Michaels hands. He picked her up and held her against his chest. "Please, babe, I love you, come back to me, please come back to me." He began mouth-to-mouth resuscitation again. "I love you, please come back to me," he said between breaths.

One of the crew looked to Anzio to see if they should stop Michael and Anzio shook his head.

The clouds parted and the sun became visible. The sunshine shone brightly through the opening and LT Connors said, "God is taking her home now... God is taking you home, Amanda, and we're going to miss you." A tear slid down his cheek.

Michael looked up toward the sun, and he could just see a woman in a long white gown coming toward him from a long way away. As she came closer, he saw an image of Amanda next to the woman in white. The light got so bright and so intense Michael could barely see them through his squinting eyes.

"Please come back to me, babe," Michael begged as he bent over and stroked Amanda's hair. "May all the angels in Heaven bring you back to me."

With a loud cough and purging of water, Amanda began to gasp for air. The crew looked away from the light toward the miracle happening before them and began to cheer at the sight of Amanda, alive.

Michael leaned over and whispered into her ear, "I thought I lost you, and I never want to lose you again. I love you."

CHAPTER 52

Six weeks later…

Michael's cell phone rang, disrupting the silence of the yellow-orange glow of the sunset over the waters of Guffins Bay, off the coast of Cherry Island. Sitting on the dock that extended sixty feet out into the water in front of the cottage, with Amanda by his side, Michael debated answering his phone.

"You should really answer that." Amanda was looking at the caller ID on Michael's phone. "He's been calling you for days." Amanda was used to her father getting phone calls from politicians, but the President of the United States was something very different.

With a sigh, Michael pushed the talk button. "Hello, Mr. President, how can I help you?"

"It's nice you hear your voice, my friend. I heard you were laid up for a while with the bends. I thought you SEALS were immune to those things." Both men laughed.

"Yes, sir, Mr. President. I'll try not to let that happen again." Michael smiled.

With a chuckle POTUS said, "I heard George Kane was able to keep your situation out of the press, and I thought I would help by scrubbing clean the Coast Guard's records, if that's all right with you."

"Yes, sir, Mr. President, I greatly appreciate that."

"How are things with Amanda? I hear she's made a full recovery."

"She's doing great sir," Michael gripped Amanda's hand a little tighter. "And, with her testimony, all charges against her brother have been dropped."

"I am glad to hear that you and Amanda are doing well." POTUS didn't comment on Jeff's situation.

"Thank you, sir, I'll let her know."

"I'll let you get back to your sunset, it looks like a good one." POTUS smiled as he looked at the satellite image of Michael and Amanda. "Get some rest and heal up. We have a developing situation that will require you and your team in the next few weeks."

Michael looked up into the sky. "Yes, sir. Until then. Thank you for calling." Both men hung up their phones.

Michael knew the time to tell Amanda about his secret life with the MFB Black Ops was coming. He waited for her to ask why POTUS was calling, and he tried to think of a plausible explanation, but they just sat looking into the setting sun.

"Do you think your brother will change his ways?"

Amanda thought about recent conversations. "Yes. My father has put a stop on new acquisitions for a while, and we all agreed no more nasty business. As for his heavy drinking, he lost Cathy over it. I think we'll see a new Jeff from now on."

Michael knew people like Jeff, and they never changed, but he was not about to say anything to Amanda.

Amanda thought about Jeff and Cathy. "Now that Jeff and Cathy are separating, I wonder if Joshua and Cathy will keep dating."

The sun looked like it was melting into the water and Michael couldn't take his eyes off it. "I really don't know either of them very well, but Cathy deserves to be happy, especially after all she's been through with Jeff."

Amanda laid her head on Michael's shoulder. "Do you think Betty can make Jeff happy?"

Michael smiled. "Betty is a kind and caring person, but she won't put up with Jeff cheating on her."

Amanda said softly, not knowing whether Michael would believe her or not,

"She brought me back, Michael. It was Louise Boldt. She said that we should be together."

"I know, babe... I saw her coming through the light." Michael looked deep into her soft brown eyes.

"I love you, Michael," Amanda whispered.

"I love you too, Amanda."

AUTHOR'S NOTES

Bray is a town of nearly 32,000 in Ireland and a seaside tourist attraction in County Wicklow, immediately south of County Dublin within the Greater Dublin Area.

The president runs Joint Special Operations Command (JSOC), which consists of Seal Team 6, Delta Force, 75th Ranger Regiment, the 160th Aviation Group, and the 24th Special Tactics Squadron.

At the end of World War II, Harry S. Truman aka POTUS, fearing leaks of top-secret security information and non-conforming political agendas, was the first president to receive his own black budget. Today, the president's black budget is estimated to be between thirty and fifty billion dollars annually. The president's black budget comes under the Department of Defense's overall budget and is labeled as the Research, Development, Test and Evaluation (TDT&E) budget. Because this budget is listed under the DOD Budget, Congress is not allowed access, and its line items contain code names like Pilot Fish, Retract Larch, Chalk Eagle, and Retract Juniper… each with amounts in the millions and under the direct control of POTUS.

Along with the president's black budget, a kitchen cabinet does exist, due to the lack of trust and numerous security leaks, which have been going on since George Washington was president. It's also true that the number one source of classified information being leaked originates from those working closest to POTUS.

It's true that some intelligence officers that work for secret military operations and intelligence agencies, as well as some generals and colonels within the military, are in positions of power for twenty years or more, and they all have their own agenda and political allies not always in line with the current president. Some of the best-known examples of secret agendas are the Iran Contra Affair, when former national security aides were caught keeping secret the sales of weapons to foreign countries from POTUS. In the 1960s during the Cuban Missile Crisis, the CIA planned Operation Northwoods, a plan to kill U.S. citizens in order to start a war with Cuba. President Nixon created a secret group known as the Plumbers Unit to plug leaks. This contributed to the Watergate Scandal. In the 1990s, a Russian military officer put a listening device in a state department office. In addition, in the summer of 2010, some U.S. war plans in Afghanistan were leaked on Wikileaks from a source inside army intelligence.

It's true that in July 15, 1863, the USS *Wyoming*, a wooden hulled screw sloop, powered by both steam engines and sails, did engage superior forces, and was outgunned in the Strait of Shimonoseki, a narrow gateway to the East China Sea off Japan. Reports described how one of the daimyos (great feudal lords), Lord Mori Takachika of the Choshu clan, sent his private navy to take control of the Strait of Shimonoseki. This action violated the Treaty of 1854 between Japan's de facto rulers, a military dynasty called the Tokugawa Shogunate, and the United States. Another treaty, the Treaty of Kanagawa, between the United States and Japan, proclaimed bilateral peace, opened two Japanese ports to provisioning for U.S. ships, guaranteed safe haven for shipwrecked sailors, and permitted the appointment of resident U.S. consuls.

Internal warring between the local warlords and Japan's emperor had led to murder and arson committed by the "Ronin" (master-less samurai) and spread to many of Japan's cities. Cmdr. David McDougal (a Mexican War vet) skippered the ship in what is known as the first battle against Japan. Commander Callaghan and his actions were my contribution to the battle. The USS *Wyoming* did sink two ships and disabled a third by using fine marksmanship. One other worthy footnote is that the *Wyoming* ran aground for a few harrowing minutes before reversing engines and escaping heavy fire.

The death of my brother inspired the scene where Mitch Connors dies. Both Mitch and my brother were recently married, their wives were pregnant, and both men were shot and killed.

The scene where Michael meets Amanda and the scene with the young calf were based on actual events that happened to me.

The California Brew Haus in Rochester, New York, is a real bar and the bar food and pool tables make for a fun night. There is a gentleman's club next door called the Mirage. Eastman Kodak is a neighbor on the other side. The scene where Ann confronts Joshua while he's playing pool was inspired by my time spent there.

The Changing Scenes Building is in downtown Rochester. The top of the building is round and turns in circles when operational.

Bayshore Estates on Pillar Point does exist, and only has one dusty dirt road that leads down to the cottages and the shoreline. It's a private road and community. I've enjoyed many bonfires there with many of my friends and as a result, I was inspired to write some of the scenes in the book.

According to my family coat of arms, the descriptions of the history of King Ceallachan and the battle of Strongbow described in Michael's secret room are fact-based.

The Boldt Castle along with the George and Louise Boldt story are real. When George Boldt returned to America, he returned to New York City and abandoned the castle. It's open as a tourist attraction during summer months.

All of what is written about the mighty St. Lawrence River is true. In addition, it's part of the largest fresh water system in the world. German U-boats during World War I sank several merchant marine ships and three Canadian warships in the St. Lawrence River. Many battles from the American Revolution and the Battle of 1812 took place along the St. Lawrence River, such as the Battle of Sackets Harbor and the Battle of the Plains of Abraham. My time spent in the area and on the *Alexandria Bell* inspired several scenes in the book.

Made in the USA
Middletown, DE
16 November 2019

78890939R00168